TERRA
The Portal Series
Book Two

Richard Bowker

Book design by eBook Prep
www.ebookprep.com

Cover design by Jim McManus. www.complexstories.com

September, 2016
ISBN: 978-1-61417-871-2

ePublishing Works!
www.epublishingworks.com

PART I

Home

CHAPTER 1

I was standing in the snack-food aisle of the 7-11 when I saw her. Somehow I knew who she was—or *what* she was, really. Even though she looked like everyone else, was dressed like everyone else. There was something about her eyes, her gaze. Something I remembered....

And she knew me, which was very strange. "Larry," she murmured. "We've got to talk."

But just then my friend Vinny Polkinghorne came up behind me and whacked my Red Sox cap off, and when I had picked it up the woman was gone. "Cut it out, Vinny!" I said, but he just grinned.

I ran to the front of the store, but she wasn't there, and I couldn't leave the store without paying for my bag of Doritos, and when I had done that and gone outside, she wasn't there either. She wasn't anywhere.

"What's the matter?" Vinny asked. "Looking for someone?"

"No, I just—nothing."

"Well, that's stupid," Vinny said. "Can I have a Dorito?"

I handed him the bag.

"Let's go hang out at the harbor," he suggested, opening the bag and stuffing his mouth full of Doritos.

"Nah, I gotta get home. I just remembered I've got a composition to write."

"Stupid homework."

"I know, right? See you."

Vinny handed the bag back to me, then got on his bike and rode off. I got on mine and searched for the woman for a couple of minutes, but I didn't spot her. So I got off my bike and sat on a bench across from the Glanbury post office. After a minute I took out my cell phone and called Kevin Albright.

I was still getting used to having a cell phone. My parents had finally relented and gotten us all phones, even my kid brother Matthew, because everyone else in the world but us had one. Also, I think they liked it that we were all getting along so much better, which was mainly due to me and the way I had matured. My parents had no idea why I had matured, of course, and I wasn't going to tell them.

"What's up, Larry?" Kevin said.

"I'm pretty sure I just saw someone," I replied.

"Someone who?"

"You know. Like the preacher. From, you know."

"The preacher? Where? Was he, you know, preaching?"

"No. And it was a woman. I saw her in the 7-11."

"Did you talk to her?"

"No. But she knew me. And she had those eyes." *Those glittering eyes...*

"What happened?"

"She knew me. She said she had to talk, but then Vinny Polkinghorne showed up and started bugging me, and when I looked up she was gone."

Kevin was silent for a minute. Then he said, "You could be mistaken. It could've been anyone."

Kevin had never seen the preacher. If he had, he'd have known I wasn't mistaken. "What if I'm right?" I said. "What if someone has come back? What if the portal is here again?"

The portal. Our secret. The invisible device that took you to other universes—like the one we lived in but different, in little ways and big ones. The device had taken Kevin and me to a universe where we'd ended up trapped for months, without cars or computers or phones, where we'd fought in a war and Kevin had come down with a strange disease and almost died. And where I found another version of my family, different from mine but somehow the same. A universe in which I had already died.

"The portal isn't here, Larry," Kevin said quietly. "Why should it be here? We've been back for months, and after we came back it disappeared—they took it away or moved it or something. That's all over now."

"I don't think it's over," I replied.

"You don't want it to be over," Kevin said.

"It doesn't matter what I want. I saw that woman. She knew my name."

"You saw someone. But that doesn't mean anything."

"Yes, it does."

"Whatever," Kevin said, suddenly sounding bored. "I'll see you at school."

"Sure."

I put my phone away. I was right; I knew that. But I was thinking about what Kevin said. *You don't want it to be over.* Was that true? Maybe. I didn't run away from that woman when I saw her; I went looking for her. That said something, didn't it?

And I knew that Kevin may have sounded bored, but he wasn't, not really. He wanted to know what was going, too.

But maybe I wanted it a little bit more.

I rode my bike home. My kid brother Matthew was playing a video game in our room. Mom was in her office, working on one of those grant proposals she gets paid to write. My older sister Cassie wasn't home; she was in the play at the high school and stayed late every day rehearsing. I sat in the living room and tried to concentrate on my homework. It wasn't any use, though.

Those eyes.

What did she want? She knew my name. *We've got to talk.*

I thought about the preacher. He had called himself simply a *traveler.* He was from one of those other universes. They used the portal to travel around to universes like ours and give sermons to people who mostly paid no attention to them. Seemed like a waste of time to me, but I guess he knew what he was doing. He had helped Kevin and me get home, which he didn't have to do, and for that I was grateful.

I wondered what universe he was visiting right now.

Dinner was the usual—Dad got home around six, and he wanted to know about everyone's day while we ate spaghetti and meatballs. Of course Cassie didn't like the meatballs, but she was more interested in telling us about her rehearsal than complaining about the food. She went on and on about who was messing up their lines and who didn't understand their character and whatnot. She didn't have a very big part, but she was convinced that she should have the lead. I overheard Dad tell Mom once that drama gave Cassie "an outlet for her histrionics." After I looked up the word, I decided he was probably right.

Matthew had a long, boring story to tell about his Social Studies project, which he was doing with his friend Zach and involved creating a display of agricultural products from different states. Or something.

And then it was my turn.

"How was your day, Larry?"

"Fine."

"What did you do?"

"Nothing much. Hung out with Vinny."

"How's Vinny?"

"The same."

What could I say? Things were kind of boring. Except for the thing that I couldn't talk about.

After supper I went upstairs and surfed the net for a while. Matthew asked me what I was doing, like he always does.

"What does it look like I'm doing?" I replied. "I'm reading."

"I know, but what are you reading about?"

"The multiverse."

I thought that would shut him up, but it didn't. "What's a multiverse?"

"There's this theory that the universe we live in isn't the only universe that exists. There are lots of other universes—maybe an infinite number of them. They call that the multiverse."

"But that's stupid. There's only one universe. How could there be more than one?"

"Well, some really smart people think that's not true."

"How do they know? Has anyone ever seen one? Has anyone ever been to one?"

Sometimes I wanted to tell Matthew about my adventure, but why bother? He wouldn't believe me. How could he? From his perspective, I had never left—the months I had spent in that other universe had passed in no time on this one. I couldn't explain how. And I couldn't explain how the portal worked, when all the scientists said that the best we could do is maybe detect another universe somehow; we couldn't actually visit one. "No," I said to Matthew, "no one's ever been to one. But no one's ever been to the sun. That doesn't mean the sun doesn't exist."

Matthew pondered that, and then moved on. "Did you know that California produces almost all the artichokes in America?"

"I did not know that, Matthew," I replied. "That's very interesting."

He looked at me suspiciously, sensing sarcasm, and then said, "Well, *I* think it's interesting."

"I'm going to look up some more artichoke facts right after I finish reading about the multiverse."

"Shut up, Larry," he said. But I knew he wasn't upset.

The next day at school Kevin cornered me in the lunchroom. "It's not here," he repeated.

"Why do you keep saying that, like you know for sure? You don't know anything. You're just—" And then I figured it out. "You're worried you'll have to make a choice," I said. "Go or stay."

"Don't be stupid," he replied.

I had been by myself when I first discovered the portal, and I didn't know what it was—just some invisible *something* that let me hide from the annoying Stinky Glover. I used it fast—found myself in another universe, spent half an hour exploring a Glanbury that was kind of like the town where I really lived and kind of not, and then I came back. It had been Kevin's big idea to go into the portal again, this time with him. And we landed in a very different, very scary place. And it was Kevin who came to regret that decision even more than I did.

"Okay, Kevin," I said. "It was probably nothing. I just got, you know, this vibe. Plus, she knew my name."

"Fine," he said. "But I don't think you're right. What are the odds?"

I wanted to argue with him. What did odds have to do with it? The woman was looking for *me*. Which meant she knew where she could find me. Which probably meant she knew the preacher.

But why was she looking for me?

I decided I didn't really want to argue with Kevin. "Yeah, okay," I said. "I agree. Sorry I even mentioned it. Let's hurry up and eat."

We hurried up and ate, and we talked about other stuff. But Kevin still looked worried.

After school I went home on the bus. I didn't really feel like hanging out downtown like I usually did. I didn't have much homework, so I went back to trying to understand the Wikipedia article on the multiverse. Like Matthew, my father had noticed me reading about the multiverse once, and he'd gotten really excited, and he tried to explain to me about Everett's many-worlds interpretation of quantum mechanics and the wave function collapse and other stuff I wasn't ever going to understand. I pretended to be interested—and I guess I was, sort of. I knew that what happened to me and Kevin was real, but it was nice to know that there was science behind it—that smart people like my Dad could possibly *believe* it was real.

Anyway, I gave up on Wikipedia after a while and I decided to take a walk in the conservation land behind our house. This was where I had found the portal back last fall. Now it was spring, and the leaves were budding on the trees and the ground was a little muddy, so my mother would probably yell at me if I didn't wipe off my sneakers before I went back in the house. She used to be really worried about me wandering off by myself in the woods, but she's calmed down a bit lately. Apparently she has decided I'm not quite as stupid as she thought.

I found the spot where I had stumbled onto the portal when I was trying to get away from Stinky Glover. I groped around to see if it was there. It wasn't. That didn't necessarily mean anything. It could be anywhere. The preacher had moved it, back in the other universe. And, like Kevin said, he—or someone—had taken it away from here sometime after we returned. What did I know about portals?

I felt a surge of disappointment, though. And I knew that Kevin was right. I didn't want it to be over.

And that's when I heard the voice.

"Larry Barnes."

It was so soft that at first I thought I was imagining it. I couldn't bring myself to answer.

"Larry," the voice repeated.

I turned. And she was there, standing among the trees, staring at me the way she had at the 7-11.

"Larry, I need your help."

CHAPTER 2

I stared at her. She was tall and slender, with short black hair. I'm not really good at telling how old people are, but I guessed she might be about thirty. She was wearing jeans and a down vest over a plaid shirt—the same outfit she'd been wearing at the 7-11. She was very attractive. She spoke English with the slightest bit of some kind of strange accent—just enough to tell you that she wasn't from America.

Stranger danger, my mother would say.

But I felt safe—safe enough, anyway. The woman's eyes told me what I needed to know. "Who are you?" I asked, although I thought I knew the answer.

"My name is Valleia," she replied.

"And…you're not from here."

She nodded. "I am not."

"Why do you need my help?"

"Do you remember sitting in a dark church last Christmas Eve? It was not far from here, but at the same time…it was not *here*. And a stranger appeared. He explained some things to you, and he told you how to get home, when you thought you would never be able to."

I remembered. The preacher. The traveler. When I first saw him, he was giving sermons to people who weren't very interested. And then there was that Christmas Eve.

Listen to your heart, he had told me when I was trying to figure out whether I should leave that other world, or stay with a family I had come to love.

"Is he in trouble?" I asked.

Valleia nodded. "He is. Do you have time to listen to the story?"

"Sure," I replied.

She got down on the ground and sat crossed-legged on the soggy leaves. I sat opposite her. She closed her eyes for a moment, and then opened them. "His name is Affronius," she began. "*Affron,* for short. Did he tell you anything about the world he came from?"

"Just a little. He was a kind of priest, he said. He and the other priests used the portal to go around to other worlds, other universes—'imparting wisdom,' he said. But they tried not to interfere, even though they knew how to cure diseases and everything."

"Well, yes, that's true, although Affron is much more interested in imparting wisdom than most of the rest of us."

"He was kind of...odd," I said. "I liked him."

"Many of us like him," Valleia replied softly.

"What's going on? Why is he in trouble?"

"Because of his oddness, I suppose. Larry, let me tell you about Terra."

Terra. I must have come across that word somewhere in my reading, because it didn't seem totally unfamiliar. But the word sounded so different, hearing it spoken by Valleia that afternoon, sitting on the damp ground in the woods behind my house.

"Terra is the name of our world," Valleia went on. "A big part of our world is ruled by a priesthood. Affron is part of that priesthood; so am I. Some of us travel to other worlds; many others stay behind and govern our empire on Terra. This has been going on for centuries—ever since Via was discovered, really."

"What's *Via*?" Like *Terra,* the word seemed familiar.

"Ah. I'm sorry. That's our name for what you call the portal. Anyway, there is a rule—Affron says he told you about it—that we are not supposed to change the worlds we visit. We don't tell them how to build weapons; we don't cure their diseases; above all, we don't talk to them about the portal."

"Is that why he's in trouble? Because he talked to me?"

Valleia sighed. "That's what he's accused of. But…it's complicated. This shouldn't really get him into trouble. Others have done far worse things, without punishment. But Affron has powerful enemies, and they see this as a way of defeating him."

"Is he on trial or something?"

"Yes, Larry. And Affron would like you to speak for him at the trial."

"You mean…go to Terra…in the portal?"

Valleia nodded. "To Terra. Just long enough to tell your story. Affron has told it to me—you were trapped in another world, cut off from your family, with no hope of return. It's a powerful story. Perhaps it will move the judges. They are not easily moved, and they are not well-disposed towards Affron, but we have to try."

"What will happen to Affron if he's found guilty?" I asked.

Tears suddenly began to swim in her glittering eyes. "We cannot let that happen," she said. "We cannot let Affron die."

"They're going to put him to death? That's ridiculous!"

"I know," she said. "And we must do whatever we can to stop it. Affron's life—and the future of Terra—is at stake."

"The future of Terra?"

"Ah, Larry, it is too complicated to explain, and we don't have much time. His trial is today. We must leave now, if you are going to help. I wanted to talk to you yesterday—to give you a chance to think about it—but I didn't have a chance. So I came back."

I could feel my pulse racing. This was the chance I'd been dreaming of—to get back in the portal and visit a different universe. The preacher's universe.

But I remembered when Kevin and I had stepped into the portal last time. What could possibly go wrong, Kevin had said. And then, of course, everything had gone wrong.

How did I know I could trust this woman? Obviously she knew the preacher—*Affron*—but so what? Should I risk my life on her say-so?

Valleia's eyes were studying me, and I suddenly understood that she was scared. Scared that I'd turn her down.

"Would I be able to come back at the exact moment I left?" I asked her.

She looked puzzled. "What?"

"You know, like no time at all passes here in my universe, even though lots of time passes in the universe I go to. That's what happened before."

"No," she said. "No. That's *not* what happens."

Now I was puzzled. "Sure it is," I replied. "I was gone for like three months before—I was in the other world from September to December—Christmas Day, actually, if you know what that is. But when I came back, it was the exact same time I left. Like I'd never been gone."

Valleia shook her head. "I don't understand—it doesn't work that way. We'll get you back here as soon as possible. But time flows at the same rate in every universe. If you stay three hours on Terra, you'll return three hours later here on Earth."

I didn't understand either. I knew what had happened to me. "Maybe Affron did something?" I suggested.

She shook her head again. "It's not possible," she stated. And then she looked scared again, like she was losing the argument with me. "You won't have to stay long, Larry. I promise."

This was weird. I had just told her it was possible. Didn't she believe me?

Knowing that I wouldn't get back at the same time I left made it even harder to imagine going with her to Terra. She could promise all she wanted, but it didn't sound like she was in control of things. If I didn't get home till late at night or next morning, my mom would be a wreck. She'd call the police. She'd issue an Amber Alert or whatever it was. Volunteers would be searching the conservation land. I couldn't do that to her, even to save Affron.

And when I finally did come back, what would I tell her and everyone else? I'd have to make up some kind of excuse. But what would it be?

It just didn't make any sense. I shook my head. "I'm sorry," I said. "I can't help you."

"A few hours of your life, Larry," she said. "To save someone who saved you." She sounded desperate.

I shook my head. "I just can't," I repeated.

We sat there on the leaves staring at each other. And then Valleia started to cry. Not in the *histrionic* way that Cassie cried, like whatever happened to her was the worst thing ever and we all had to pay attention—no, these were silent tears leaking out of her eyes. Like she couldn't help herself.

She didn't wipe them away.

I thought: maybe she's in love with Affron. But that wasn't *my* problem, was it?

I thought about my family. Matthew would be playing his video game, just like yesterday. Cassie was at rehearsal; Mom was in her home office; Dad was at work. Pretty soon Mom would start making supper and Dad would come home, and we would talk about the day in the same old way. Just like yesterday. Just like tomorrow. I hadn't realized how much I loved my family until I almost lost them, back in the fall when Kevin and I were stuck in that other universe.

The universe that Affron had rescued us from. Shouldn't I rescue him?

That wasn't what made me decide. And it wasn't Valleia's tears. And it wasn't curiosity, exactly. What was Terra like? I'd love to find out, but…

It was the sudden sense that right here, right now, I was deciding my entire future. I could go home and live my life in the usual way, and maybe it would be a great life. Maybe

I'd be rich and famous and happy and never cause my mother to worry.

...and I would regret forever that I didn't take this one final risk.

I had this dizzying sense of choices being made everywhere, by everyone—universes splitting and splitting again as people decided which kind of Doritos to buy, whether to bike to the harbor with Vinny or go home and write my composition, what show to watch, what college to go to, who to marry, where to live.

So many choices. So many chances for regret. I had to close my eyes to keep from falling over under the weight of the choices.

When I opened them, Valleia was still staring at me, puzzled. She had wiped her tears away. What had happened? I sensed that maybe a lot of time had passed.

"Are you all right?" she asked.

I felt okay, I thought. Maybe a little weird. "Did you just...do something to me?" I said.

She shook her head. "I did nothing, Larry. You seemed to go into a trance."

I'm not sure why, but I believed her. This had all been inside me somehow.

It is only by living in doubt that we can reach certainty, the preacher—Affron—had told me.

It is only by setting out that we can finally return home.

I still didn't know exactly what he had been talking about in his sermons. But I know that he had been talking to me when he said: *Listen to your heart.*

I stood up. I still felt a little dizzy, but I wasn't going to lose my balance. I was going to be all right.

I brushed some twigs off my pants, and then I said, "Let's go."

"Let's go?" Valleia repeated.

"To the portal," I said. "To Terra."

"Are you sure?"

I nodded.

She got up from the ground, smiled, and hugged me.

"Thank you," she whispered.

Then she led me silently through the woods. Finally she stopped in a clearing.

"Is it here?" I asked Valleia.

She nodded. "It's here."

She walked slowly forward. She let go of my hand, and then she stretched both of her hands out in front of her.

Something glowed a light blue beneath them.

This wasn't what had happened to me when I entered the portal. It had been completely invisible from the outside.

The blue light faded after a second and a long dark shape appeared, extending down to the ground.

"Are you ready?" Valleia asked.

Was I ready? No, of course not. I would never be ready. But I nodded.

She went first, and I followed, leaving the woods, and my universe, behind.

When I had used the portal by myself, or with Kevin, its interior had been all foggy, like a bathroom after you've taken too long a shower. But this time I thought I could make out curved walls, a little out of focus. The air inside the portal was a little warmer than the air in the woods.

Valleia made some motions with her fingers, as if she was typing or playing the piano, using invisible keys. The opening we had walked through disappeared. On the opposite side of the portal, another opening appeared.

She touched my arm. "Thank you, Larry," she said again.

And then she reached out her hand to me. I took it. She led me out the opening in the far wall of the portal, and into her universe.

PART II

Terra

CHAPTER 3

Always before, when I left the portal I was in a place that looked more or less like where I had entered it—outdoors, in the woods. Not this time. This time I was inside.

This time I was in a church.

Not the kind of plain wooden church my family goes to in Glanbury, but a huge cathedral-like place, with a high ceiling and a balcony and large windows that let the sunlight shine down on us. Valleia and I were standing on a marble platform—an altar?—surrounded by masses of flowers and lighted candles. I smelled the flowers and something smoky and woody. Incense?

To the side of the altar, beyond the flowers, a man that I couldn't see spoke a few words in a foreign language.

Two women walked up a few steps onto the altar. They were dressed in thin, white short-sleeved robes cinched with red cloth belts, and each had black hair that was twisted into a kind of circle on top of their heads. They bowed to Valleia, who returned the bow, smiled, and said a few words to them in the foreign language.

Then she turned to me. "Wait here, Larry," she said. "I have to bathe and change. It's a ritual that I can't skip."

She followed the women around the portal, down a few stairs, and into a small room. I stood nervously next to the portal. I looked around.

The portal had a shimmering light-blue color all over it now. It looked like a large dome hovering a few inches above the marble floor. The cathedral's ceiling was also a dome, as if mimicking the portal's shape. High on the wall behind the portal were these words:

HAEC EST VIA

I tried to figure out what they meant—I recognized *VIA*, but I couldn't understand the other two words. Finally I gave up and looked around some more.

The floor in front of the altar was empty; carved wooden benches lined both sides of a long central aisle. A balcony extended all the way around the cathedral, maybe thirty feet above the floor. A white-haired old woman wearing a brown robe was tending the flowers. She glared at me, like my clothes offended her or something. To my left a fat, bald man, also wearing a brown robe, was seated at a large wooden desk, writing something in a huge book that lay open on the desk. At the far end of the cathedral was a pair of huge doors.

"Here I am, Larry," Valleia murmured.

I turned. Valleia was now wearing a purple robe with long, flowing sleeves. It was fringed with deeper purple, with a lighter purple band up the side; a dark belt was tied around her waist. She looked beautiful.

"What does that mean?" I asked, pointing behind her to the words on the wall.

"You never studied Latin, did you?"

I shook my head.

"That's the language we speak here on Terra—a version of it, anyway. *Terra* means 'the Earth' or 'the World.' Those words mean 'This Is the Way.'"

"You don't have a word for 'the'?" I asked.

Valleia smiled and shook her head. "Latin is similar to English, but there are many differences. That's one of them. But come, we must hurry."

She led me down the steps at the front of the altar, and we stopped before the fat man seated at the large desk. He bowed; she bowed. She spoke to him in Latin, I guess. He pointed to me, and she spoke some more. Finally he took a quill pen, dipped it in an inkwell, and wrote something in the book.

Then we walked quickly down the central aisle. Two brown-robed men stood by the huge doors. They bowed and opened the doors for us, and we stepped outside into sunlight. The doors were flanked by soldiers wearing helmets and breastplates and red capes, with swords in scabbards by their sides. Was this ancient Rome? I wondered. It looked like a version of it, anyway. Did that mean I wasn't in Glanbury, or America?

I wanted to ask Valleia, but she hurried me past the marble columns and down a long set of steps. The steps led to a huge cobblestoned plaza filled with people and surrounded by large buildings. At the bottom of the steps was a large statue of a man pointing up towards the cathedral. Valleia gestured at a long building, three stories high, on the far side of the plaza.

"That's the *palatium*," Valleia said. "The palace. We're going there."

We crossed the plaza. Everyone was wearing a robe of some sort. They all bowed to Valleia as they passed. Most of them looked at me like: *Who is this kid in the weird clothes?* But they didn't say anything. "Is that where the trial is?" I asked.

Valleia nodded. She looked nervous now. "Yes," she replied. "We must go quickly."

We entered the palatium through a large wooden door and passed through an entranceway that led to a curving marble staircase. On both sides of the staircase were painted statues of men and women wearing robes and staring nobly into the distance. The walls were covered with paintings—I later learned that they were called *frescoes*. Smaller statues looked out at us from recesses in the walls. The floor was marble, interrupted by occasional tiled mosaics.

Someone bowed and spoke to Valleia, but she just shook her head, as if she didn't have time to talk.

"Upstairs," she murmured to me.

We went up the staircase. At the top was a large open room with big windows that looked out on the cathedral, or whatever it was. At the far end of the room were two ornate doors, guarded by soldiers.

A few people were standing by the windows, talking quietly. They all fell silent when they saw Valleia and me. A tall blond man in a purple robe like Valleia's walked over to us, He shook hands with Valleia—well, not exactly: they grasped each other's forearm briefly. Valleia spoke to him in a low voice and gestured to me. The man responded.

The conversation went on for a bit. Finally Valleia broke it off and turned to me. "This man's name is Gratius, Larry," she said. "Stay with him while I go inside and see about the trial."

"Okay."

"And Larry? When they question you at the trial, don't say anything about returning home at the same moment you left."

I nodded, still puzzled by what that was all about.

Then Valleia walked over to the ornate doors, spoke to the soldiers guarding it, and went inside.

"Welcome to Terra," Gratius said to me in English, with the same hint of a foreign accent that Valleia had. "I am very grateful that you agreed to come."

"Do you know, um, Affron?"

He nodded. "Everyone knows Affron."

"Is he really on trial for his life?"

He nodded again. "Terra is on trial for its life."

He fell silent, and we waited. Eventually the door opened again, and Valleia motioned to me. I walked past the guards and into the room.

The room was smaller and darker than the room I had just left. The floor was covered with thick carpets; curtains covered the tall windows, and tapestries lined the walls. A couple of brown-robed men were sitting at desks writing by lamplight. At the far end of the room, a small old man sat on a large carved-wood chair set on a small platform. He wore a white robe with a blue collar—the color of the portal. On his feet he wore blue slippers instead of the sandals everyone else was wearing. He was bald except for a few wisps of white hair, and he had a small white beard. His hands trembled a little. His dark, penetrating eyes were trained on me.

It was hard to break away from that gaze, but I did. Two other old men sat in chairs on either side of him, on slightly lower platforms.

Affron sat at a table to their left. He, too, was gazing at me. He looked thinner than I remembered him, and very tired. He was wearing a purple robe like Valleia's. He smiled at me and nodded. I nodded back.

And it was only then that I noticed the tall, brown-haired man sitting at a table in the corner, next to a fat purple-robed man with graying hair. He was the only other person in this room not wearing a robe. He was, in fact, wearing faded jeans, running shoes, and a sweatshirt with a New England Patriots logo on it.

It was Carmody. Lieutenant William Carmody—the soldier who had befriended Kevin and me on the world that the portal had brought us to, and then tried to keep us there so we could continue to work for the United States of New England after we helped them win the war. When that didn't work, he headed off in the portal to our world so he could bring back information about all our fabulous weapons and inventions. Kevin and I looked for him when we got back home, but we never found him. Had he managed to return to his world? Or was he stuck in ours, as much out of place as we had been? We never found out.

And now he was here on Terra, staring at me across the dim room.

"Please sit down, Larry," Valleia murmured to me.

We both sat down at a table on the other side of the door from Carmody. Then Valleia said something in Latin to the men at the front of the room. The old man in the middle replied. His voice was cracked and harsh. His eyes were cold.

Valleia turned to me and quietly explained. "This man is named Tirelius, Larry. He is the pontifex—the chief priest, the most powerful man on Terra. The other two men are his vice-pontifexes. They want you to tell them everything that happened between you and Affron."

I nodded. And so I began, with Valleia interpreting what I said after every couple of sentence. It seemed like such a long story. But as I began telling it, it turned out that I didn't really have that much to say. In the first world I had visited—the one with Burger Queens and Dairy Kings—I had seen Affron giving a kind of sermon in a park in Glanbury. In the world Carmody came from, I had seen him giving another sermon in Boston; afterwards I talked to him for a minute, and he gave me his coat because it was cold out and some kids had stolen mine. And then there was the time Valleia had mentioned, when I met him on Christmas Eve in the dark Glanbury church, where he finally told me a little about what he was doing, where the portal was, and how Kevin and I could get home.

And then the next morning: one final glimpse of him, one brief conversation—before he stepped into the portal and disappeared.

And that was it.

When I was done telling my story, the room was silent for a moment. Then one of the vice-pontifexes—a little younger than Tirelius, with gray hair and cloudy eyes—asked me a couple of questions to get straight which worlds I was talking about. I knew that was a bit confusing.

When he was done, he nodded and said something to Tirelius.

"He doesn't see a problem," Valleia murmured to me. "That's good. He understands that this is a sham—Affron did nothing wrong."

Then Tirelius asked a question.

Valleia translated. "Larry, he wants to know if Affron ever talked to you about the gods."

"Gods? What gods?"

"Any gods, Larry. Did Affron ever mention gods?"

I shook my head. "No, I don't think so."

She gave Tirelius my answer. Then he repeated: "You must be certain. Did he mention gods? The gods who created Via."

"Well, I guess he mentioned that the portal—Via—came from some other universe. That it hadn't been invented here. But he didn't say anything about gods."

"Did he perform any feats of magic?" Tirelius demanded.

"I don't understand," I replied, when Valleia had translated.

Tirelius gestured impatiently with a trembling hand. "He gave sermons. He lent you his coat. He explained something about Via to you. What else?"

Valleia looked worried as she translated. But I remained baffled. Was this about returning home the moment I left? Was that the magic Tirelius was talking about? "Nothing else—honest," I said.

"Why did Affron have to tell you where Via was?" the other vice-pontifex asked suddenly. He was short and totally bald. He looked like an egg with eyes.

"Well, because he moved it," I replied. "To make it harder to find, I guess."

When she heard me say that, Valleia looked over at the fat man sitting next to Carmody. He sighed and folded his arms. Then Valleia turned back and translated what I said, softly, in a monotone.

Tirelius barked something out when she had finished.

"He moved it, Larry?" Valleia asked me softly, like she didn't really want to ask the question.

"Yeah. I mean, he was just trying to help, right? To keep it out of people's way. Because it's dangerous."

"Of course," she replied. "He was just trying to help."

And then she relayed my words to the rest of the room.

When he heard them, Affron smiled and nodded to me.

Then the pontifex and the other guys ignored me and started asking Affron questions. They seemed angry. Affron seemed unconcerned.

Valleia did look concerned.

Finally, abruptly, all the conversation stopped. The two vice-pontifexes nodded to Tirelius. He stood up shakily and said something to the brown-robed men taking notes. One of them left the room and returned with the guards, who took hold of Affron.

Then Tirelius said a few things more—to the fat man, and then to Valleia.

And that's when everything changed.

Valleia stood up and began shouting angrily at Tirelius. Tirelius stared at her with his cold eyes while she shouted, and then he gestured once again to the brown-robed man. Before I knew it more soldiers had arrived and were dragging Valleia out of the room. She was in tears now. "I'm sorry, Larry," she called to me in English. "But I'll save you! I'll save you all!"

I watched them take her away, and then I turned back to see what was going on the room. Carmody was standing; the fat man next to him was scratching his head. Affron was being led out by the other soldiers. "Thanks for coming, Larry," he murmured to me as they led him past. "It will be all right."

Then I looked at Tirelius. He had sat back down and his head was slumped to one side, as if he had used up all his energy. The vice-pontifexes rose and helped him to his feet, down the couple of steps to the floor, then out a door to the left. None of them looked at me or Carmody. The brown-robed men took up their papers and followed.

We were now alone in the dark room with the fat man in the purple robe.

"Well, then," the fat man said in English.

CHAPTER 4

"First, let me introduce myself," he went on, looking at me. "My name is Hypatius. And I must apologize for my English. It is nowhere as good as that of Affron or Valleia. They are un—er, incomparable at learning languages. Also, I am quite out of practice. There is a time for traveling among worlds, and then comes a time when one moves on to other things. I am only here because I do have some small competence in your language."

His accent was strange—the "V" in Valleia sounded more like a "W", for example. There was so much I didn't know, but I decided to start with Carmody. "Why are you here?" I asked him. "What's going on?"

"Because Valleia asked me to come," Carmody replied. "She is a very persuasive woman. I wasn't much use at the trial, though. As for what's going on now...I think we need to find that out from Hypatius. But obviously this trial didn't turn out for Valleia—or Affron." He didn't seem happy about that.

"Well, is the trial over?" I asked Hypatius. "Can I go home?"

He sighed and scratched his head. "You see, things have taken an unexpected turn, I'm afraid. It seems, er, that neither of you will be going home."

He spoke that last sentence a bit like it was a question, which was very confusing. "What do you mean?" I demanded. "Valleia said I could go home after Affron's trial."

"Yes, and it was going quite well," Hypatius said. "But then some things were said that concerned Tirelius and the others. So I'm very sorry to say that you will have to stay here on Terra—with me, actually."

"Stay here? For how long?"

"Ah, well, that was not decided."

"I have to go home!"

Then Carmody said something to Hypatius—in Latin, it appeared. Hypatius responded quickly. They went back and forth for a minute, and then Carmody spoke to me. "It appears that your testimony suggested that Affron was some kind of danger to Terra," he explained. "And those judges seem to think we have been contaminated by him somehow. Although how this applies to me is certainly unclear. I never even met the man."

"I'm sure you will be able to appeal," Hypatius said. "If there has been an un—injustice, the pontifex will address it."

"You need to address it *now!*" I demanded. "Valleia said I could go home right after the trial!"

"I fear that promises made by Valleia are of no interest to the pontifex," Hypatius replied.

"Before they carried her off she said that she was going to destroy the pontifex and everything he stands for," Carmody added. "It was really a very powerful speech."

Hypatius rubbed his cheek. "It is a speech for which she'll pay dearly, I fear. But come—I offer both of you my hospitality. I live simply but comfortably, not far from here. It is an inconvenience for you to be here on Terra, I know, but we shall have to see what the future brings."

See what the future brings? How had I let this happen to me again? "It's not just an inconvenience—my family is going to be looking for me," I pointed out. "The police…everyone. You could go to the portal—to Via—

right now and take me home, couldn't you? What's stopping you?"

"I'm afraid you understand nothing of using Via," he replied. "Or of what happens if one disobeys Tirelius. There is, of course, much that you don't know. I can perhaps explain some things to you, if you are interested. But again, let us go to my home. You must be hungry. I offer you a fine meal and excellent wine. You will be well treated while you are here, and perhaps soon this will all be resolved."

Hypatius pushed himself up with difficulty from his chair. I looked pleadingly at Carmody. But what could he do? He simply shrugged. "I believe we have to accept his invitation, Larry."

So we followed Hypatius out of the room. The outer room was almost empty now. Those who were left bowed to Hypatius as he passed and gave Carmody and me the usual puzzled looks. Hypatius moved faster than I'd expected for someone so overweight. We went down another staircase, and then out another door. It was twilight now; Mom would already be getting worried.

We were on the other side of the palatium. We walked along a small path to a large circular drive where open horse-drawn carriages were lined up. Hypatius motioned to the driver of the first one. It pulled up, and the driver got down to assist us. He was a short, stocky man wearing a yellow robe and a straw hat. He bowed separately to each of us.

"It is a fine evening for walking," Hypatius said, "but I think perhaps a ride will be pleasant. I haven't the energy I used to possess."

Hypatius struggled a bit getting up into the carriage, but with the driver's helped he settled himself in the back seat, and Carmody and I sat facing him. The driver got up and started off. We went along a wide, straight road lined with trees. A few people were walking on a path by the side of the road. Beyond the road on both sides were more buildings.

Hypatius waved a hand. "This is the City," he said. "*Urbis*, in Latin. The home of Via. The beating heart of Terra. The center of our lives. You were here last night, William—may I call you William?"

Carmody nodded. "I stayed with Valleia."

"Excellent. A wonderful woman. Devoted to Affron. As you saw, perhaps too much so. Did she tell you about Urbis?"

"A little."

"Well, perhaps I should repeat a bit of its history, for Larry's benefit."

Carmody shrugged. "As you wish."

So Hypatius told us the story of the beginnings of Urbis.

It began centuries ago. A simple peasant named Hieron was climbing a hill when he came upon Via. A magical, invisible portal that led him to other worlds, many filled with wonders beyond his imagining. Hieron could, of course, have brought back some of those wonders—an invention, perhaps, or the cure for a disease—and used them to obtain wealth and power on Terra. Or, he could have stayed in one of those worlds and left his hard peasant life behind.

But Hieron was not such a person. He believed that the portal had been left there by the gods—not for his benefit, but for the good of everyone on Terra.

Terra in those days was filled with warring nations. Roma, where Hieron lived, had been powerful for a long time, but it was in danger of being overrun by nomadic tribes from the north and powerful empires to the east and south.

"There was a Roman empire in my world," Carmody pointed out. "And in Larry's, too, I imagine."

I nodded. "But I thought it went away a long time ago."

"Yes," Hypatius replied. "That was the case in many worlds we have visited. But hardly in all. In some, the Roman empire did not collapse, but stayed strong and vibrant for many centuries, as it did here. But always there was war here, generation after generation. Everyone was tired of war and worried about the future. Everyone was looking for an answer.

"In our world, Via was the answer."

Hieron slowly brought others into the secret, Hypatius explained. Like Hieron, these men and women were wise and interested in the good of others. They decided they would learn what they could from the other worlds they visited, and try to apply that knowledge to making Terra a better place. This was a project they knew would last much longer than their own lives, but they dedicated themselves to it.

And gradually Hieron's vision transformed his world. The priests of Via gained ultimate power in the Roman empire, and they built Urbis as the center of their power. The empire was peaceful and happy, thanks to Hieron and the gift the gods had given him.

"The statue in front of the temple of Via," I said. "That's Hieron?"

"It is indeed," Hypatius replied.

"And they took power without using weapons from the worlds they visited."

This had been Carmody's idea in coming to my world. His world had primitive muskets, which would have been no match for the guns you could buy all over the place in America. Bring some of those guns back, and the United States of New England would have had no trouble defeating its enemies.

The comment seemed to make Hypatius uncomfortable. "Yes, Hieron and his followers did not use such weapons," he replied. "That was not their way. They relied on persuasion, on making life better for people. They did not want to rule by force, but by virtue."

"That's not an easy thing to do," Carmody noted.

"Yes, of course," Hypatius agreed. "But they were remarkable men and women. They were not without their flaws, of course, and neither are we, who have followed in their footsteps. But I have traveled to many other worlds, and none are as successful as ours."

"Valleia seems to think that your current leaders are destroying Terra."

Hypatius scratched his head. "Well, of course we can't pretend that there are no disagreements here, no controversy. We have learned much since Hieron, and we face far different problems. The solutions are not always obvious. But we do our best."

"Where does Affron come in?" I asked. "Why are they so upset with him?"

"Yes, Affron," Hypatius replied. "There is a certain…magic associated with Affron."

"Magic? Tirelius asked me about magic."

"Hmm, yes. Some say he has been touched by the gods. Some say he has been to the world of the gods—the gods who gave us Via."

"Do you believe that?"

"Ah, such things are unposs—impossible to know. He is certainly an interesting and powerful person. Many expected him to be the next pontifex, even though he is quite young for such an honor."

"What will happen to Affron and Valleia?" I asked.

"I cannot say. They are in trouble, of course. But as for punishment…I don't know. They have many supporters here in Urbis. It might be prudent to be merciful, to work out our differences."

"Valleia said that the future of Terra was at stake. Is that true?"

Again Hypatius scratched his head. "Some say so. Tirelius wants to take the empire in a different direction. Others disagree with his plan. Who is right and who is wrong—that is not for me to say."

We turned onto a side road. Soon we were in what looked like a town center with a small park in the middle, and a plaza surrounded by small shops. In the park someone was playing strange-sounding music on a flute-like instrument. Beyond the park were narrow streets lined with single-story houses. The carriage pulled up in front of one of them.

"Here we are," Hypatius said. The driver helped him down, and Carmody and I followed him. Hypatius produced a couple of coins from his pocket and handed them to the driver. "Let us enter my home and leave our cares behind," he said, gesturing at the house.

Fat chance I was going to leave my cares behind. My mother would be totally freaking out by now. She'd have called Kevin and Vinny and all my friends. She'd have called Dad, and probably the police. And I was supposed to relax.

We went inside the house. We walked through a small entrance way, filled with frescoes and little statues in niches in the wall, and into an interior courtyard filled with plants and flowers, with an opening in the roof and a fountain below it in the center of a pool. The other rooms were off this courtyard, which Hypatius called an atrium. He led us to seats in the atrium, next to the fountain. The place would have been pleasant enough, if I'd been in the mood.

"Now wine!" Hypatius exclaimed. He called out something in Latin. In a few moments a girl about my age appeared with a tray on which were a couple of jugs and three cups. She set the tray down on a table and poured red wine from one of the jugs into the cups, followed by water from the other jug. Then she bowed to each of us as she handed us a cup.

The girl was thin, with short blonde hair and gray eyes. She was wearing a simple dark green robe. She stared openly at Carmody and me—taking in our faces and our odd clothes—until Hypatius spoke sharply to her. She bowed to him again and went back inside.

"Palta will have dinner for us shortly," he said. He raised his cup. "Meanwhile—to Via!" And he took a long gulp of the wine.

I took a sip from my cup. I had never drunk wine before. It tasted a little sour, but it seemed to warm my blood, and maybe calm me down a bit. I decided I better not drink very much of it.

"What do we do while we're here?" Carmody asked Hypatius.

"Ah, first we will find you more suitable clothing—you can't go around looking like that. People will find it confusing, perhaps even distressing. Then..." Hypatius shrugged. "You will be guests of Urbis. We will want you to stay in the city of course, but really, there is no reason to leave. Everything you could want is right here."

"How large is Urbis?" I asked.

"Ah, large enough. It has grown over the centuries, and we have had to move the city walls more than once. We are in inner Urbis—the temple of Via is at the center, of course. It is surrounded by official buildings and residences—the palatium where the trial was held, of course, and the pontifex's residence, and the schola, where the best students in the empire prepare for their roles in our priesthood. The military barracks are nearby, and other such buildings. Beyond this area are little castella— villages, neighborhoods—like this one, where we officials reside. And then there is outer Urbis—the castella where the rest of our residents live: the carpenters and masons and wheelwrights and seamstresses, and so on. Wonderful people, so devoted. This is a lovely city."

Hypatius nodded and poured himself more wine. This time he put only a little water into it.

"I can see why you might not want weapons," I said. "But why don't you have electricity and automobiles and stuff like that?"

He nodded knowingly. "Yes, you come from a world filled with such things. So many wonderful inventions— marvels of human ingenuity! Is *ingenuity* the word I want? When Hieron visited such worlds, at first he thought the people who lived in them must be gods. But you know better, don't you, Larry? And eventually Hieron did, as well. Ingenuity is not wisdom. Inventions do not necessarily increase happiness. There is much to be learned from other worlds, but that was perhaps Hieron's most important lesson. He took what mattered, and left all the rest behind. And that included electricity and automobiles. And even medicines—ah, that was a hard choice, and one we still debate. But come, dinner must be ready. Palta!"

Hypatius heaved himself up out of his chair, took the wine jug, and led us into what was apparently the dining room. Torches were lit on the walls, and in the center was a low, three-sided table surrounded by couches. Apparently you reclined while you ate, because Hypatius got carefully down onto a couch, lay on his side, with pillows propping up the top of his body, and gestured to us to do the same. I did it, but I felt stupid and uncomfortable. Palta brought in a plate of fruit, and we ate some grapes and figs. This was followed by slices of roasted pork and fresh bread, which we were supposed to dip into a dish of olive oil, followed by a dessert of roasted almonds. There wasn't any silverware; there weren't any napkins. You took what you wanted from the plates, and you wiped your mouth with your hand, or your sleeve.

Palta served us in silence. She didn't make eye contact; she didn't stare at our clothes. Her expression never changed. Meanwhile Hypatius kept drinking wine and praising Terra, and Via, and Hieron—and himself. He was a *viator*, like Affron and Valleia. A viator was a traveler, someone who used Via to go to other worlds; only viators wore those purple robes. It was the most prestigious role in the entire priesthood of Terra; only the most talented, most dedicated people became viators. They were the ones who brought back wisdom from other worlds, and tried to provide wisdom to those worlds in turn, like Affron with his sermons. But Hypatius thought the role had outlived its usefulness. "We have the wisdom we need," he said. "Better to stay here on Terra and implement that wisdom. That is what I have chosen to do. And, of course, traveling to other worlds is not without its risks. Some viators never return from their journeys, alas. And that is such a waste of talented people."

He then started talking about his important role in overseeing trade regulations or something. I couldn't follow any of it. Maybe it was me, or maybe it was him—after a while he sounded pretty drunk. When Palta came to take away the nuts he pulled her down onto the couch next to him and patted her thigh. "Palta is a good girl," he said to us. "But quiet." He turned to her. "You should make some noise once in a while, my little sparrow."

Palta removed his hand from her thigh, stood up, and left the room without saying a word. Hypatius sighed. "So young," he murmured. "So..." he didn't finish the sentence. He got to his feet and stood unsteadily by the couch. "Nothing to be done," he muttered. "But I must show you your cubiculum. Bedroom, as you say in English. It has only one bed, but I hope it will suffice." He bellowed something to Palta, and she returned with a lamp. He led us back out into the atrium, then into a small, plain room with nothing in it but a bed and a low table. "Very nice," he murmured, "very nice. Toilet across the atrium over there," he said, waving his hand vaguely.

He left the lamp on the table, then staggered out of the cubiculum and into another room towards the front of the house. We could hear him muttering to himself as he went.

Carmody and I stood there, listening to him.

"Well," Carmody said finally. "We meet again, Larry."

"Why did Valleia want you here?" I asked.

He shrugged. "She found me while looking for you—I'm not sure how. At first she thought I could help persuade you to come here to Terra—you're the person Affron wanted. That wasn't likely, I explained to her. But I also explained to her about my other problem."

"You were stuck in my world, once the portal disappeared."

"Indeed. I was living in a cheap motel in the next town over from Glanbury, working as a laborer and cursing my decision to use the portal."

"Did she offer to take you back to your world?"

"She suggested that it might be possible. What did I have to lose? But you, Larry—you had a lot to lose. You were home with your family, weren't you? Safe and sound, at last. Why are you here?"

Why? I couldn't begin to explain it. "I guess I wanted to help Affron," I said.

Carmody shook his head. "That can't be all, can it? I expect you were bored, after all your adventures in my world. You wanted something more than your ordinary life, something different."

"I suppose it's something like that."

"I fear you've gotten more than you bargained for."

"You, too."

"Yes, perhaps."

Carmody went off to use the toilet, and I thought about what he had said. Had I been bored? Maybe, just a little. But that wasn't it; that wasn't why I had stepped back into the portal. Was it?

Carmody came back a few minutes later. "Indoor plumbing was certainly one advantage of your world compared to mine, Larry," he said. "I'm pleased to see Terra has it as well."

"I kind of got used to chamber pots and outhouses."

"Well, in your world I got used to flushing toilets and hot showers."

I went to the bathroom myself, and it made me homesick. No light switch; no shower stall; no toothbrushes. Instead I saw a couple of gross little statues of a naked man and woman. As I crossed the atrium I heard activity from a room at the back of the house; it was Palta cleaning up, I supposed. Back in our cubiculum, Carmody had found a thin blanket that he he'd placed over the bed. He was sitting on the edge of the bed and taking off his running shoes.

"What do you think will happen to us?" I asked.

"I haven't the slightest idea. I'm worried about Valleia—and Affron, I suppose. She explained a bit about the turmoil here. This man Hypatius seems eager to minimize it, but it's serious. It turns out there are weapons here—very powerful weapons—and Tirelius and his followers want to use them to expand the priests' empire to cover all of Terra. Valleia, Affron, and others are opposed to this. And that seems to be the reason Affron was put on trial."

"That doesn't sound like what Hieron wanted."

"No, it doesn't. But we seem to be on the losing side at the moment. Which may make it difficult for us to get back home."

Carmody got into bed. I took my shoes and pants off. I felt my cell phone in my pants and took it out. I tried calling home—and how stupid was that? Nothing happened. Here my phone was just a hunk of metal and plastic.

I got into bed next to him. The mattress and pillow were thin. But I was used to that sort of thing from Carmody's world. I was used to sharing a bed with someone. I was used to a lot of things that a kid from Glanbury shouldn't have been used to.

We talked a while longer, and then I turned off the lamp. After a while I heard Carmody starting to snore, but I couldn't get to sleep. The noise from the kitchen had stopped. Back home, was Matthew asleep? How had Cassie's rehearsal gone? What was Kevin doing? And Vinnie Polkinghorne, and Nora Lally, and Stinky Glover, and all the other people I knew in Glanbury?

Were they worried about me? Did they miss me?

Somehow I didn't feel the same sense of...desolation that I had felt that first night with Kevin when we were in Carmody's world, stuck in a refugee camp in Boston and then later in a jail. *You wanted something more than your ordinary life, something different.* I thought about that dizziness I had felt sitting on the ground with Valleia as I tried to make up my mind whether to leave with her. It was as if my mind had actually gone away someplace on its own—somewhere out into the multiverse—and found it hard to come back.

I loved my family.

But here I was.

I must have fallen asleep eventually, because I had the sense of waking up and wondering where I was, what was going on.

Then I remembered about Terra, and Valleia, and Carmody lying on the other side of the bed, and my heart sank.

Something else was different, I realized. And then I understood what it was.

A figure was standing silently in the doorway to our room, staring in at us.

It was Palta.

I sat up in bed, my heart pounding, and stared back at her.

"Whatever you do," she whispered in English, "do not trust Hypatius."

And then she disappeared.

CHAPTER 5

I fell back asleep then, and when I awoke it was daylight, and I was alone in the bed. I got up and found Carmody and Hypatius in the dining room, eating breakfast.

"Ah, there you are," Hypatius said. "Salve! *Good day*, that is. You are just in time." He gestured for me to sit down. His eyes were bloodshot, but otherwise he seemed okay after all the drinking he'd done the night before. "Eat," he said, gesturing at the fruit and cheese and bread. "And then we go to the baths."

I looked at Carmody. He shrugged.

"We shall have to see about new clothes for you," Hypatius went on. "We'll visit a shop after we bathe."

"Can't we wear our own clothes until we find out if they'll let us go home?" I asked.

"No, no, that is not possible. These clothes—" he gestured at us—"so confusing. Not for the priests who understand about Via—they will find you unusual, but not inexplicable. Is *inexplicable* the right word? But ordinary people—those who live in outer Urbis, for example—they think of Via simply as a source of wisdom from the gods. They wouldn't know how to make sense of you."

"Why don't you tell people the truth?"

Hypatius sighed. "It is much simpler this way, you see. For everyone."

"*We* could just tell people the truth," I pointed out. "Carmody and me."

"They wouldn't believe you. They'd rather think you came to Urbis from Barbarica."

"What's Barbarica?"

"Oh, I beg your pardon, the lands beyond the Roman empire."

"Where barbarians come from," Carmody said.

"Precisely."

We ate breakfast. I missed drinking orange juice—just like I had in Carmody's world. But otherwise the food was great. I wondered if Palta had risen early to bake the bread, or had she bought it somewhere?

Soon we got up and prepared to leave. While Hypatius was in the bathroom I looked into the kitchen. It was a small room with an open hearth in one corner and a sink in another. Palta was sitting at a table in the middle of the room, chopping a carrot. She stared at me and said nothing.

"What did you mean last night—about Hypatius?" I asked.

Her eyes moved towards the bathroom, and then back to me. She didn't reply. Finally I turned away.

So we left her in the house and walked to the baths, which were in a large, ornate building just off the central plaza of the castellum; the central plaza was called a forum, according to Hypatius. I had heard of the Roman Forum in World History, but apparently every neighborhood had its own forum.

At the baths we went first to a changing room, where we got out of our clothes and wrapped towels around ourselves. From there we entered a room sort of like a sauna, where everyone sat on benches and relaxed. On the walls were frescoes of people having sex; I tried not to stare at them, but I caught myself looking at them more than once. Hypatius greeted everyone and gestured at us, presumably explaining who we were. Then he sat down and chatted with his neighbors.

"There were public baths like this in ancient Rome," Carmody said to me. "Everyone used them."

I tried to remember more of what I'd learned about Rome in World History. Julius Caesar, gladiators, aqueducts, roads…not much. "Did they have all these dirty pictures and statues in ancient Rome?"

"I believe they did, Larry. Sexual practices were far different back then."

I didn't know whether I liked that or not.

After a few minutes Hypatius led us into an even hotter room, more like a steam bath. "So refreshing," he murmured, closing his eyes.

And it was. After that we went into a room where I got the first massage of my life, and from there into a large open-air pool. No one was swimming, though; they just stood around and talked while musicians played in the corner. Again, the music sounded weird—like the harmonies weren't quite right. Finally we got out, dried ourselves, and returned to the changing room. "Now we can face the day," Hypatius said. "Come, then, and we will dress you suitably."

We walked to the forum and entered a shop with a sign above it that said *Vestimenta.* Inside, a little man with a fringe of gray hair bowed deeply to Hypatius from behind the counter and gave us the usual puzzled look. Hypatius spoke to him and gestured to us, and he came out from behind the counter to measure us. Then he went into the back room of his shop.

"I told him that you are newly arrived from Barbarica," Hypatius explained, "and you need new robes—you need to look like normal Romans."

While we waited, Carmody asked, "Why does Barbarica still exist? Why don't the priests take it over, the way they took over the Roman empire?"

Hypatius shook his head. "That's a complicated question, you see, and one on which there is much disagreement. There are limits to communication in a world without the wondrous inventions Larry talks about. This makes control difficult over long distances. We could rule those far-off places if we chose, but it would be quite difficult."

"What if people in Barbarica come up with those inventions?" Carmody asked. "What if they invent guns in China and invade your empire?"

Hypatius waved the question away. "We have our ways of ensuring that such things don't happen. The barbarians all fear us, even if we do not rule them. They know when they go too far."

The shopkeeper came out of the back room then with an armful of robes and sandals. The robes were plain dark brown and made of cotton, I think. We tried them on right there. My robe and sandals fit well enough, although I felt like I was wearing a costume.

Hypatius nodded his approval when we were done. "That is much better," he said.

"Do the color of the robes signify anything?" Carmody asked.

Hypatius shook his head. "Some colors are reserved, like the purple of the viator. But these robes are suitable for anyone."

"We can keep our regular clothes, right?" I asked. "For when we go back home."

"If you must," he sighed.

He said something to the shopkeeper, who provided us with a satchel into which Carmody and I put all the clothes from my world. "I trust I'll never have to wear those things again," Carmody muttered.

"Didn't you become a Patriots fan?" I asked, pointing to his sweatshirt.

"I couldn't begin to understand the game they played," he replied. "I bought that at a used clothing shop because it was cheap. People in your world have far too many clothes."

Hypatius gave the shopkeeper some coins. The man bowed deeply to all of us, and we left his shop. "Now I must go to the palatium," Hypatius said. "I will return for dinner this evening. Till then you are welcome to do whatever you like in Urbis. Do you know the route back to my house?"

Carmody nodded. That was a good thing, because I had no idea.

"Fine, fine. Palta will prepare your lunch—if she is at home. I fear that she likes to disappear during the day when I'm not there. Doing what, I have no idea. She's a troublesome little sparrow, but quite lovely."

Then he walked away, signaling to a carriage driver. That left Carmody and me on our own. We sat on a bench at the edge of the forum and stared in silence for a while at a fountain where water jetted up through a statue of naked boys.

I thought about home. The search parties would definitely be out now. My photo would be on the news. My mother would be a wreck. She'd be blaming herself—she should never have left me out of her sight. What would Kevin say? Would he tell anyone about the portal? They wouldn't believe him if he did. And if I didn't return, there would be no relief for my family, no answer to the mystery. Ever.

And it was all my fault. What was the matter with me?

But also: why was Valleia so surprised when I told her I had returned home at the instant I left. Why didn't she not want me to talk about that at Affron's trial? If I had done it once, why couldn't I do it again? Or was that an example of Affron's "magic"?

I had no idea. I glanced at Carmody. Lieutenant William Carmody, soldier in the army of the United States of New England. Key aide in the nation's successful war against the forces of Canada and New Portugal. I didn't like him very much. But I didn't really dislike him either. He had taken care of Kevin and me when we first arrived in his world, but he had also used us. And now he was my only friend here on Terra.

I realized I didn't know much about him. Was he married? Had he left behind a wife and kids? Did he miss his friends?

"Very strange, eh, Larry?" he said. "To be in this world, wearing these clothes?"

"Yeah," I agreed.

"Do you want to explore Urbis?"

"Not particularly."

"I suppose I could start teaching you Latin, although I might get a lot wrong."

"I don't want to learn Latin."

Carmody sighed and then pointed. "Look," he said, "we can see the temple from here."

I looked where he was pointing, and he was right. The temple of Via loomed above us on a hill in the distance. The portal was so close—maybe a couple of miles away. But soldiers were guarding it, and even if we managed to use it, we had no idea where it would take us. I really didn't want to end up in some totally different universe. Maybe I'd have to learn Chinese. Maybe I'd have to deal with dinosaurs.

We fell silent. Finally Carmody stood up. "We can't sit here all day," he said. "Let's go."

He started walking, and I followed, carrying the satchel with our old clothes in it. My sandals seemed a little too big for me, but they were comfortable enough. Carmody led us directly to Hypatius's house. It was empty; Palta wasn't there. "What do you think Palta's story is?" I asked Carmody.

"She's likely just a servant," he said. "But I wonder, are viators celibate? Do they take wives and husbands? Do they have children?"

"Palta's too young to be Hypatius's wife," I pointed out. "She's my age Also, she knows how to speak English." I told him what she had said to me in the middle of the night.

Carmody nodded. "Yes, I think it's wise not to trust Hypatius. Or anyone, really."

We spent the day in the viator's house. It really was small, compared to our house in Glanbury. And there wasn't much *stuff*. Very little furniture except for tables, no closets filled with clothes, only a few books—and they were hand-lettered. Didn't they even have printing presses here?

I looked into Palta's room, though I didn't go inside. It was a tiny cubiculum next to the kitchen. One brown robe hung on a hook; a hairbrush lay on a table next to her narrow bed. And that was it.

I spent most of the day just sitting in the atrium. When we got hungry, Carmody and I ate some cheese and fruit we found in the kitchen. He went out exploring after that, but I didn't go with him. Later in the afternoon Palta returned, carrying a satchel filled with food. She stared at my new outfit, but she didn't say anything. Instead she silently went into the kitchen and set to work making dinner. Carmody came back next. "I watched the soldiers drilling," he said. "They use swords and lances. If they have special weapons, I didn't notice any."

I shrugged. "Maybe they just use them for special occasions."

He slumped down in a chair. "It's folly," he replied.

Hypatius arrived a while later. He looked upset. He nodded to us and then called out towards the kitchen: "Vinum!" Then he sat down and folded his arms.

Palta came in after a couple of minutes with the tray filled with jugs and cups, as she had the night before. But it wasn't fast enough for Hypatius, apparently. He spoke to her viciously as she set the tray down next to her and slapped her face.

I tensed, ready to jump up and defend her if he did it again. But he didn't. Palta silently bowed and went back to the kitchen.

"My apologies," Hypatius said. "Palta is insufficiently trained, and sometimes rather insolent. Please, have some wine."

He poured the wine and water into cups and handed us each one. "To Via!" he intoned, and then he downed his drink in one quick gulp.

"Is everything all right?" Carmody asked quietly, taking a sip from his cup.

Hypatius rubbed his cheek and poured himself some more wine. "Ruling our empire is a complicated business," he replied. "One must make many difficult decisions. I don't envy the pontifex."

"What does that mean?"

Hypatius simply shrugged. "So much to be done," he murmured. "Very difficult decisions." And he drank his second cup of wine.

The evening went like that. The food was delicious, but I wasn't hungry. Palta served it in silence and didn't make eye contact with anyone. Hypatius had little to say—he was more interested in the wine than in us. He stumbled off to bed before Palta brought us dessert, and I was glad to see him go.

"I wonder what's up with him," I said.

"I never quite understood that idiom when I heard it in your world," Carmody replied, "but yes, his behavior was unexpected. And I have no idea why."

"I don't like the way he treats Palta," I said.

"Nor do I."

When she returned to take away the plate of nuts and fruit, Carmody spoke to her in Latin. Palta stared at him for a moment, and then muttered something quickly and returned to the kitchen.

"What did she say?" I asked.

"*Hypatius diabolus est*," Carmody replied. "Hypatius is the devil."

"Oh. That seems about right."

"Indeed."

There didn't seem to be much to talk about then, so after a while Carmody and I went to our cubiculum. As before, he got to sleep before I did. I listened to him snoring, and Hypatius snoring in his room off the atrium, and Palta finishing up her work in the kitchen. And again a wave of homesickness came over me. I shouldn't be here, wearing this stupid robe, lying in this uncomfortable bed.

Like the night before, I must have fallen asleep eventually. And like the night before, I awoke to see someone standing in the doorway.

But this time it wasn't Palta staring at me. This time it was Gratius, and he was holding a gun.

CHAPTER 6

"**D**on't be afraid," he whispered. "We must rescue Affron and Valleia."

I poked Carmody, who was instantly awake.

Gratius repeated what he had said. He motioned with the gun. "We must go. Now."

"Where are they?" Carmody asked him.

"In prison. In the palatium. Come."

"I suggest we obey him, Larry," Carmody said. "What have we got to lose?"

We quickly got out of bed and put on our sandals. In the moonlight coming in through our small window I got a better look at the gun. It was strange—the shape wasn't quite right. It didn't seem to have a trigger, and the barrel was a little too thin. And the metal glowed a soft blue in the moonlight.

Was this the weapon Valleia had told Carmody about?

When we had our sandals on, Gratius led us out into the atrium.

…just in time to see a lamp come on in Hypatius's cubiculum. He appeared in the doorway a moment later. His hair was messy; his robe was rumpled; his eyes were bloodshot. He set the lamp down on a table in the atrium and stared at Gratius—stared at the gun.

"Oh dear," he said. "Oh my."

He and Gratius started talking to each other in Latin. Gratius gestured with the gun; Hypatius shook his head.

"I forbid it, my friend," Hypatius said finally in English. "It cannot be done. It isn't right. I know that this business with Affron is not proceeding the way you would like, but you will destroy us all."

It was at this point that I noticed Palta, her arms folded, standing in the shadows of the atrium just outside her cubiculum. Gratius had his back to her, and Hypatius didn't notice her because Gratius was in the way. She was listening intently to their conversation.

And then she started walking slowly forward, towards Gratius.

I stared at her. Should I say something? Should I try to stop her? She glanced at me, and then looked back towards Gratius.

She was staring at the gun in his hand. In her own hand was a small knife.

The argument between Gratius and Hypatius lapsed back into Latin and continued. Gratius looked upset. Hypatius looked frightened. Gratius began to speak…

And then Palta leaped forward and stabbed his hand. Gratius yelped in pain and dropped the gun. She grabbed it and scampered back away from him, brandishing it at us. She said something to Gratius and motioned to him to move aside. He did as he was told.

She aimed the gun at Hypatius.

Hypatius extended his hands and spoke to her in Latin— gently, as if explaining to her the mistake she was making. His face was sweating; his hands were shaking.

"Diabolus," she hissed. And then there was a brief low hum, an even briefer flash of light from the barrel of the gun, which turned a deep blue. Hypatius's body glowed a brilliant white for a moment, hands outstretched, mouth open to reply….

And then his body disappeared.

There was a bitter smell in the air. On the tiled floor of the atrium where Hypatius had stood was a small heap of ashes.

He was gone. Totally gone.

We all stared at Palta. Gratius slumped into a chair. Palta placed the gun down on a table next to him and went into the kitchen. She returned with a narrow strip of wet cloth. He looked up at her and fumbled for the gun. She bowed and offered the cloth to him. Finally he put the gun down and held out his injured hand to her, and she wrapped the cloth around it.

"That weapon is not like anything from your world, is it, Larry?" Carmody murmured to me.

"I've never seen anything like it."

"Palta says Gratius can kill her if he likes, but she did what she had to do," Carmody went on. "Now she wants to come with us to rescue Affron. Apparently Affron and Valleia are both going to be executed at sunrise."

"Executed?" I said. "Is that what Gratius and Hypatius were talking about?"

"Yes. I didn't understand all of the conversation, but as you heard, Hypatius was trying to persuade Gratius not to involve himself in this."

Palta had wrapped the cloth around Gratius's hand, and now she was kneeling next to him, waiting.

"Why did you do that?" Gratius demanded in English.

"Why were you arguing with him?" Palta replied. "Do you think you could have left him alive? Do you think he wouldn't have done everything he could to stop you?"

"No, I suppose not. But that isn't why you killed him."

"No," she admitted. "It isn't."

Gratius sighed and stood up. "Very well," he said. "We have no time to waste." He picked up the gun in his left hand and motioned for Palta to rise.

"What is the plan?" Carmody asked.

"When Valleia and I talked before the trial," Gratius said, "we agreed that if Affron were sentenced to death, we would try to rescue him. And save you two, if Tirelius wouldn't let you go home. We did not expect that Valleia herself would be imprisoned. I think now perhaps our plan should be that we all use Via to leave this world. It is the only way we can ensure Affron's safety."

"How do we help?"

Gratius shook his head. "I think your help will not be necessary." He looked down at his gun. "It is not a good thing to use such a weapon. But now we have no choice."

Palta went and put out the lamp, and then we all left Hypatius's house. And we left his ashes behind. I wondered briefly if we should do something about those ashes, but no one seemed interested. And I wondered why Palta had killed Hypatius. But I guess I knew. I remembered how disgusting it was when he had pulled her down onto his lap. How would he act when there was no one else around?

The night was cool and silent. All the houses around us were dark. Gratius led us in the opposite direction from the main road, into thin woods beyond the castellum. My mind was filled with the image of Hypatius just…disappearing. Alive one second, a small heap of ashes the next. Like in a video game, only real. I could still see the pleading look on his face. I could still smell the bitter odor in the air afterwards. What kind of gun was that?

I sneaked a glance at Palta as we walked. If she was upset about killing Hypatius, she didn't show it.

I tried not to think about his death. Instead I thought: once Gratius rescued Affron and Valleia, we were going home. That was the plan, right? Would it really happen? That meant I'd show up in a robe and sandals. Well, so what? I'd be home. My parents wouldn't care about what I was wearing; they wouldn't care about the explanation. They'd only care that I was safe. I hadn't known that before I went to Carmody's world and learned something about the love parents feel for their children; I knew it now.

We kept walking. I could make out the temple of Via on a hill in the distance. Buildings loomed off to our left. I stopped thinking about home and started thinking about what was about to happen. How far away was the palatium? How dangerous would it be to rescue Valleia and Affron? Were they locked in cells? How many people would we—would Gratius—have to kill to get them out?

Did the guards have these strange guns too?

I noticed that Palta was walking beside me. "Are you all right?" I asked.

She nodded.

"You're not from here—from Terra."

She shook her head.

"Shhh," Gratius said, waving at me to be quiet.

I stopped talking. And then the palatium loomed ahead of us. We were walking towards it at an angle; only a large park separated us from it. A few dim lights shone in random windows, but mostly the huge, long building was dark.

Gratius took us around to the side of the palatium, onto a narrow path between it and another building. Then he led us down a set of stairs that led to a door. He opened the door, and we went inside.

We were standing in a long corridor. In the distance a torch or lamp was burning. Gratius waited a moment while our eyes got used to the dim light, and then he led us quickly down the fresco-lined corridor towards the light.

The light came from a torch flickering in a bracket on the wall next to another door. Gratius opened the door, and we walked down a flight of stairs. Now we were in a cold and featureless passageway, without the tapestries and statues and frescoes of the upper floors. Gratius paused, as if he was uncertain which way to go. Finally he headed left, and we kept going until we reached a large pair of metal doors. Gratius paused again, and this time I got the sense that he was gathering up his courage.

Finally he whispered, "Stay here. Away from the doors."

We moved to the side. Finally Gratius twisted the knob, opened one of the doors, and strode through.

We waited. I heard voices being raised, sounds of an argument. And then silence. After a moment Gratius opened the door. He had the gun in one hand, a ring of keys in the other. I could smell the bitter odor I had smelled after Palta killed Hypatius.

Gratius led us inside. We were in a cold, bare room with a table at the far end of it. A lamp and playing cards of some sort sat on the table. Next to the table were two small piles of ashes.

I glanced at Gratius. He was sweating, despite the coldness of the room. "Quick," he said. He motioned to Carmody to pick up the lamp. Then we went through another door and into a small, foul-smelling passageway, with prison cells on each side; each had a metal door with a small barred window at eye height. Gratius looked into a couple of them and then whispered, "Salve, Valleia."

He fumbled with the keys until he found one that fit. He opened the door, and inside Valleia was standing up, wide awake, still wearing her purple robe from the last time I'd seen her, when the guards dragged her away after Affron's trial. Gratius went inside, and the rest of us stayed in the passageway. He and Valleia embraced and had a brief conversation. Then she came out of the cell with him.

She touched Carmody on the arm in the narrow passageway, which I thought was odd. Then she bowed to me and Palta. She gave Palta an odd look, as if unsure why she was there. "Welcome, all," she said in English. "Now let us save Affron."

He was in the last cell on the right along the passageway. Gratius handed Valleia the keys while he held the gun. She found the right one, opened the door, and went inside.

We waited. I caught a glimpse of her kneeling beside Affron's hard-looking cot, talking urgently to him. Finally she led him out of his cell.

He looked worse than he had at the trial—gaunt and tired and a bit confused. "So nice of you to come," he murmured. And he put a hand on my shoulder and stared at me with those glittering eyes of his. "You look very odd in that robe, Larry," he murmured.

Then Palta prostrated herself on the damp floor in front of Affron. Why did she do that? With some difficulty Affron bent over and brought her to her feet. He smiled and whispered something to her. And then he said to

Valleia and Gratius, "I do not understand the plan."

"We must leave Terra," Valleia said. "Anything else is too risky."

Affron sighed. "I suppose you're right. But I fear the gods will not look with favor on this plan."

"The gods are not interested in us, or our plan. Let's go."

We headed back down the passageway to the room where the guards had been playing cards until a few minutes ago. Affron smelled the air, looked at the piles of ashes on the floor, and sighed. "This is not good," he said. "Why do we struggle against Tirelius, if we turn into him?"

"It had to be done to save you," Valleia replied.

"Nothing has to be done."

She looked a bit exasperated.

Gratius motioned with his good hand that we had to hurry.

We went through the doors and back out into the main passageway, then up the stairs. Valleia led the way, carrying the lamp. Affron could barely keep up; I grabbed one of his arms and Palta grabbed the other as we climbed the stairs. "Sorry," he muttered. "Not a lot of exercise lately."

But we made it, then hurried along the corridor that led to door we had used to enter the palatium. Valleia left the lamp there in the corridor, and we went back outside and up the steps to the narrow path between buildings.

But something was different.

We heard noise now. Shouted orders. Marching feet.

We crept along the side of the palatium, then looked out at the forum and beyond, at the temple of Via.

A scaffold had been erected in the forum. Behind it, soldiers were arrayed all along the steps of the temple. A man on horseback holding a torch was supervising the arrival of more troops.

The place was getting ready for the executions.

"Too late," Gratius murmured. "I'm sorry."

We retreated back along the path, down the steps, and into the palatium. We all looked at each other.

"We could circle around by the schola," Valleia suggested. "Use the side entrance to the temple."

"All the entrances will be guarded," Gratius said. "Tirelius will take no chances."

"Then we can kill the guards."

Everyone turned to Affron. He slowly shook his head. "I cannot do it," he said. "We should not have killed those guards. It isn't right."

My heart sank.

"We must save you," Valleia insisted.

"Not like that."

"Then don't leave Terra," Gratius said. "We have been waiting to start the revolution. Let's start it tonight. We can go to the armamentarium. The guards have only swords—this is known; they scarcely know what they are guarding. And we have a gant. I know we may end up killing people, but how else are we to succeed? I risked my life to obtain this gant. We seize the other gants that are there, arm your followers, and take over Urbis. Tonight."

Gant? Was that what they called Gratius's weapon?

Again we looked at Affron.

And tears leaked out of his eyes and coursed down his cheeks. "I cannot," he said. "I'm tired. You need a better leader."

"There is no one else," Valleia said. "You know that."

He shook his head. "Not me. Not now."

"What are we to do, then?" Valleia exclaimed. "The scaffold is for *us*, Affron. You don't like death. Do you want us to die? Gratius? These children?"

"We can escape," he replied. "Leave Urbis. Make our way to Roma. There we can disappear among the masses, or find a ship that will take us to Barbarica."

"Tirelius will track us down and kill us," she replied. "You know he will."

"His reach doesn't extend as far as you think. We can survive."

"But how do we get out of Urbis?" Valleia demanded. "How do we get to Roma? In an hour or less Tirelius will know we have escaped, and then nowhere in Urbis will be safe for us."

Affron turned his gaze to Palta.

"I can get us from Urbis," she said quietly. "I know how to do this."

"What do you mean?" Valleia asked.

"Palta likes to explore," Affron explained. "She probably knows more about Urbis than we do."

How did Affron know about Palta? Why had she prostrated herself in front of him in the jail cell?

"Are you sure?" Valleia asked Palta. "How do we do it?"

"There is tunnel," Palta replied. Her English didn't seem quite right, I noticed.

"The Egorinthine tunnel? That's just a legend."

Palta shook her head. "It is deep below us. It leads beyond the walls."

"How do you know that?"

"I found it. I walked its length. I came out of tunnel and saw walls of Urbis—from outside. Come."

Valleia folded her arms and looked at Affron; she didn't seem convinced.

"If we're going, we need to go now," Carmody said.

"All right," she replied. "It seems to be our only choice."

But Gratius raised his bandaged hand. "I will stay," he said. "You will need a friend in Urbis."

"Will Tirelius know you helped us?" Valleia asked him.

"No. Perhaps he will suspect. But he won't be able to prove anything. Hypatius is dead, by the way." Gratius gave Palta a look.

"All right, then. We are very grateful to you, Gratius."

He and Valleia talked for a moment in Latin. He took out some coins out of a pocket and gave them to her. And then he handed her the gant.

They grasped each other's forearms. Then Gratius bowed deeply to Affron, and nodded to each of us. "We will meet again," he said. And he walked quickly out of the palatium.

"You have many friends," Valleia murmured to Affron, gesturing to Gratius as he departed.

"I am grateful to all of you."

He nodded to Palta. She picked up the lamp Valleia had left there and motioned to us to follow her.

She led us along the corridor, then through a door and down a flight of stairs. And another flight of stairs, and another. The air was cold and smelled musty. Palta opened a large wooden door, and we seemed to be in a storage room of some sort. We made our way past broken tools, wooden crates filled with dishes, statues and rolled-up tapestries, spare cart wheels.... The place reminded me of the basement of our house in Glanbury, only way bigger. A mouse skittered past my feet, which made me jump. I wondered what other creatures lived down here.

Also, I was cold and tired and scared and depressed. Home had seemed close for a while, and now it was further off with every step we took away from the portal. Now we had killed people, and soldiers were about to start chasing us. Maybe they were already chasing us. Before I had seemed to be a kind of guest on Terra; now I was an enemy.

Finally Palta stopped and held up the lamp for us. "Here," she said.

I didn't see anything.

She got down on her knees, pushed a box out of the way, and pulled on a small iron ring. The ring was attached to a square door, which opened with a creak. She shone the lamp into the opening—we could make out a ladder descending into the darkness below. The air now smelled damp and earthy. Palta handed the lamp to Carmody and scrambled down the ladder. Then she called up to us. "Come!"

Valleia went next, then Affron, then me. It was scary descending the ladder into darkness, but hands grabbed me after about a dozen rungs, and I landed safely on the ground. Finally Carmody came down, holding the lamp and closing the door behind him.

We started walking. The tunnel was damp, narrow, and muddy; water seeped up through the ancient cobblestones and down through cracks in the ancient walls. Rats scurried away from us whenever the lamp's light reached them. As we walked, Valleia explained briefly to Carmody and me where we were. "Hieron discovered Via on the outskirts of Roma. As Via became famous, the city grew out towards it. That's when they built Urbis and put up walls around it, closing off Via—and its priests—from the public. The great pontifex Egorinthus didn't like this; he had this tunnel built so that he could sneak out at night and listen to what ordinary Roman people had to say. It was his way of ensuring that he got accurate information from his advisers. After Egorinthus, the priests decided that Roma should not be so close to Urbis, so they tore down the new neighborhoods that had been growing up around it and moved the people elsewhere. The tunnel was no longer needed, and eventually it was forgotten."

"So are we in, like, Italy?" I asked.

"That's what it would be called in your world, yes."

"I thought the portal—Via—was always in the same place. In my home town. In America."

"No, it can be anywhere. You were just lucky that the portal found you."

I think she was kidding.

We fell silent as we trudged through the tunnel. It seemed to go on forever. I was exhausted. The air was stale and hard to breathe. I had lost all track of time. I really needed to pee. And meanwhile, Affron was not in good shape. He started to have difficulty walking, and Carmody and I held him up. "Sorry," he whispered.

Then the lamp flickered and died, and we were in utter darkness.

"We can't be far from the end," Valleia said. "The tunnel is starting to slope upwards—did you notice? Move forward slowly and stay together."

We didn't really have much choice. But what if we fell into a pit? What if the tunnel split and we went in the wrong direction? What if we managed to make our way out of the tunnel, and soldiers were waiting for us?

Valleia took out the gant, and its blue light was better than no light at all.

"It will be all right, Larry," Affron whispered to me, as if he could sense my fear from the way I was gripping his arm.

And then Palta said simply, "Ladder."

We stopped. There was some conversation, and we decided that Carmody should go up the ladder first and see what was at the top.

He went up, and we could hear him pushing against something. "It's another door or hatch of some sort," he called down finally. "But I can't move it."

"There is latch," Palta said.

"Ah, yes." Suddenly the hatch opened. I felt a rush of fresh air. Dim light filtered down from an opening above us. Carmody scrambled outside, and then popped his head back into the opening. "It's safe," he whispered, "but make as little noise as you can. We're not far from the city walls."

One by one we ascended the ladder and scrambled out onto the ground. We felt cool air; we saw brightening sky.

And a hundred yards away, the walls of Urbis, looming high above us. I saw torches on the parapets, and cloaked soldiers striding slowly back and forth.

We were on a flat plain outside the city. And if any of those soldiers happened to spot us, we were doomed.

CHAPTER 7

"L et's go," Valleia whispered. "Quickly."

We crouched and ran—even Affron, although Carmody and I still held onto his arms in case he stumbled. At first the ground was flat. Then the terrain gradually got rougher and hillier. I could see the outline of trees in the distance. If we made it to the trees, surely the soldiers on the walls wouldn't be able to see us.

Affron's breathing became harsh and ragged as we started to climb. And then he stumbled and fell.

"Can't go…on," he gasped.

Carmody and I immediately picked him up, and we kept going. Did I hear shouts in the distance? Had the soldiers noticed us? I couldn't tell; I was breathing too hard myself. I didn't know how much more of this I could take. My legs felt like jelly; my bladder felt like it was going to burst. We struggled forward towards the trees, and when we finally made it and the walls were out of sight, we all collapsed on the ground once again.

"They saw us," Valleia said. "At least, they saw something. We need to get down to the river and find a boat. Horsemen could easily have reached the walls by now with news of our escape."

"How far is the river?" Carmody asked.

"Half a mile, perhaps."

"How do we get a boat?"

"That will be the least of our worries." She looked at Affron, still stretched out on the damp ground. "Are you all right?"

"Sorry," he said. "Just...tired."

I wondered if he had been tortured while he was in prison.

I went behind a tree to pee. When I was finished, I noticed Palta squatting nearby, her robe up around her thighs, doing the same thing. She nodded to me; embarrassed, I nodded back and quickly turned away.

"Is everyone ready?" Valleia asked when Palta and I had returned to the group. "Let's go."

We helped Affron up and set out again. I felt better, but not much. The soldiers had seen us. How could we hope to outrun them?

The river, when I finally looked up and saw it, was beautiful, flowing calmly in the pre-dawn light. A few boats bobbed gently on the water or were tied up at the end of docks; on the shore were a few small shacks.

"Do we steal one of those boats?" Carmody asked.

Valleia shook her head. "No need. These people will do whatever a priest tells them to do. One look at my robe will ensure obedience."

We walked up to the first shack. Outside it a man with long, greasy hair and a scraggly gray beard was mending a net by the light of a small oil lamp. Next to him a black cat with yellow eyes glared at us. Near the shack a boat was tied up at the end of a short dock. When the man saw us, he dropped the net, stood up, and bowed deeply. He looked terrified, especially when he noticed Affron, who could barely stand up.

And then he saw Palta, and he became even more agitated. I don't know when it had started, but Palta was standing there, her arms tightly folded, trembling from head to foot. She looked like she was closer to collapsing than Affron. What was going on?

Valleia walked up to the man and started speaking to him rapidly in a commanding tone I hadn't heard her use before—like Hypatius giving orders to Palta. She gestured at the boat at the end of the dock. The man said something back. Valleia repeated what she had said. She took out one of the coins Gratius had given her and tossed it to him. The man caught the coin and bowed again, even more deeply this time. Then he hurried down to the boat.

"I told him we needed to take Affron to Roma for medical care." Valleia murmured to us in English. "And if he doesn't get us there fast enough, we'll blame him." She noticed Palta. "Are you all right?"

Palta said nothing. It looked to me like she couldn't speak.

Valleia shrugged. "Come, then. We cannot delay."

We followed the man down to the boat and got on board. The small vessel rode low in the water with so many of us in it, but it didn't sink. It stank of fish. The man used a pole to push off from the dock and then raised a single square sail. We moved out onto the water, and the current started to take us.

"Keep your heads down," Valleia whispered. "Soldiers are coming."

I took a quick glance, and on the shore I glimpsed torches and men on horseback. I hunkered down in the boat. Would the soldiers spot us? Would they be able to find a boat and overtake us? Would they be waiting in Roma when we arrived?

The bottom of the boat was wet. I was lying next to Palta. Her eyes were squeezed shut, and she was still trembling. What was the matter with her? She buried her face in my chest. That felt nice, but I was too worried to enjoy the feeling. Also, the rocking of the boat was making me a little seasick. I put my arm around her, and gradually her trembling quieted down.

Affron was lying with his head in Valleia's lap. She was gently stroking his hair. Carmody sat next to them with his arms folded. The fisherman stood up while he steered the boat; occasionally he would look down at the five of us and quickly look away, as if merely gazing at viators and their friends was forbidden.

Finally the rocking of the boat must have put me to sleep, because the next thing I knew Carmody was shaking me awake.

I opened my eyes to bright sunlight and seagulls wheeling overhead.

"Roma," Valleia murmured.

PART III

Roma

CHAPTER 8

I knew about as little about Rome's geography as I knew about its history. I remembered that it was the capital of Italy, of course, and Italy was shaped like a boot, but where on the boot was Rome located? No idea. And in any case, I had no idea if the geography of Terra was the same as the geography of my Earth. In the multiverse, there was no reason it should be.

Anyway, now it seemed like I was going to have to live in Roma, in hiding. Maybe for the rest of my life. I couldn't begin to imagine what that might be like.

I looked around. The river was wide and muddy here. Stone walls lined both banks; beyond the walls were hills crowded with buildings. In the distance was a stone bridge across the river. A couple of wagons were crossing the bridge; a few boats were sailing down the river ahead of us. No one seemed to be chasing us.

Palta had fallen asleep and was now leaning against my shoulder. Affron was still sleeping in Valleia's lap. The frightened fisherman sat in the stern, his hand on the tiller.

"Wake up the girl," Valleia murmured to me.

I shook Palta a bit. She opened her gray eyes and looked around. Then she shut them again. "What's the matter?" I asked.

"Water," was all she said; the "w" sounded almost like a "v". Just speaking that single word seemed to take something out of her.

Valleia said something in Latin to the fisherman, who bowed in response but looked puzzled. He steered the boat towards the left bank of the river.

"Just past that bridge there are steps that lead up from the river to the bank," Valleia said to us. "We'll get off the boat there and head into the city. Affron and I need get out of these robes—they are far too conspicuous; that will be our first task. Then we'll have to find a place to stay. That will be more difficult, but we need to get indoors before every soldier in the Roma starts looking for us."

"And what happens after that?" Carmody asked.

Valleia shrugged. "We will rest first and then decide. But we need to take care of Affron."

"Will he be able to walk?" I asked.

She stared down at Affron with concern. "He will have to," she replied. "We can't carry him through the streets."

She bent over and whispered into Affron's ear. He opened his eyes. He looked confused and uncertain for a moment, and then struggled to sit up. "I can make it," he said.

He didn't sound like he could make it.

We passed underneath the bridge finally, and just beyond it were a few steep, narrows steps, just like Valleia said. The fisherman maneuvered the boat up to the bottom of the steps and tied a line to an iron ring next to them. Then he helped each of us out of the boat and onto the steps. When he did this for Valleia, she reached out and laid her hand gently on the top of his head and whispered something to him. The guy looked like he was going to faint from happiness.

We climbed the steps. At the top was a narrow walkway along the river, and past that was a line of trees that paralleled the path. Both stopped at the bridge, which led into a wide road with a few wagons and carts on it. Beyond the trees was another road that intersected the bridge road.

We crossed the path and stood among the trees, which managed to hide us a bit from the traffic.

Valleia said something in Latin to Palta, who was looking a lot better since we were out of the water. They had a brief conversation, after which Valleia handed her some coins. Palta bowed and headed off by herself along the road.

"She will buy us robes and food," Valleia said. "Her Latin is good enough."

"What was the matter with her in the boat?" Carmody asked.

"She's afraid of the water," Valleia replied. "But she won't say why."

Carmody just shook his head. I don't think he was frightened by much of anything.

So we waited for Palta to return. Affron sat down and leaned back against a tree, closing his eyes.

And my fears returned. How could we hide or escape if every soldier in the city was going to be looking for us? What if Valleia decided it would be easier if there was just her and Affron? How much did they care about me or Carmody or Palta?

And even if I wasn't captured, how could I possibly find my way home?

"You really will have to learn Latin now, I'm afraid," Carmody said to me.

And I supposed he was right.

I realized I was hungry, in addition to being worried. What if Palta got lost, or was captured? There was so much to worry about. Finally she returned, carrying a loaf of bread and a package containing two plain pale-gray robes. We made a circle around Valleia and Affron while they changed into the new robes. Then Valleia handed the old ones to me. "Throw them in the river, Larry," she said. "First make sure no one is looking."

So I balled them up and took them across the narrow walkway to the river. A boat was coming out from under the bridge. I waited till it had gone past, and then I tossed the robes into the water and watched them float slowly downstream. Then I returned to the others.

We ate the bread Palta had bought while Valleia outlined the situation and what we had to do. The soldiers would eventually find and interrogate the fisherman and learn where he had dropped us off. So we had to get away from here. We had to find a place where he would have a chance to rest and recover. But we didn't have much money—only the remaining few coins from what Gratius had given her. And Affron wasn't going to be able to travel far.

Affron seemed a little better after resting in the boat, at any rate, but he was clearly still exhausted. Didn't matter, apparently. We headed off onto the streets of Roma. Valleia, Palta, and Affron went first—looking, I guess, like a regular Roman family. Valleia held onto Affron's arm as if she were an affectionate wife, although she was really helping to prop him up in case he stumbled. Palta walked on his other side, holding his hand.

"Ready, Larry?" Carmody asked me.

"Sure."

"No English where we can be overheard, right?"

"Okay."

Carmody and I headed off after the others, hanging back but keeping them in sight. We stayed silent. The narrow cobblestone streets were alive with people. Women walked by with wicker baskets on their heads. Blind and crippled beggars blocked sidewalks holding out bowls with a few coins in them. Occasionally we saw men carrying a curtained litter on their shoulders with what I assumed was some rich person inside. People didn't have to be told to get out of their way. We passed countless food stalls selling fish and sausages being cooked over open fires, and little outdoor markets where you could buy flowers and birds in cages. It was hard to keep Valleia and the others in sight as we made our way through the crowds.

The streets were lined with multistory wooden apartment buildings that looked like they might fall over in a strong wind. We headed uphill at first, and towards the top of the hill the houses got more substantial, and the people were better-dressed. But things deteriorated again, and maybe got worse, when we started down the other side of the hill, further away from the river. Finally Valleia, Affron, and Palta disappeared into one of those large apartment buildings. Carmody and I stood across the narrow street and looked up at it.

On the first floor were a few small shops, including what looked like a bar or tavern. There were four stories above the shops. The building was made out of wood, and some of the planks looked like they were rotting. There were small curtained openings in the walls; no glass windows, no shutters. And no chimney that I could make out, just a hole in the roof. Next to the building, naked, dirty children were playing in a small alley.

I could feel a familiar lump growing in my throat. I remembered my first night in Carmody's world, stuck first in a cold refugee camp and then in a jail cell. That seemed like paradise to me now. Would I ever see my bedroom in Glanbury again? I looked at Carmody. His face showed no emotion. But he murmured a sentence in Latin that I thought I understood. "Hoc est pessimum." *This is very bad.*

Eventually we saw Palta come out of the building and look around for us. When she saw us, she motioned for us to join her.

"Eamus," he said to me. *Let's go.* And we crossed the street and followed Palta inside.

Palta led us into a small courtyard behind the building, then up a narrow, rickety staircase. The interior of the building was dark and smelled of vomit. We passed a couple of men going down—one was missing an eye, the other had a withered arm—and both of them stared at us suspiciously. Palta and Carmody ignored them. She led us up to the fourth floor and opened a door into a dim, hot room. I noticed a couple of low benches, a table, and a few stools; in the corner was a toilet—I was surprised it wasn't a chamber pot. We walked through this main into a small, windowless cubiculum, separated from the main room by a curtain.

In the room, Affron was lying on a narrow bed, and Valleia was kneeling next to him, holding his hand. She looked up at us, and I saw tears on her cheeks. "We must keep Affron alive," she said. "If he dies, then none of this matters."

CHAPTER 9

Carmody went over and put a hand on Valleia's shoulder.

And Palta knelt in front of Affron, with her head touching the floor.

I stood in the doorway and felt lost. I didn't know the language. I didn't know the world. And I didn't know these people, or why they were acting the way they acted.

Finally Affron stirred. "Just need...to rest," he murmured. And then he fell back asleep.

This seemed to rouse Valleia. She rose from her knees and murmured, "Enough." She saw Palta and said, "Girl, we will need supplies for the insula—food, water, wine, candles. Can you do it?"

Palta scrambled to her feet and bowed. She pointed to me—"Can I take Larry?" I liked it that she remembered my name.

"I suppose." Valleia handed her a couple more coins. "Don't waste money. We have little enough. Speak only Latin. And stay away from soldiers."

Palta and I left the apartment—the *insula*, Valleia had called it. The heat was blistering now. I was afraid we'd get lost as we traveled through the narrow, twisty streets, but Palta didn't seem concerned. Nearby we found a small forum with a fountain in the middle, another open-air market at one end, and shops lining the cobblestoned plaza. At the market we bought bread, cheese, figs, olive oil, and a jug of wine, and then went into shops to buy more items; Palta haggled strenuously with everyone. Then we sat on a bench near the fountain; I noticed for the first time that colored flags were flying everywhere. Children splashed in the fountain's water. "Festival is approaching," Palta said. "Some kind of games, I think." I figured we should be getting back, but Palta didn't seem in any hurry. "Affron will not die," she stated.

"Why not?"

"Because he told me he would take care of me."

"Should we be speaking English? Valleia said—"

Palta made a disgusted face. "That woman is no one."

Was she jealous of Valleia? Or did she know something I didn't? Valleia certainly hadn't been very nice to her. I felt nervous about speaking English, but I wanted to learn more about Palta. "Tell me about where you came from."

"It is called *Gaia*," she replied. "It is not happy place. Affron saved my life there and brought me here. I served him until they put him in prison. Then that pig Hypatius took me for his own. I was so happy to kill him."

"How did you know how to use that gun—that *gant*?"

"Because gant comes from Gaia. Gant is why it is not a happy place."

"So you don't want to go home?"

She shook her head. "No. I want to serve Affron, that is all."

"Oh."

We sat in silence for a while, and then Palta asked me about my world. I started describing it, but I got choked up talking about my family and had to stop. She looked at me, and then nodded as if she understood. "Eamus," she murmured.

We bought a jug and filled it with water from the fountain, and then made our way across the forum.

That's when we saw soldiers for the first time. A pair of them were tacking a notice to a large wooden board while a few others stood by. We didn't stop to see what the notice said. Instead, we hurried back to the insula with our purchases.

The apartment felt like an oven, although no one seemed to mind the heat as much as I did. Affron was still asleep. Valleia and Carmody were sitting together in the main room, talking. We told them about the soldiers as we set the food and supplies out on the table.

"We cannot stay here," Valleia said. "It's far too dangerous. In a building like this, everyone knows everyone else's business. But we need more money to go anywhere else."

"Can we steal it?" Carmody asked.

"Perhaps, but I hardly know where, or how."

"We have the gant," he pointed out.

"We could use the gant, of course. But it could draw attention to us."

We heard movement from the bedroom. Affron pulled the curtain back. "Don't use the gant," he said. "I can get the money we need."

Valleia rushed over and hugged him; Palta knelt at his feet. He still looked tired and a little out of it.

"How do you feel?" Carmody asked.

"Hungry," he replied.

We led him over to the table, where he sat while we served him. I noticed that there weren't any couches as there had been in Hypatius's house; apparently ordinary people in places like this just used chairs and benches when they ate. That was fine with me. When we had taken care of Affron, the rest of us sat down and ate with him.

"How can you get money?" Carmody asked Affron finally.

"I shall have to steal it, I'm afraid," Affron said.

"But how?" Valleia pressed him.

Affron made a vague gesture. "Don't worry. There is no risk. But I will do it tomorrow. Today I must rest some more."

Valleia looked like she wanted to press the issue, but she didn't. Instead she said, "If we have money, what shall we do? We could bribe a ship's captain—"

"We should stay in Roma," Affron replied.

"Why? It will be more dangerous for us here than somewhere in Barbarica."

"But it will be easier to defeat Tirelius from here."

Valleia's face brightened. "Do you mean that? Are you ready to fight against Tirelius?"

"I don't see how we can avoid it. We can't run from him forever."

"But how will you do it? How can we defeat him?"

Affron shook his head. "I don't know. I just need some time to recover. I don't even know where we can stay."

Valleia considered. "Here is an idea. The Roman Games are starting soon, yes? Rich families will already be fleeing the city for their villas by the sea. I expect we could rent one of the houses they have vacated. Pretend to be a wealthy family from abroad, here to experience the Games. Such a house will give us privacy, running water, soft beds—it will do until we have a plan."

"Ah," Affron replied. "That is good. Yes, we could do that."

"But such a house won't be cheap," she pointed out.

"You find the house, and I will find the money."

When Affron had finished eating he went back to bed. Palta went in and sat on the floor next to him. Valleia continued to sit at the table, looking worried. Carmody and I went over by the windows, where we could get a breath of air. "Are you all right?" he asked me.

"I'm okay, but I wish I knew what was going on," I replied.

"We'll find out before long, I think."

"You and Valleia…" I began, but I didn't know how to ask my question.

Carmody knew what the question was, though. "We met in a world that wasn't mine, wasn't hers," he said. "But there was an immediate attraction that transcended space and time. Do you think such a thing is possible, Larry?"

"I don't know. I guess so."

Carmody looked at me like I was too young to know what he was talking about. Which I guess I was. "She didn't really have to bring me back here to Terra," he said, "but I am very grateful that she did—even though our circumstances are now less than ideal."

"Things will get better, probably," I said.

"Let us hope so."

No one said much for the rest of the day. When it got dark out, Palta went into the bedroom and lay on the floor next to Affron. Valleia and Carmody lay down together in one corner of the main room, and I got as far away from them as I could, lying down next to the table.

It was too hot and noisy and uncomfortable for me to fall sleep at first. I wished I had a pillow—how could you sleep without a pillow? People were shouting drunkenly at each other in the apartment below. I heard wagons passing by on the street, the distant sound of music.

And then finally a breeze came up and the room started to cool off. I must have fallen asleep finally, because I dreamed I was having one of my typical arguments with Cassie. I couldn't even tell what it was about, just that I was mad at her. I started to stomp out of the room. And then I heard her start crying. She came up and embraced me from behind and sobbed, "Don't ever leave us, Larry. Don't ever leave."

And then the dream turned into something different, and I could *feel* the embrace. And I could feel the hard floor beneath my side as I lay on it. I was awake. It was still dark, and the room was silent except for the sounds of people breathing. I turned my head, and I saw Palta, snuggled up to me, fast asleep.

It felt good, the way her head on my chest had felt good in the boat. But why was she here beside me? Why wasn't she back on the floor next to Affron?

I forgot about Palta, though, when I noticed something else. Affron was sitting cross-legged in front of the small windows. He was making strange motions with his hands in the air, like he was trying to describe something, or he was conducting an orchestra, or doing those Chinese exercises I saw people doing once on the common in Glanbury.

I sat up, and he must have heard me, because he put his hands down and, without turning around, he murmured, "I'm sorry you're in this mess, Larry. When I left you before, I thought you'd be safe."

"I was safe," I replied, keeping my voice low. "But Valleia said you needed my help."

"Valleia worries about me a great deal. But I am grateful to you for coming as you did. And I will do my best to make sure you're able to return to your world."

"Something happened back in my world," I said. "Valleia told me not to talk about it to anyone, especially at your trial. When I returned home that final time in the portal, it was at the exact moment I left. I think maybe that also happened the first time I used the portal, although I'm not so sure about that. But anyway Valleia said that's impossible. Time passes at the same rate in every universe, or something like that."

While I was saying this Affron turned around so he was facing me. "That's very interesting," he said.

"Did you set up the portal to do that?" I asked. "I mean, it sure saved me a lot of explaining when I got back home."

"No, no—I wasn't responsible for that."

"Then what happened?"

"I have no idea, Larry. But I remember seeing you that first time…in a world not terribly different from your own."

"The Burger Queen world."

"Is that how you think of it? Yes, that world. And…you stood out."

"I was dressed funny—for that world, anyway."

"Yes, but it wasn't how you were dressed. You were different. That's why I asked Valleia to bring you here. I didn't really think you could help me at the trial. And it turns out I was right."

I didn't know how I felt about that. I liked the idea of being different; but I didn't feel different. "Do you think I could do it again?" I asked him. "Go back home the instant I left? That would be so much better for my family, for me, for everyone. A lot less explaining to do, a lot less worry for everyone."

"Yes, I understand. All I can say is—if it happened once, it can happen again."

That gave me some hope, although it was still very puzzling. I asked another question. "Hypatius says people think you've visited the world of the gods—the gods who created Via. Have you?"

"People think a lot of things about me, apparently. But no, I haven't visited the gods. I don't really know if there are such beings."

"But when I talked to you in that church—back in Carmody's world—you said that some, you know, advanced race created the portal and then disappeared."

"Yes, I did say that. But it's just a theory that many of the priests have. And now I wonder—I wonder if that theory is correct."

"Why? And why do people think you've been visited by the gods, if you haven't?"

Affron sighed. "Too many questions, Larry, too late at night. I will show you something tomorrow that may help you understand. When we go to steal the money. Now let's get back to sleep."

He stood up and returned to the bedroom. I lay back down on the floor, snuggled up to Palta, and tried to do as I was told. But it was hard. What was he going to show me? And he had said: *When* we *go to steal the money.* Did that mean I was going with him? Why?

And what had he been doing in front of the windows?

I fell asleep finally, and when I awoke it was daytime, and Palta was no longer by my side.

CHAPTER 10

Everyone else was already awake. Palta had gone to buy food. When she returned, we sat down to eat breakfast. That's when Affron announced that was taking me with him.

"Isn't that a risk?" Valleia pointed out. "He knows no Latin."

"He'll be fine."

"But what are you going to do? If it's dangerous, you should take William with you."

"There is no danger, Valleia. I just need some company."

Valleia looked like she wanted to argue with Affron, but she didn't bother. I noticed Palta looking down at the table. She wanted to go with Affron, I realized. Why did I get to go? She had already done more to rescue us than I could ever have done, by leading us out of Urbis. Why shouldn't she continue to help?

I didn't know.

Affron and I left after breakfast. "The first thing to do, Larry," Affron said when we were out on the street, "is to get rid of this beard of mine. I'll be sorry to see it go."

So we found a barber nearby, and Affron came out a few minutes later clean-shaven. He looked very different without his black beard.

"Aren't you worried that the barber will remember you?" I asked.

"Roma is a big city," he replied. "Do you know how many men are having their beards shaved off today because of the heat? Too many to track, even with the soldiers searching for us. This isn't your world, Larry. There is no photography, no television. We should be safe unless someone who actually knows me happens to run into us. We will be fine."

"What about speaking English? Should we do that?"

He shrugged. "People from every part of Terra are arriving in Roma for the Games. You will hear a lot of foreign tongues being spoken here. English will sound like just one more of them."

That made me feel a lot safer.

We walked through the city. Affron seemed to be looking for something, or someone. While he searched, he started talking about Terra. "I suppose you've learned a little about this world by now," he said.

"Hypatius told us a bit."

Affron nodded. "Hieron had a wonderful idea when he discovered Via: take the brightest minds in the world, send them off to every other world—and bring back the best ideas about how to organize society. And the priests have done many great things. Women have equal rights with men. Slavery has been abolished, except when you commit a crime—then you work for the state instead of going to prison. We prevent disease with good sanitation and hygiene and sewage systems—even in wretched insulae like the one where we are staying. We don't have advanced medicines, but that is perhaps a reasonable choice—to have them, you need to create a world of factories and mass production, with the accompanying dehumanizing labor and pollution. We give up some things, but we gain much more."

"What's the problem, then?" I asked. "Why are you and Valleia and Gratius opposed to Tirelius? Is it gants?"

"Yes, gants. Fifty years ago, there was a revolt against the priests. It was led by King Harald of Gallia—that's France in your world, more or less. The priests thought that Gallia was loyal; they were wrong. They thought the revolt would be easily put down by our soldiers; again, they were wrong. Before they knew it, Harald and his army were headed for Urbis, and there weren't enough soldiers to stop him. The soldiers were off guarding the borders with Barbarica. No one thought they were needed to protect Urbis itself."

"What happened?" I asked.

"Ah, Larry, we sold our souls. You have seen the gant's power. You have seen its—well, its *cleanliness*. Your victim is there in front of you, and then he is gone. Not like swords or arrows or gunpowder. They are all messy and brutal. The gant makes death seem almost pleasant: you don't suffer; you are here, and then you are not. The priests knew where such weapons existed, but they had ruled their empire without them—until King Harald threatened it. Then viators were sent to the world that produced them."

"Gaia," I said.

"Yes, Gaia. Palta's world. Poor, wretched Gaia. The viators brought back gants. And the Roman soldiers used them on the Gallic army as it approached the walls of Urbis. And as a result that army simply disappeared—like Hypatius, like those poor guards at the palatium. A few stragglers survived, to bear witness to the power of the priests."

We walked in silence for a moment. "But the priests had to do it, right?" I said finally. "Or all the good you did would have been lost."

"That is the argument. But once you use such weapons, it is hard to stop. The temptation is too great."

"But why do you need to use them again? Didn't people learn their lesson?"

"The people of Gallia have learned their lesson, perhaps, although I'm sure they will never forgive the priests for what they did. Some nomadic tribe invading from the east in search of better pasture land—who knows? But that is not the real problem. The real problem is how easy the gant makes it for the priests to expand their empire. Before, there were limits on expansion. We didn't try to conquer the peoples of the Far East or the Americas, or even of northern Europe. But the gant makes conquest easy. And once you betray Hieron's vision in that way, why not in others? Why not import medicines that cure diseases? Why should we stand by and watch people die in agony, knowing we have the power to cure them? Why should we ourselves die in such a way? Many priests say it is time to move on. That is what Tirelius thinks. Others think we should be faithful to Hieron and what he taught us."

"You think the priests should be faithful to Hieron?"

Affron shrugged. "Let's just say that there is a reason Tirelius wants to put me to death."

"How can you defeat him?"

"I'm not sure, Larry. Some of us used to think that Tirelius would simply die before he could implement his vision. I would be voted the new pontifex, and then things could change back to the way they used to be. But now it seems clear that he is not going to delay any further. He is getting rid of his enemies, stockpiling gants, drawing up plans. It is distressing." He stopped walking and looked around. "And it is clear, to me at least, that I am not the right man to defeat Tirelius."

"Why not?"

"It doesn't matter, Larry. Anyway, we have found the place I was looking for." We were on a narrow, dark side street, and Affron stopped in front of a windowless brick building. There was no sign in front of it; only three yellow balls hanging from a bar next to the door.

We went inside. We were in a long, dark room filled with random objects—pots and paintings and furniture and clothing; statues and swords and daggers. A bald man wearing an eyepatch and a dirty robe stood behind a counter talking to a nervous woman. Finally he open a drawer in the counter and took out a few coins, which he handed to the woman. The woman put them in her pocket and left hurriedly. Then the bald man picked up a bracelet from the counter, took out a key, and unlocked a large wooden cabinet to his left. He put the bracelet inside and locked the cabinet. Then he bowed to Affron and me and said something in Latin. Affron walked over to him, and I followed. Affron gestured at the cabinet. The man took out a key and unlocked the cabinet once again. I could see that the cabinet was filled with tray after tray of jewelry.

"I don't remember: Do you have pawn shops in your world, Larry?" Affron asked me in English.

"I've heard of them, I think," I replied. "I've never been in one."

"They are entirely worthy establishments, filling a social need, and I'm sorry I have to do what I'm about to do. It may—well, I don't know what it will do to you."

What did that mean?

Affron turned back to the bald man. The man had placed a tray on the counter. Affron picked up a gold ring. And then...

And then something happened. I saw the bald man drop to the floor. At least, I think I saw him. But my senses weren't working right, my mind was swirling, and then it spun out of control. I saw everything. Or nothing—just...emptiness. The black emptiness of a million empty universes. Emptiness that showed how trivial and worthless and meaningless I was, we were, everything was. I was just a speck in a speck in a speck. And even that speck existed in a million versions, alive and dead, good and evil. Why did I care about anything? Why did I worry and struggle? Why did I even bother to breathe?

And then I noticed that Affron was holding on to me, keeping me from falling. "Are you all right?" I think he asked.

"I don't know," I think I said.

"I'm sorry," he said. "That affected you more than I expected."

"What was it? What happened?"

"It is—I don't know. It is the gods inside me, Valleia might say. It is my power, my curse."

"It...reminds me."

"Of what?"

"I felt something like this...just a bit...when I was trying to make up my mind to go into the portal with Valleia. To help you. I think I blacked out for a few seconds."

Affron stared at me, and then shook his head. "Very strange. But we must hurry, before the poor pawnbroker regains consciousness."

He stepped around the counter and over the bald man, who lay sprawled on the floor. I followed. "Will he be all right?" I asked.

"I think so," Affron replied. "But I don't really know. I wish I didn't have to do such a thing. But we need the money, and I didn't want to destroy him—or anyone—with the gant." He opened a drawer in the counter that was filled with coins. He emptied them into a sack and handed the sack to me. "This should be enough," he said. "If it isn't..." He shook his head. "Let's go."

As we left the pawn shop, we heard the bald man start to groan as he lay on the floor.

We hurried back out onto the busy main street. Soon I was totally lost in a maze of streets and surging, restless crowds. I still felt dizzy and confused. "Have you ever experienced this?" I asked Affron. "This feeling, like—like you just experienced the entire multiverse in an instant?"

"Is that what it feels like to you?"

I nodded.

He considered. "I experience that all the time," he murmured.

"Have you done this before—what you did to that man? Do other people know you can do it?"

"A few times—unintentionally, when I was angry or frustrated. I am not proud of that. But it's part of why I have this reputation, I suppose."

"About knowing the gods."

"Yes. The gods."

"But where does the power come from? How come you have it, and no one else?"

"If I knew that, Larry..."

He didn't finish his answer. I kept thinking about what had happened, about what I had felt, and I continued the interrogation. "When you were in prison—in the palatium, waiting to be executed—why didn't you do this to the guards? Why didn't you use your power to escape?"

"I'm not sure it would have worked—I wasn't in the best of shape back there. Besides, I don't enjoy doing this to people, Larry."

"But they were going to kill you."

"I didn't really know that. And, you know..." He shook his head. "Perhaps I wasn't sure I wanted to escape."

"Why not?"

"Because I don't want to be the next pontifex. I'm not sure I know how to solve what's wrong with Terra. When you have visited universe after universe, seen the same problems over and over...greed and ignorance and lust for power...anyway, give me a coin, Larry. One of the smaller ones. I'm tired. Let's get something to eat."

I took a coin out of the sack and handed it to him. It was heavy, and I noticed it had an engraving of Via on one side. We found a sort of outdoor café at the edge of a forum, and Affron ordered some kind of cold pasta for us. It was served on a single plate for the two of us, with something like chopsticks to pick up the food. Soldiers strolled by, but they ignored us. On the other side of the forum jugglers and acrobats were putting on a show.

After a while Affron's energy seemed to return, and he began to talk about himself. "The priests seek out talented children at a young age," he said. "I was such a child. My family was very proud, but I was taken away from them—a bit like you and your family, I suppose. I was sent to a special schola, and I was the best student there. And when I graduated I was sent to another schola, and I was the best student there, as well. And eventually I ended up at the schola in Urbis, with the best of the best."

"You became a viator," I said.

He nodded. "It is an odd role nowadays," he went on. "More of an honorary title for someone like Hypatius. If you explore new worlds, you may find something wonderful—but, more likely, you will catch a disease or be eaten by a strange beast or buried in molten lava, and you never return. So most viators go only to worlds we have already visited. I have chosen to explore. That has also been part of my reputation, I suppose."

"That guy in the temple at the desk next to the portal—he keeps track of where you go?"

"Yes, that is his job. But he only writes what we tell him. That is how Gratius got his gant—he secretly went to Gaia and obtained one. That was very brave of him."

"Do a lot of viators visit my world?" I asked.

Affron shook his head. "I am the only one who has visited your world. To be honest, Larry, it isn't particularly interesting. But of course every world has its share of interesting people—like you."

He seemed serious about the compliment. That pleased me a lot. "What are we going to do next?" I asked. "I mean, after we find someplace safe to stay. What happens then?"

A cool breeze suddenly sprang up. Across the plaza the crowd, applauded as the jugglers and acrobats finished their show. Affron sighed and pushed around the remaining pasta on the plate. "I suppose," he said, "we shall have to try to save Terra."

CHAPTER 11

B ack at the insula, an old man wearing a thin tunic was standing on the steps, waving a fan in front of his face. He nodded to us as we passed; Affron nodded back.

"He knows who we are, I expect," Affron murmured to me as we continued up the steps. "I expect that everyone in the insula does."

"How do you know?"

"We stand out too much. The neighborhood is small. People talk."

"Will they turn us in?"

"Probably not. People in the poorer castella have no love for the priests."

"Why not?"

"Because the priests take them for granted nowadays. They take Roma for granted. They think all that Romans want is their games in the summer and free grain when they're old. It's not enough for many."

"But there's a reward for our capture."

"Yes," Affron agreed. "That does complicate matters."

Back in the apartment, people was hot and worried. Flies buzzed over the toilet; everyone and everything stank. Affron placed the sack of money we had stolen onto the table and then went back to bed.

Everyone looked at me for an explanation.

"How did you get the money?" Carmody asked me.

I shook my head. "Affron doesn't want me to say."

"He used his magic, I suppose," Valleia said.

"What magic?" Carmody asked.

Valleia shrugged. "It is said that he knows some kind of magic. What it is I cannot say."

Carmody looked at me to explain the magic, but I just shrugged too.

He looked annoyed. And Palta looked annoyed because Affron had taken me and not her. We were all annoyed. We had to get out of this place. It was too hot, too small; and, if Affron was right, one of our neighbors would turn us in to the priests eventually.

"When can we find a bigger place to live?" I asked.

"William and I will find a place tomorrow," Valleia said. "Right now, you two go out and buy us food."

Palta and I left the apartment with a few of the stolen coins. She was quiet at first, and I thought she was mad at me. But then she perked up. She quizzed me about what had happened with Affron, and I told her some stuff that I hadn't told Carmody.

And then she said, "I know his magic."

"Really?"

She nodded. "It is how he saved my life."

"Here? Or on Gaia?"

"Gaia. One night I was on street I should not be on. My tribe had sent me out for food, and this was fastest way back. They were not bad people usually, but sometimes they beat me when I'm too slow. But still—I was stupid girl to go down that street. I saw them too late—big men, long beards, faces painted every kind of color. I know that kind of men—they are evil. I ran—I am fast runner—but I tripped, and they grabbed me. They took my food, of course. I said: 'You have my food. Now let me go.' But they were not going to let me go. You know how it is."

I supposed I did. "What happened?"

Palta folded her arms up tight. Her gray eyes were moist. "One of them had gant, I saw. So I say to him: 'Just take food and shoot me, please, but leave me alone.' Much better to be pile of ashes, right? But they all just laughed. 'Don't worry, we'll shoot you later,' one of them said. And they laughed some more."

"And then what?"

Palta smiled. "Then someone says, 'Excuse me, I think I'm lost.'"

"Affron?"

She nodded. "Men turn. I was still on ground, but I see him standing there. He nods to me, like he knows all about me, like this is no trouble at all. One man tells him to go away. He shrugs and doesn't move. Man raises gant. He still doesn't move. And then man screams and is on ground next to me, sobbing. I grab gant and start shooting. One, two, three of them disappear into ashes. Then Affron says to me, 'Enough,' and I stop. Rest of them run away. I turn and kneel before Affron. He tells me to get up. Then he says: 'Stay, or come with me?' He explains a little about where he is going, but I don't understand. I don't care. I say: 'I want to come with you.' As we leave, that first man was still lying there in street, sobbing. Affron did it to him just by looking. By being Affron. That is his magic."

"He brought you back here to Terra, in Via?" I asked.

"Yes. Terra was much better than Gaia. Much, much better. Until they took Affron away, and that pig Hypatius made me his slave."

She fell silent. I thought about her story. "When Affron did that," I said, "when he made that man fall down sobbing—did you feel anything?"

"What do you mean? I was happy, of course. Relieved. Who wouldn't be?"

"No, I mean—did you feel what Affron did, what made the man fall down and start sobbing?"

Palta shook her head. "Of course not. Affron was doing his magic on that man, not on me."

"Okay. I understand." But I didn't, not really. *Affron's magic.* Why had I felt it—suffered from it—and not Palta?

"He did that to someone here today, yes?" Palta asked. "To get money."

Affron had told me not to say anything, but he hadn't mentioned that Palta already knew about his magic. "He did something like that," I said.

She nodded. "They say gods have visited him."

"Maybe. I don't think his magic makes him happy."

"We must help him be happy."

We bought bread and cheese and dates and olives and brought them back to the insula. Palta tried to teach me some Latin on the way—what the shop signs meant, how to say simple things like "Good morning" and "How are you?". Learning the language seemed to come easily to her. It was harder for me, but I thought I could get the hang of it. It was weird that her version of English didn't seem to have the words "a" or "the"—just like Latin.

People hanging around outside the insula stared at us as we walked past them. A fat woman said something to us, and Palta gave her a brief reply.

"She wanted to know where we come from," Palta said. "I just told her: not from here."

Affron didn't get up for dinner. We ate in silence, and after the sun went down the room finally started to cool off, as it had the night before. There wasn't anything to do in the darkness, so I tried to go to sleep on the floor. I wondered if Palta would join me.

She didn't. But in the middle of the night I awoke and saw Affron sitting cross-legged once again in front of the small windows, making those strange motions in the air. I watched in silence for what seemed like an hour. Finally Affron stopped and stood up. He turned and nodded to me. "Go to sleep, Larry," he whispered.

"What were you doing?" I asked.

He shrugged. "Magic," he replied. "Except the magic isn't quite working."

And then he went back to bed.

* * *

In the morning Valleia and Carmody left to find a house. He would pretend to be a rich merchant from Britannia, the most distant part of the priests' empire. He was in Roma with his wife to see the Games, and needed a suitable place to stay while he was here. Valleia would be his Roman-born wife; she would do most of the talking. With the money Affron had stolen, they would be able to rent an entire house in a fancy castellum.

In the meantime, Affron sent Palta and me out to buy the day's food. Without refrigeration, you couldn't have more than one day's food at a time, especially in the summer, so people were always shopping for it.

As before, Palta wanted to explore, not just do our task and return to the insula. I was beginning to understand a bit about Roma at this point, even though I had a hard time keeping the geography straight. It seemed like there was an endless series of neighborhoods—castella—some poor and run-down, like the one where we were living, others much nicer. The nicer ones were up in the hills, where the air was cooler. All of the castella seemed to have shops surrounding a central forum with a large fountain in the middle. In the poorer castella you'd see women washing clothes at the fountain and naked kids playing in it; beggars and drunks were everywhere. In the nicer ones there'd be outdoor cafes, like the one Affron had brought me to, and beggars were nowhere to be seen.

We were mostly silent as we explored, but suddenly Palta grabbed my arm and whispered, "Priests." She gestured with her head to two blue-robed men strolling through the plaza, maybe twenty yards away from us. I didn't recognize them, but Palta evidently did, because she turned around and quickly led me down a dusty side street.

"Are they from Urbis?" I asked.

"Yes. I have seen them in palatium. Maybe they have seen me too."

We kept walking, losing ourselves in the crooked streets the way Affron and I had done the day before. Eventually we found a bench in a small park and sat down. I was afraid to go back to the insula now, as people grew more suspicious of us, and I was afraid to walk around out in the open.

I wanted to go home.

We sat silently on the bench for a while. Then I started explaining to Palta about "the" and "a".

"I have heard those words from you and the rest," she said. "But they are stupid. They mean nothing."

"Maybe, but I can't seem to speak English without them."

She shrugged. "Then I will give them try. *A* try." She laughed. "And you learn the Latin."

"I'm trying."

"Try harder." She stood up. "Come. Let's go and buy the food."

We bought food and made our way back to the insula. On the way, she silently slipped her hand into mine.

The same people were staring at us outside the insula, but this time no one spoke to us.

When we arrived, Valleia and Carmody had already returned, and everyone was worried about us, especially when we told them about the priests. "We must leave tonight," Valleia said. "We cannot wait."

"You found a place for us?" I asked.

"We did. In the Parioli castellum. It is secluded and very wealthy. The house is smaller than I'd like, but it has a wall and a gate. We will leave here after dark."

Valleia had bought us all new robes, so we wouldn't look out of place walking through a rich neighborhood. I was happy not to be wearing my sweaty brown one anymore.

"Our robes aren't as fine as yours," Palta pointed out to her.

She shrugged. "We need to have servants, or people may be suspicious. You, Larry, and Affron will be the servants."

Palta didn't seem happy about this, but Affron just bowed to Valleia and said, "We will strive to give you satisfaction, Domina."

"It's just for show," Carmody said to Palta.

Palta shrugged. She seemed to be okay with it because Affron was okay with it.

We ate our last meal in the insula, cleaned up, and left the place, braving the suspicious gaze of the neighbors one last time.

Valleia and Carmody went first, and we "servants" followed, carrying our few possessions. This was the first time I had been in the city at night, and I was glad I wasn't alone. The streets were dark, lit only by occasional torches and the glow of lights from houses and taverns. "Rich people go nowhere at night in Roma without their bodyguards," Affron said to Palta and me. "And things will be worse when the Games start. Then every pickpocket and thief in the empire will be here."

But he didn't sound worried.

Parioli was up on one of the hills, and the city seemed quieter, cooler, and safer when we reached it.

The house was on a little side street lined with trees. The gate was locked, but Carmody had a key. He went inside, lit a torch in the entranceway, and we all followed him in.

It had the same basic layout as Hypatius's house, but it was far larger and more ornate. Every room was bigger, and we each had our own bed to sleep in; the atrium was enormous, and there was a large garden beyond it—a *peristyle*, Valleia called it. The best part was that the place had a wide pool made of marble. No need to go to the public baths; no need to stink in the summer heat inside your apartment. When Palta saw the bath, she immediately took off her robe and sandals and got in.

"Different customs here, eh, Larry?" Carmody murmured to me, watching Palta naked in the water.

"And on Palta's world," I replied.

Then Affron and Valleia took their clothes off too, so Carmody and I joined them, and we were all naked in the bath. I tried not to look at Palta or Valleia, but my eyes kept returning to them. And I couldn't help becoming aroused. If they noticed, they didn't seem to mind. Valleia's body and breasts were bigger than Palta's, but Palta was cute in her own way. I noticed Carmody looking at Valleia too, although he ignored Palta.

Valleia looked back at him and smiled.

Affron said nothing and looked at no one, closing his eyes and letting the water wash over him.

After bathing Palta and I went out and bought the food and wine for dinner, and we ate in the dining room, reclining on couches the way we had in Hypatius's house. The wine made me sleepy—and happy. I wasn't back home, but it was better to be here than in the insula; it was good to have my own room for a change. I went to sleep right after dinner.

When I awoke it was daylight, and Palta was snuggled up beside me.

CHAPTER 12

We were safer here, but we needed a plan. After the Roman Games our lease would end, the owners would return, and we would need someplace else to stay. Or we would have to leave Roma entirely.

Day after day we could hear Valleia and Affron talking in his room—it was Valleia talking, mostly, and sounding more and more frustrated. Obviously Affron wasn't agreeing with her ideas, or coming up with any of his own. At dinner, they both started drinking a lot of wine.

Palta and I were still in charge of shopping for food. It was good to get away from the arguing, and with Palta's help I started picking up some Latin. It was like something finally clicked, and the sounds suddenly began to make sense.

On our way home one day I decided to ask Palta about why she snuck into my bed every night.

"Do you not want me to?" she replied quickly. "I'll stop if you don't want me to."

"No, no—it's fine. It's great. I just—wondered why."

She slowed down as she considered her answer. Her eyes glistened with tears. "On Gaia, we survive by being part of tribe. *A* tribe. In my tribe, we all slept close together. For safety. For warmth. I'm used to feeling other bodies next to me when I sleep. I wake up in the middle of the night and I miss it. It makes me scared. It seems like you don't mind."

"No, of course I don't. Do you miss a lot about Gaia?"

She shook her head. "Gants destroyed everything on Gaia. It was too easy to kill, too easy to die. My mother, my father—all my family was dead. It was too hard just staying alive to notice any good things."

"It sounds awful. No wonder you want to—"

I didn't have a chance to finish, because suddenly we caught sight of Gratius walking along the busy street.

He had already seen us and was making his way through the crowd in our direction.

"We should run," Palta said. "I don't trust him."

But I didn't want to run. "He saved our lives," I pointed out. "And he'll know what's going on back in Urbis."

Palta looked dubious. Gratius was wearing the purple robe of a viator, which meant that everyone bowed to him and got out of his way. When he reached us, he turned and pretended to look into a shop. "Follow me," he said in English, and he strode away from us.

We followed him through twisty side streets into a dark alley, empty except for a mangy dog, who slunk away when he saw us.

Gratius turned to face us. "Affron and Valleia—are they all right?" he asked.

"Yes," I replied.

He let out a sigh of relief. "Where are they?" he asked. "No, don't tell me—I don't want to know. You must tell them there is no time to lose. They must act soon, or else leave Roma. Tirelius has spies everywhere. He knows they are still here. And he will know where to look for them. It is only a matter of time before they are caught."

"We can tell them," I said. "But—"

"*Tell them,*" Gratius repeated. "Tell them that many priests still support Affron, but he must act. He must do something to make those priests believe he will stop Tirelius. Or the pontifex will win, and everything that Hieron worked for will be destroyed."

Then Gratius turned away from us and walked quickly out of the alley.

Palta and I stared after him. I felt an icy fear in my heart. "Very bad," she murmured.

"Yes," I said.

We hurried back to our house in Parioli. We found Affron, Valleia, and Carmody sitting in the peristyle drinking wine. Birds were chirping in the trees. The fountain gurgled. In the distance I could hear a band playing. It was such a lovely place.

We told them about our meeting.

Valleia looked at Affron. "Do you see?" she said. "We cannot delay."

"Gratius gets nervous," Affron pointed out. "Perhaps he is being too—"

"He is telling the truth!" Valleia exploded. "We can't simply sit here and drink wine while Tirelius and his spies hunt us down. We are safe now, but will we be safe tomorrow, or even an hour from now? It is time to act."

Affron nodded slowly but didn't speak.

"Well?" she demanded. "We may have enough money left to hire a ship that will take us to Barbarica," she said. "If not, you can steal some more. We can go to Persia, or India, or Scotia—anywhere that is not part of the empire. We don't have to stay and fight, if you don't want to. But we must *decide*."

He sighed. He rubbed his cheek. It looked like he still wasn't used to being clean-shaven. He poured himself a cup of wine. "I will fight," he said finally.

"How? With Marcus Decius?"

He nodded. "As you say. With Decius."

"Who is Decius?" Carmody asked.

"He is the governor of the Roman province," Valleia replied. "Not a friend of the priests, especially Tirelius."

"Why not? Doesn't the pontifex appoint governors?"

"It's complicated. The different provinces that make up the empire are allowed considerable autonomy, as long as they follow the policies that the priests set down. Decius has criticized Tirelius for many things. But he is highly popular, so Tirelius has been reluctant to move against him."

"Why does he criticize Tirelius?"

"You have seen Roma," Valleia said. "Much of it is beautiful. But you have also experienced the wretched insulae, the beggars, the poverty. Decius says the priests do not do enough to help the poor of Roma. And he is right. Other provinces have wealth—gold and iron mines, rare spices, rich, fertile land. Roma doesn't; it has land, but not enough to feed its citizens. So the Roman people suffer, and Tirelius doesn't seem to care. It is where the empire started, but he is too interested in expanding his power elsewhere. The people look to Decius to help them."

"All right," Carmody said. "What is the plan? You make an alliance with this man?"

Valleia nodded. "Yes. He knows about Affron. He will support us."

"But how?"

Valleia looked at Affron, who said nothing. "We have a gant," she said. "It is not much, but it may be enough. The rest of the gants are held in an armamentarium not far from the soldiers' barracks in Urbis."

"Yes, you talked about going there after we rescued Affron."

"Yes. Well, we have worked out a plan—or rather, *I* have. There's no reason why we can't return to Urbis the way we left it. At night, through the tunnel; it won't be guarded. The armamentarium will be guarded, but the guards aren't trusted to have gants. That means we can capture all the weapons it holds. Once we have those gants, Tirelius loses the main advantage he has over us."

"But where does Decius come in?"

"There are only five of us," Valleia pointed out. "Even with those gants, even with our supporters among the priests, it's not clear that we could defeat Tirelius and his soldiers."

"Not without killing many, many people," Affron said.

"But Decius could provide you with soldiers?" Carmody replied.

"Yes, he has soldiers who are more loyal to him than to the priests. With them, we can take over Urbis. Once we are in control of Urbis, we can control the empire."

"And Larry can go home."

"Yes, Larry can go home."

I noticed that Carmody didn't mention going home himself.

He seemed dubious about her plan, though. "You don't think Tirelius will guard against someone sneaking into Urbis? The walls are patrolled, after all. Presumably they know we used the tunnel to escape. What makes you think they won't guard that, as well?"

"Perhaps they will," Valleia replied. "But there are other ways into the city. And again, the guards won't have gants. No, the key is to get to the armamentarium undetected. And I think we can do that."

"This will need to be carefully planned," Carmody said.

"We will rely on you to help with that, William." Valleia turned back to Affron. "You and I will track Decius down tomorrow and lay the plan in front of him," she said. "I'm sure he will agree."

"I would prefer to go with Larry," Affron replied.

And that caused Valleia to explode again. "Why?" she demanded. "Why do you need Larry? He adds nothing. He is just a boy. He can't even speak Latin."

"I can speak it well enough," I protested—in Latin. Not that I was particularly interested in going to meet Decius.

Valleia glared at me. But Affron wouldn't change his mind, and he wouldn't explain himself. "Larry comes," he said. "You can come too, of course."

And that was that.

Through all the discussion, Palta said nothing. After the plans had been made she went off to the kitchen to prepare dinner. We ate in silence for the most part, but afterward, in my room, I asked her what she thought.

"I like it here," she said. "In this house, with Affron, with you. I want to stay here forever."

"But we can't—you know that. We have to leave at the end of the summer, even if Tirelius doesn't track us down."

"I know that, of course. But I worry about Affron. He doesn't want to do this. He doesn't want to go back to Urbis. The woman is forcing him into it."

"Then why didn't he agree to go to Barbarica instead? That would have been safer."

"Maybe he doesn't know what he wants."

That seemed pretty likely to me.

"This will let you go home," she noted.

"Yeah." She didn't sound happy about that. And that made me happy. I hadn't been thinking so much about home in the past few days. But just hearing Palta saying the word made memories come flooding back. Doritos. Cell phones. The Internet. Cassie's play—I had missed it, of course. Matthew's school project about California. Almonds. In this world, there wasn't even a California. I realized that I didn't even know the date anymore. School was out by now. In the summer I was supposed to be a counselor trainee at Glanbury's town day camp—my first real job. I had been so excited when I got that job. Now, none of that mattered.

I suppose Palta could sense my emotions, because she reached out and squeezed my hand. "Affron will get you home," she said. "I know it."

I hoped she was right.

I didn't sleep well. Again, Affron wanted me to go with him. Why? Why did I feel it when Affron used the power of his mind, and Palta didn't?

Why did he want Valleia to bring me to Terra, even if he knew I wouldn't help him during his trial?

I had no answers. In the morning Valleia was excited, but Affron was his usual calm self. "Decius will be surrounded by aides and soldiers," he said. "But we will see what can be done."

"Does he knows what you look like?" I asked.

"I doubt it."

"He knows your reputation," Valleia pointed out. "He knows why Tirelius is so interested in finding you. We just need to find a way to talk to him."

We had breakfast and a bath, and then we were ready to go. "Bona fortuna," Carmody said to us. *Good luck.*

Palta gave me a quick, hard hug.

Valleia put the gant in a pocket of her robe.

The day was hot, as usual. We walked quickly out of our shady neighborhood and onto the busy, crowded streets. And we made our way to the real, central Roman Forum, which was lined with buildings even larger and grander than those of Urbis.

"Before Hieron, before Urbis, this was the center of the Roman empire," Affron said.

He pointed at one of the largest buildings, a great stone edifice with a long set of steps leading up to an entrance supported by massive columns. "That's the headquarters of the provincial government. I expect that Decius has an office somewhere inside."

"We shouldn't all go in," Valleia said. "Let me find out if he's there."

Affron shrugged. "As you wish."

We watched her climb the steps and disappear into the building. Then we found a place to sit on the steps of another building where we could see her when she reappeared. Affron said nothing.

"Why do you bring me with you?" I asked after a while. "To the pawnbroker, and now here. I don't mind, but I don't understand it."

Affron rubbed his clean-shaven chin. "Because I need company," he said. "Because no one else seems to feel what I feel, experience what I experience."

"You mean like the feeling I had at the pawnbroker's shop? Like I was experiencing the entire multiverse at the same time?"

"Yes. Something like that."

"But I'm just a kid from an average world. I wasn't trained to be a viator or anything Why am I the only one?"

"Terra was an average world—until Hieron came along," Affron responded. "It's not training. Or not *just* training, perhaps. In an infinity of universes, there are bound to be people who are different. Perhaps they are not even aware of that difference—they just need to be made aware of the *possibility* that they are different. There is so much locked inside the human mind, Larry. Some people remember every event of their lives as if it just happened to them. Others can multiply six-digit numbers in their brains without a thought. Others invent gants. Others...are somehow in tune with the multiverse."

"I don't understand any of this."

"Well, neither do I. But I do know that it was not my doing that the portal brought you back to your home at the instant you left. And it was not my doing that you can feel this—this—" He groped for the right word.

"I think of it as *speckness*," I said. "This sense that you're just this tiny speck of nothingness inside the multiverse."

"Yes, that is good. Your *speckness*. That is what is inside you."

I pondered this. And then I asked: "What do people believe here—about the portal, about the multiverse? Do they know the truth? Or do they think it's all, you know, magic, or miracles, or something?"

Affron pointed to a large, dome-shaped building on our left. I realized that it looked familiar. It looked like the temple of Via; and it had the same large statue of Hieron standing in front of it. "That is the Roman temple," he said. "As you can see, it is built on the model of the temple in Urbis. There are such temples throughout Terra. They are where ordinary people go to worship Via. Most people believe that the gods gave Via to the priests as our means of contacting them, of receiving wisdom from them. And the priests are content to have people believe this. Even highly intelligent men—Decius, for example—probably have only a vague understanding of what Via really is, even though there have been renegade priests over the years who have tried to explain the truth. It is impossible for the average person on this world to really comprehend the multiverse. I know how astounded I was when I was finally brought to Urbis and learned the truth."

I contemplated this. "But couldn't there be something more to Via than even the priests understand?"

"Yes," Affron agreed softly, "perhaps there could. Perhaps there could."

"What do you do at night, Affron—when you sit in the dark making those strange motions in the air?"

He shook his head. "Ah, Larry, I don't really know. I think it's my way of trying to understand just how different I am."

"That doesn't make any sense," I pointed out.

"You're right," he replied. "I couldn't agree more."

It was clear that he didn't want to say anything more about it. We fell silent, sitting in the hot sun and waiting for Valleia to return. I kept thinking about being special, about being different. It just didn't seem right. But…here I was in another world, plotting to oust its rulers. This was not the summer day camp in Glanbury.

Finally we saw Valleia come out of the government headquarters and descend the steps. We walked over to meet her. "He wasn't there," she said. "He's at the Circus Maximus, inspecting it for the Games."

Affron sighed. "Let's go, then. I hope we don't end up chasing the man all over Roma."

We set out once again. The Circus Maximus was a short walk from the Forum. The place was huge—bigger than any football stadium, bigger than the Roman Colosseum, which I'd seen pictures of. It was made of concrete, and sat in the middle of a broad plaza filled with fountains. Multicolored flags were flying everywhere. Workmen were busy putting up booths and signs.

"We'll never find him in this place," I said.

"And if we find him," Valleia added, "he'll be with a dozen other people."

"Let's go inside," Affron replied.

We walked through a long tunnel underneath the stands and out onto a dirt track that surrounded a large grass field. On the field athletes were practicing—at one end men were throwing javelins; at the other end they were doing the long jump. All of them were deeply tanned, heavily muscled, and naked. More workmen were painting seats and setting up awnings. "I don't see him," Affron said after a while.

"Shall we look underneath the stands?" Valleia asked.

"Yes, I suppose so."

We went back into the tunnel. I was getting hungry, and the midday heat was blistering. Being under the stands was a little cooler than being out in the sun, at least. We turned left, into a long concourse lined with booths for selling food and drinks. They were all closed. I heard shouts and hammering. Laughter and curses. We passed naked athletes, their bodies slick with sweat, guzzling water from buckets. We passed bored-looking soldiers guarding doors.

We didn't see Decius.

I could tell that Valleia was starting to get worried. How was the plan going to work, if we couldn't even find the guy? I recalled my first night in Carmody's world, where Kevin and I talked our way out of a refugee camp and into a jail cell by showing the guards his calculator watch. "Maybe we should get ourselves arrested," I said.

Affron stopped walking. "What?"

"Do the soldiers here report to Decius? Maybe we should just let one of them arrest us, and he'd bring us to him."

"Yes, they report to him," Affron said. "But how would we—"

And then he stopped. A couple of soldiers were approaching us, deep in conversation. "Run," he murmured to us. And he turned and ran. Valleia and I hesitated for a moment, and then we took off after him.

"Sistite!" I heard one of the soldiers shout. *Halt!*

We didn't halt. I heard them come after us. Affron slowed down. Valleia and I slowed down behind him. I couldn't run that fast anyway, in my sandals, in the heat. And I knew what Affron was doing. A hand grabbed my shoulder and spun me around. One of the soldiers had a hold of me. He was tall and dark and sweating and looked like he wanted to punch me. The other soldier had hold of Valleia and Affron. He was broad-shouldered and had close-cropped gray hair. We were all panting.

"Venite mecum!" the gray-haired soldier said. *Come with me!*

The soldiers marched us down the concourse. One of them said something to the other; I couldn't quite understand it, but I heard the word *viator*.

Had they recognized us? Success, I guessed. But it was a risk. Except we had the gant. And Affron. The soldiers brought us into an empty room and shoved us onto a bench. A little light filtered into the room from an opening high up in one wall. The room stank of sweat and stale urine. Obscene graffiti and drawings were scrawled all over the walls. Filthy towels were piled up next to a toilet in the corner. Beside the toilet was a bucket of water. Was this a locker room? The tall soldier stood in front of the door, and the gray-haired one left.

"Well," Affron said to us in English. "Let's hope this works."

"Latine loqui!" the soldier barked at him. *Speak Latin!*

Affron shrugged and fell silent. He crossed his arms. Valleia fingered the pocket of her robe that contained the gant. We waited. My stomach started to growl.

After maybe twenty minutes there was a knock on the door; the tall soldier opened it and stepped aside. The older soldier walked in, followed by a man in an expensive-looking white robe. I knew instantly that this was Decius. He wasn't tall, but he held himself in a way that made you know that he was in charge. He was bald, with a fringe of gray hair on the sides of his head. He had piercing gray eyes, and he held himself very still. He was the only one of us who didn't seem to be sweating. He stared at us for a moment with those gray eyes, and then he bowed to Affron.

"Salve, Affronius," he said quietly.

Affron bowed in return.

Then the governor greeted Valleia and me by name. It was odd hearing him call me "Larry."

"I find this unusual," he said. In Latin, of course. I was pleased that I could understand most of what he said, although often I lost track, especially when he spoke quickly or the sentences got too complex. "It seems you wanted to be captured," he went on. "Why?"

"To meet you, obviously," Affron replied.

"Again, why?"

"It would be better to talk in private."

Decius slowly shook his head. "The soldiers stay. By the way, give me the weapon."

"What weapon?"

He didn't respond. Affron and Valleia looked at each other, and Affron shrugged. We had gone this far; we couldn't stop now. Valleia took the gant out of her pocket and handed it to Decius. He hefted it, stared at it. The soldiers stared at it too—at the polished metal with the faint blue glow. They had never seen anything like it before, of course. Did the soldiers have any idea what it was? Decius clearly did. "Very interesting," he said. "This little thing. The gods are indeed wonderful." And he put the gant into a pocket in his robe. I expected Affron or Valleia to complain, but they didn't. "You know," he went on. "I expected you to get in touch with me, if you were still in Roma. If you didn't show up, I would have had to pay you a visit myself. But I didn't expect to see you here." He gestured at the room where we were sitting.

"We're running out of time," Affron responded.

"Time for what?"

Affron glanced at the soldiers, sighed, and said: "Time to reach an agreement with you, in our areas of mutual interest."

"Why should we reach an agreement on anything? Why shouldn't I return you to the priests, as I am supposed to? Perhaps they would even give me the reward."

"Because I can help you far more than Tirelius can, or will."

"How do I know that? In fact, Tirelius has already promised increased support for the Roman province if I helped track you down."

"But you don't believe him, obviously. Nor should you. He doesn't care about your province."

He shrugged. "Possibly, but why should I believe you?"

"Because Tirelius is interested in expanding the priests' empire; he is interested in Barbarica. I, on the other hand, am not. And that is why I had to flee from Urbis. I understand your legitimate concerns about the needs of the people of Roma, and I am prepared to meet them."

"These are just words," Decius responded. "Tirelius is very interested in you. I could simply hold onto you until he meets my demands. Why wouldn't that work?"

Affron rubbed his chin. "You should understand, Decius," he said finally, "that you will never be able to return me to Tirelius. This will not happen."

Decius seemed amused by Affron's statement. "What do you mean, 'this will not happen'? I have my soldiers. I have your weapon. You are in my power."

Affron shook his head. "No, governor, I am not."

Valleia looked at Affron, puzzled. But I wasn't puzzled. I could feel it coming this time, the way you can feel a thunderstorm in the air. A sudden coldness in the humid room. A prickling at the back of my neck.

And then it happened. I felt it like the shock wave from an explosion. Like I was spiraling down into a black hole, infinitely dark and infinitely deep. I was unable to breathe, unable to feel, except for the one overpowering feeling of *speckness*. I am nothing. My life is nothing. Everything is nothing.

And then, somehow, I came out the other side, and I was back in the grimy locker room in the bowels of the Circus Maximus on Terra, still alive, still conscious. In front of me, the two soldiers and Decius lay crumpled on the hard concrete floor. And I saw fear in Valleia's eyes as she stared at Affron.

Now she had seen Affron's magic.

CHAPTER 13

"Take the gant back from the governor," Affron ordered Valleia. "Make sure they're all alive." He turned to me. "Are you all right, Larry?"

"Uh, I guess so. I'm a little weak. It was like before."

He nodded. "I'm sorry. I wasn't sure I was going to have to do that. But I think I had no choice."

"Do what?" Valleia asked. She had gone over to Decius and taken the gant from him.

"He's alive?" Affron said.

"Yes. But what—?"

"Check the soldiers."

She did as she was told. "They are still breathing," she reported. "Now, please tell me what happened. Is this your magic?"

Affron looked tired, resigned. "Yes," he said. "My magic. I thought it was important to show Decius just where the power lay here. He seemed to be under a misapprehension."

"You did this with your mind," Valleia said.

Affron nodded. "Did you feel anything?"

"No." She looked at me. "And you did?"

I nodded. "I don't know why," I said.

She came back and sat down next to us. "What will happen now?" she asked.

"Now we wait for them to come back to consciousness," Affron replied. "They should be all right. And then the conversation will continue."

So we sat there and waited in the heat. Finally Affron pointed to the bucket of water and said, "This is taking too long. Larry, let's see if we can wake up Decius."

I got the bucket and threw the water onto the governor's face. He groaned and opened his eyes. Then he sat up and wiped his face with the sleeve of his robe. He noticed the two soldiers on the floor. Then he felt for the gant. And then he looked at us.

"Call your men to come help those soldiers," Affron said. "Then let's find a more pleasant place to talk. It's hot here, and we need some lunch."

Decius hesitated, and then he got up, opened the door, and called out into the passageway. In a few moments more soldiers rushed in. He pointed to the bodies on the floor. "Take them away," he ordered. "And tell Iduma I need him."

The soldiers looked baffled, but they picked up their comrades and carried them out of the room.

"Will my men survive?" Decius asked Affron.

"Yes, they will be all right. I'm very sorry I had to do that to them, but otherwise they might have gotten upset when I did what I did to you."

"That was you? It felt like—"

"It felt like a horrifying madness had descended upon you. But yes, that was me. That is what you are facing, Decius—a mind that is also a weapon."

"Could you have killed me?"

"I believe that I could. Or, at least, I could have made that madness permanent. Which, really, would be worse than death—certainly worse than the kind of death that Valleia's weapon offers—instant, painless oblivion."

"And you can do this to anyone?"

Affron shrugged. "It seems so."

There was a knock on the door. Decius opened it, and a short fat man entered. He gave us a puzzled look, but said nothing. "Bring my carriage immediately," Decius ordered. "Have luncheon ready for the four of us in my peristyle. No one is to see us there. Understood?"

The fat man nodded. "Yes, Dominus." He scurried away, and Decius shut the door behind him.

The governor turned back to Affron. He rubbed his forehead; I bet he had a headache. "What is this power?" he asked. "Does it come from Via? Do others have it?"

"The power is mine alone, as far as I know," Affron replied. "As for Via...perhaps everything comes from Via. Perhaps nothing. I do not know."

"There is much that you do not know, apparently. You speak in riddles, like all the priests. What exactly do you want from me? What is the agreement you spoke of? Or is that a riddle too?"

"It is simple. We want you to help us take power from Tirelius. In return, we will improve the lives of your people and make you the most successful governor the Roman province has ever known."

"But why do you need my help? With your power—"

"There are limits to my power," Affron said. "There are limits to how we can use this weapon. We will need the support of your soldiers and your people to succeed."

"You have a plan?"

Affron nodded. "We have a plan."

The conversation was interrupted by another knock on the door. It was the fat man again. "Ready, Dominus," he said to Decius. We all rose and followed him through the tunnels to the plaza outside the Circus Maximus, where an ornate closed carriage pulled by two brown horses was waiting for us. "Inside," Decius instructed us. "Quickly."

We climbed inside along with Decius; Iduma shut the doors, and the carriage started up. The seats were comfortable; there was some kind of fruity scent in the air. The heat was unbearable. "No one should live in the city in the summer," Decius muttered.

We didn't respond. My stomach growled again.

Soon the carriage stopped. We were in an alley behind a

large house on one of the fancy hills. We got out and went through a door in a long wall, and we found ourselves in a peristyle filled with fountains and flowering plants. I felt a slight breeze, for which I was very grateful. Decius excused himself to see about lunch.

"How do you think it's going?" Affron asked in English.

Valleia was staring at him. I realized that she was still trying to understand what he had done to Decius and his soldiers. Affron's "magic."

"He is terrified of you," she stated.

"Well, that's good, then."

"But you should have told me that you might do this."

"I'm sorry. But now it is done, and we must make the best of it."

"Do you think he knows where we live?" I asked. "He talked about coming to visit us if we didn't visit him."

"It's possible," Affron replied. "He is likely to have more spies on the streets than Tirelius. All the more reason to reach an agreement with him."

Decius returned in a few moments followed by Iduma, who was carrying a platter of food—fruit and cheese—and jugs of wine and water.

Iduma left, and we ate in silence for a couple of minutes. I had my first orange since arriving on Terra, and it tasted wonderful.

"Now," Decius said finally, "explain your plan."

Affron nodded to Valleia. She explained what we had gone over the night before: the plan to sneak into Urbis, seize the rest of the gants in the armamentarium, and take over Urbis—with the help of Roman soldiers.

Decius asked some questions, and finally he shook his head. "It's not good enough," he said.

"Why not?" Valleia demanded.

"I cannot simply order soldiers to do my will when it comes to Via," Decius explained. "The soldiers are ordinary people, and ordinary people might not like the priests, but they fear them. They must believe in their cause, and they must believe they can win. The people know nothing about Affron. He is just a name and a description posted on walls across the city. Someone who has apparently committed unspeakable crimes against Via."

Valleia looked annoyed. "What do you suggest, then?"

Decius pondered the question. "We must change the way people think about Affron," he replied. "Imagine demonstrations springing up against Tirelius, demanding improvements in the lives of Roman citizens. Imagine graffiti on every wall protesting Tirelius and praising Affron. Rumors sweep the city that Affron is being hunted down because he dared to stand up to Tirelius in favor of Roma. The rumors say that the Tirelius has lost favor with the gods and must be replaced."

"You can do this?" Valleia asked.

"Of course I can."

"Won't Tirelius find out and demand that you control your people?"

"Of course he will. I will try, but I can only do so much. I am unable to comply with his demands. The demonstrations are too large to suppress. We arrest the leaders, but more rise up in their place. As soon as we clean up one wall, new graffiti appear on a dozen others."

"I don't see how this helps," Valleia said. "Our plan relies on secrecy. What you are proposing may get the soldiers on our side, but it will also put Tirelius on alert—he will expect an attack and prepare for it."

"I think Decius has a different plan in mind," Affron said, pouring himself a cup of wine and drinking it down.

"Indeed," the governor murmured.

Valleia looked from one to the other. "And what is that plan?" she asked.

"What is the highlight of the Games?" Affron responded.

"The chariot race, of course," Valleia answered.

"And who is always at the race to crown the victor, in front of two hundred thousand cheering citizens?" Decius asked.

Valleia finally seemed to get it. "The pontifex," she whispered.

"Of course. It is the one time he appears in Roma, along with his vice pontifexes. And what if, at that very moment, the gods strike him dead?"

We fell silent, contemplating this idea.

Finally Decius continued. "Now the people are triumphant. Their prayers have been answered! Rumors sweep the city that Affron is still alive, that he will become the new pontifex. The people *demand* Affron. Affron's many supporters in Urbis are emboldened; opposition to him crumbles. He comes out of hiding, is acclaimed pontifex, and a new age dawns for Terra. No need to sneak into Urbis. No need to worry about the soldiers. No need to kill anyone—except Tirelius. And, I suppose, his cronies."

"Or, perhaps, I merely drive them mad," Affron said.

Decius shrugged. "Madness might be better," he replied. "The judgment of the gods would be even clearer."

"But what if Tirelius decides it is too dangerous to show up?" I asked.

He glanced at me darkly, as if wondering why I dared to speak to him. I realized he probably thought I was just a servant. "Tirelius will have to show up," he replied. "The pontifex always comes. To stay in Urbis would be an admission of weakness."

Valleia looked at Affron, who stared down at his wine cup. "I don't like it," she said.

"Why not?" Decius asked.

"It puts too much pressure on Affron."

"To do what he did back in that room to me and my soldiers? Was that difficult, Affron?"

Affron rubbed his chin. "No," he said finally. "No, it wasn't. I wish it were difficult."

"Can you do it in the stands at the end of the chariot race? Do you need to be close to Tirelius? Will the presence of tens of thousands of people bother you?"

He shook his head. "No, they shouldn't be a problem. Nothing should be a problem."

"If this is going to be difficult," Decius persisted, "we must discuss it now. Once we agree to this, once I set the plan in motion, you cannot fail me. I don't care what powers you possess. If you fail me, I will hunt you down and destroy you."

Affron raised his eyes from the wine cup and stared at Decius. And then he bowed ever so slightly. "We are all taking risks here," he said in reply. "I know what I can do. You have felt my power."

"Very well." Decius raised his wine cup to him. "So long as we know where we stand."

And then they started in on a long discussion of what exactly Decius wanted from Affron once he became pontifex. I didn't follow much of it, partly because the Latin got complicated, partly because I wasn't that interested. Affron didn't seem interested either, so Valleia did most of the talking for us. They discussed tax revenues, and medical care, and rebuilding the neighborhoods where the poor lived. They talked about improving the port and increasing grain shipments from Egypt. Decius became very animated when he brought up these issues; he really seemed to care. Valleia also cared, and the two of them seemed to agree on practically everything.

And as they talked, I realized that it was finally going to happen: Affron would defeat Tirelius and become the new pontifex, and I could return to Urbis and use the portal to go home. At last.

At some point I must have fallen asleep from the heat and the wine, because the next thing I knew Affron was standing over me and shaking me awake. "Time to go, Larry," he said. Valleia and Decius too were standing up. I got to my feet. It was twilight, and a couple of torches had been lit in the peristyle.

"Go out into the city as little as possible," he was warning them. "Tirelius will only search harder for you when he sees what is happening."

"We understand," Valleia replied.

"Very well. We will not see each other again until after it is done."

Affron bowed to him. "We will not disappoint," he said.

And then we left the peristyle the way we had entered it, by the small door in the rear wall.

Outside, the carriage was gone from the alley.

We said little as we walked back to Parioli; Affron and Valleia both seemed tired. At the house, we were greeted with hugs. But Carmody was puzzled when Valleia described the new plan. "Do you think that can really work?" he asked.

"Yes, if Decius can do what he has promised."

"And Affron," Carmody pointed out.

"I have now seen what Affron can do with his magic," Valleia said. "And it is amazing. Three men, suddenly almost dead—simply through the power of his mind."

Carmody shook his head. "I don't understand it."

"You are a soldier, William. You understand a different kind of weapon. It will be fine."

"Many lives will be saved if we don't have to attack Urbis," Affron pointed out.

"And that is all to the good, of course," Carmody admitted. But he still didn't look convinced.

Palta wasn't convinced either, but she didn't say anything about the plan in front of the others. "I don't like it," she said to me later that night, when we were alone in my room.

"Why not?"

"This magic—Affron says he doesn't understand it. And I know that he doesn't like it. He is risking too much."

"What is he risking? I've seen him use his power twice. It tires him out a bit, and he doesn't like doing it. But I don't think he's risking anything."

"You just want to go home," Palta said. "You'll do anything to go home."

"That's not fair, I also don't want to be captured and then executed on that scaffold in the Urbis forum. We've got to do *something*."

Palta couldn't argue with that. So she just shrugged and went off to her room, and the next morning I woke up alone.

CHAPTER 14

A nd then we waited.

Palta and I were the only ones who left the house now, and only to get food. We went to different shops every day, so that we wouldn't become too familiar to people. And that meant we could report back on what was happening in the city.

Things changed almost immediately. We started seeing drawings and graffiti on the walls of buildings, even in the Parioli district—caricatures of the pontifex, making him look like a doddering old fool, with "Tirelius non curat!" scrawled underneath. *Tirelius doesn't care!* And stick figures of what was supposed to be Affron, along with the phrase "Affronius pro pontifice!"–*Affronius for pontifex!* In the markets where we shopped, we now heard people complaining about how unfair the priests were, how Roma and its people were always being taken for granted, how it was time for a change. And why were they persecuting that wonderful viator Affron, who only wanted to help the Roman people? Shoppers talked of seeing protests against the priests—protests that the governor's soldiers did nothing to break up.

So Decius was holding up his end of the bargain. But in the meantime...Affron sat for long hours in the peristyle, speaking to no one, just staring off into space. At dinner, he would drink wine until Valleia ordered Palta to take the jug away. "What is the matter?" Valleia asked him one night.

"Nothing is the matter," he replied. "I am just contemplating what I will do when I become pontifex."

"I don't believe you."

He shrugged. "It will all be fine," he said. "No need to worry."

But the rest of us worried.

"He is our weapon," Carmody said to me after Affron had gone to bed one night. "One shouldn't go into battle with a weapon that hasn't been tested."

"But the rest of us have seen him use his magic," I pointed out. "Everyone but you. It works. It's powerful. He can do this."

"He is not acting like he can do it."

I couldn't argue with that. "Should we talk to Decius?" I asked Valleia.

"And say what?" she demanded. "Decius has made it clear what will happen if we don't go through with this." She looked at Carmody for support.

He nodded. "We are committed to the plan," he said. "We must make it work."

Palta said nothing.

And then, finally, the Roman Games opened. Banners and flags flew from every building. Even in our quiet castellum the main streets were filled with dancers and musicians and revelers. Everyone seemed to have a jug of wine; everyone seemed happy.

Inside our house, though, everyone was quiet and tense.

Affron spent most of the day sitting motionless in the peristyle. I sat next to him, hoping we'd have another one of our conversations, like we'd had after he'd stolen the money from the pawnbroker, but he stayed silent.

The chariot race was to be held on the afternoon of the second day. It was always the highlight of the Games.

I didn't sleep well the night before. I couldn't imagine anyone else did, either.

We were all up early the next morning. The day was hot, overcast, and oppressive. Valleia had decided that she, Affron, and Carmody would be the ones to go to the Circus Maximus. They were going to leave early to ensure that they got seats close enough to Tirelius. Valleia didn't want Palta and me to come. "We can't all march in there together," she pointed out. "It will be too obvious. We don't want to be captured now, when we're so close to victory."

This time Affron didn't insist on taking me. He didn't say anything.

"Then Larry and I will go by ourselves," Palta announced.

"As you wish," Valleia replied. "But you'll be safer here."

Palta gave her a look that said: *I don't have to obey you.*

"Be careful," she said to Affron before they left. He smiled at Palta and me and kissed each of us on both cheeks; Carmody shook our hands, and then the three of them headed off.

Palta pulled at her earlobe as we stood in the atrium. She did that a lot when she was tense or thinking hard. "We can't stay here," she said. "We must see what happens."

"But it'll be hours before the chariot race. Do you want to sit out in the heat all day?"

Then abruptly she sat down and started to cry. "I don't want this to happen," she said finally. "If it fails, it will be bad. If it succeeds, it will be worse."

"Why will it be worse?"

Her gray eyes looked up at me. "Because then you will go home."

I didn't know what to say to that. So I sat down next to her, and I took her hand in mine. We stayed there for a while before we silently stood up and left.

Everyone was headed to the Circus Maximus. Jugglers and dancers and even magicians were out on the streets to entertain the crowds. Most women had garlands of flowers on their heads, so Palta bought a cheap one from a street vendor and put it on. She looked pretty, and the garland seemed to make her a little happier. She grabbed my hand.

As we approached the Circus Maximus the crowds got even bigger. And that's where we saw the demonstration: a large, milling mass of people had gathered in the plaza outside the stadium and were shouting at a bunch of soldiers who stood in formation, shields raised, keeping the crowd from advancing any further. I could hear people chanting: "Tirelius non curat! Sacerdotes non curant! Affron pro pontifice!" *Tirelius doesn't care! The priests don't care! Affron for pontifex!* Occasionally someone threw a rock at a soldier, but he would fend it off with his shield without even flinching.

"Those soldiers are well trained," Palta remarked.

"Decius will claim he's doing all he can to stop the protestors," I said.

"But it's obvious he could do more, isn't it?"

"I suppose he could order the soldiers to attack the people. But he could claim to Tirelius that that would just make things worse."

"What if Tirelius doesn't come?"

"Decius was sure he'd come."

I realized that this idea gave her hope. If Tirelius didn't show up, then everything would be okay—for a while, anyway.

We circled around the protestors and soldiers and made our way to one of the entrances. From inside I could hear the roaring of the crowd and the blare of trumpets. I thought about gladiators fighting lions in ancient Rome; this wouldn't be like that, I was pretty sure. But people sure sounded excited.

Admission was free to the Games, and there was no such thing as reserved seats. You just pushed your way through the crowds into the stadium and tried to find a place to sit.

We walked along one of the long torch-lit tunnels, elbowing past people—some entering, some leaving, some just standing around and drinking cups of wine. Palta held onto my arm to keep us from getting separated. A couple of drunks tried to pinch her, and she spat out curses at them.

And then, finally, we were inside. The huge place was packed with cheering people. Out on the field a burly, long-haired man was winding up to throw the discus. He had a big chest and thickly muscled arms and legs. He twirled a couple of times and let the discus fly; it soared into the air and landed a long way down the field. But apparently it wasn't good enough; the man shook his head and turned away, and there were scattered boos from the crowd.

We climbed up into the stands, looking for empty spaces in the long concrete rows. There weren't any. We kept climbing, both of us sweating in the humid air. Finally we pushed our way into a row near the very top. I was right up against a fat guy in a stained robe who stank of body odor and garlic. We were so high up we could barely make out the athletes on the field.

"Have you ever seen anything like this?" I asked Palta. "You know, sports events?"

She shook her head. "I have seen stadiums on Gaia, but they were always empty, ruined. No time for sports."

In the stands near the middle of the field I spotted several empty rows of seats covered by a purple canopy. And in the middle of the seats were three thrones. I pointed to them. "I bet that's where Tirelius and the rest of them will sit."

Palta nodded. "It is so far away. Will people even notice what happens?"

"Decius will make sure people find out."

"I can't see Affron and the others. Can you?"

I shook my head. "I'm sure they're over there somewhere."

Down on the field, more naked, burly men threw the discus. Before long I became bored. When would the chariot race start? When would Tirelius show up? Sweat poured down my body. Eventually the discus competition ended. There was a ceremony on the field, like in the Olympics. A bunch of trumpeters came out from beneath the stands and played. Someone on the field—it looked like a priest—put a laurel wreath on the victor's head. Then he ran around the track, waving to the crowd. People stood and cheered.

And then the discus throwers left the field, and the javelin throwers came out and started their contest. The fat guy next to me went off and came back in a few minutes with a cup of wine. He seemed to enjoy farting, and the smell was just about unbearable. Palta and I bought figs from a passing vendor. The sky became overcast; I felt a few drops of rain. The javelin competition seemed to last forever. The crowd didn't seem to mind. Maybe I had watched too much sports on TV, but I thought it was really boring. I wanted to see the chariot race. I wanted to see Tirelius start to crown the victor with a laurel wreath. Then I wanted to see him fall to the ground and start writhing in agony as the crowd gasped in horror.

I wanted to step into the portal and step out of it into Glanbury—back when I left it, if possible. Or whenever. I wanted my family, my friends, my school. I wanted to be a counselor-in-training. I wanted to go to high school. I wanted to eat Doritos.

Morning turned to afternoon. The javelin throwers finished, one of them was crowned with laurel, and then there was a spectacular interlude when dancers and gymnasts performed while a huge band played weird music. It was like a halftime show in a football game, except the music on Terra never sounded quite right to me—the harmonies didn't make sense, the melodies never seemed to go anywhere.

After that, men in pants and tunics came out to prepare the field for the chariot race. The crowd cheered and then became quiet. The men seemed to take forever. Palta and I bought bread and cheese. I went to pee, and it was hard to get back to my seat. People were sitting in the narrow aisles now and pushing to make room in the already cramped rows. All around the stands people were waving flags and banners.

And then, finally, the chariots appeared, emerging through a large opening in the stands, on the opposite side of the field from the seats with the purple canopy. The chariots themselves weren't much to look at, really—they were basically small wagons with open backs and platforms for the drivers to stand on, with a couple of wheels underneath them. But the four horses that pulled each chariot were gorgeous. The charioteers waved to the crowd as they came out. Unlike the other athletes, they weren't naked; each of them wore a different-colored tunic and a leather helmet. The crowd cheered for all of them.

"Do you have chariot races in your world?" Palta asked me.

"We used to, I guess." I told her a bit about horse racing, but I didn't know that much about it, and anyway, chariot racing looked like it was going to be much more exciting. The chariots made a slow circuit of the track. Then the drivers got down and took care of their horses for a while. A long while.

"Tirelius isn't going to come," Palta said suddenly. "They're waiting for him, and he isn't coming."

"He'll come," I replied. But what did I know?

We waited. The crowd was on its feet, but quiet. The rain was heavier now. "Rain means many deaths," the fat man next to me said. He seemed pretty excited by the idea.

Finally there was a stirring. The charioteers lined up their chariots on the track; soldiers marched out onto the field and made a double line extending to the purple-canopied seats. A half-dozen trumpeters played a fanfare. Then a bunch of people came out, walking in pairs. I guessed that they were Roman officials; I thought I saw Decius in his white robe in among them, and the crowd gave a loud cheer when he appeared.

They were followed by purple-robed viators, and that's when the booing started. And then, finally, a litter emerged, carried by six men. On the litter was an ornate chair, and on the ornate chair sat Tirelius. Even from this far away I recognized him.

Boos echoed around the stadium. "Tirelius non curat!" the fat man next to me shouted, waving his fist in the air.

"Affronius pro pontifice!" someone behind us added.

The soldiers extended their right arms towards Tirelius as he passed.

Tirelius made a little gesture acknowledging them.

Just seeing him at a distance gave me a creepy, frightened feeling. This was the man who wanted to capture Palta and me and put us to death. I remembered his icy stare during Affron's trial. I wondered for the first time if he might have some kind of mental power like Affron's. What if he could sense our presence in the midst of the huge crowd? What if he could do something to us?

I shivered.

The litter-bearers lowered Tirelius and his chair in front of the far stands. All the other dignitaries were standing, waiting for him. The pontifex got off the chair and slowly walked up to the throne in the middle of the seats. The two vice-pontifexes sat on either side of him, as they had at Affron's trial. He sat, and then the dignitaries sat. The boos eventually subsided and turned to cheers as the charioteers got up onto their chariots and were strapped in. Someone with a megaphone started announcing stuff from the middle of the field. I couldn't hear any of it; the crowd was roaring now.

And then I guess there must have been a signal that I didn't notice, because suddenly the horses leapt forward, and the race began.

I've been to sports events before, but I never saw or felt anything like this. The crowd gave out one long, loud roar of noise; I was probably shouting myself. The chariots flew around the track, passing close to each other at a big wooden post on the turns as they tried to get the inside position. The lead went back and forth. Finally on the third or fourth lap two chariots collided. Their horses got all tangled up with each other in the mud, and I couldn't see what happened to the charioteers, although they had to have been seriously injured, if not killed. I expected the race to stop but it didn't—the remaining chariots just veered around the wreckage and kept going. The fat man next to me jumped up and down and screamed advice at the remaining charioteers.

I had no idea how long the race was supposed to last. Some kind of big pole in a corner of the track looked like it was keeping track of the laps, but I couldn't make any sense of it. Anyway, the crowd seemed to know exactly what was going on. After a while the charioteer in blue pulled away a bit from the others, and the stands shook with excitement as people urged him to go faster as the red guy started to catch up to him. There was another crash; more wreckage to swerve past. And the red guy was nearly up to the blue guy...

And then, suddenly, it was over.

The chariots that hadn't crashed slowed to a stop. The crowd kept roaring. The blue guy raised his arms in triumph; the red guy slumped over. People raced out onto the track to take care of the charioteers and horses from the crashes. The charioteers, covered with blood and mud, were carried off on stretchers; the crowd didn't seem to pay any attention to them.

"What do you think?" I asked Palta.

"I have never seen anything like it in my life," she replied.

Neither had I.

And now the moment was approaching. Affron was somewhere in the stands. He would be getting ready. He would wait until all eyes were on Tirelius. And then it would happen.

A few people were starting to leave, I noticed, but most were still in their seats. Torches had been lit on the field, and a platform had been wheeled out. It was raining harder now; I saw flashes of lightning in the distance.

The charioteers lined themselves up on the platform. The trumpeters played a fanfare. Tirelius and the two vice-pontifexes made their way slowly down from the stands, across the field, and up onto the platform.

The crowd started booing once again, although not as loudly as before. The fat man next to me looked like he was almost passed out. Maybe a lot of people were like that—there had just been too much excitement, too much wine consumed. Affron can't wait too long, I thought, if he wants to get a reaction from the crowd.

Tirelius and the other two old men were standing on the platform now. Someone had handed him the laurel crown. The charioteer in the blue tunic came up the steps and knelt before him.

Now, I thought. *Now!*

Tirelius bent over slowly and placed the crown on the charioteer's head. The crowd cheered. The charioteer rose and waved to the crowd. He stepped aside, as the vice-pontifexes and then Tirelius walked down the steps.

And that was all. It was over. And nothing had happened.

Palta was clutching my arm.

"He couldn't do it," she whispered.

I shook my head in disbelief.

"Perhaps now Valleia uses gant..." she said.

But no, Valleia wouldn't use the gant; no one would use the gant. It was over. Tirelius got back onto the chair, and the litter-bearers picked him up and carried him through the lines of saluting soldiers. I heard a few boos, but now everyone was too busy leaving before the thunderstorm arrived. The torches flickered in the rain. Tirelius disappeared into the tunnel, followed by the priests and the other officials. I supposed Decius was among them. And he would be furious.

I didn't move. I couldn't move. It was over, and with it my hope of ever returning home. The fat man staggered past us, along with everyone else in our row. It was dark now, except for the occasional flashes of lightning.

I couldn't imagine what would happen next. I didn't even want to think about it. Now Decius was our enemy, in addition to Tirelius. And what had happened to Affron? Was it that he couldn't use his power on Tirelius, or that he wouldn't?

Palta was still clutching my arm. She was worried about Affron, I knew—and maybe about me, I realized. And she had every reason to be worried about me.

"Come," she said. "There's nothing for us here."

She was right, but was there anything for us back at the house in Parioli? Or anywhere?

I stood up.

Palta took off her soggy wreath of flowers and flung it away, and then we went down the long set of steps past the few people remaining in the stands. I looked around for Affron and the others, but I didn't see them; I hadn't expected that I would. The passageway leading out of the Circus Maximus stank of pee and vomit. In the plaza outside no one was demonstrating; I just saw drunken fans waving blue flags and banners in the rain. A few wet and bored-looking soldiers remained to stare at the people streaming past.

We saw a flash of lightning and then heard a thunderclap close by.

"Gods are angry," Palta said. "*The* gods."

I didn't argue with her. I wondered what she had thought about gods back on Gaia. Did she blame them for everything that had gone wrong on her world? We started walking towards Parioli. But then Palta suddenly pulled me off the main street. "Where are we going?" I asked her.

"Nowhere," she replied.

And then we were running, as the thunderstorm raged. Running through the streets of Roma, past the crowds, past the drunken fans and the beggars and the prostitutes. Running nowhere, just because we had to do something. Because if we stopped, we'd have to think about what was going to happen tomorrow, and the day after that, and the rest of our lives.

Finally we paused in a long colonnade lit by a couple of torches, and we leaned back against a column, catching our breath as the thunderstorm raged. We were both soaked to the skin, but the night was warm, so it didn't feel so bad.

"I used to love being in places like this during a storm," Palta said, pushing her wet blond hair back off her forehead. "It would make me feel safe, even if the gods were angry. They weren't likely to be angry at *me.*"

"Me too," I said. "My mother was terrified of thunderstorms. She was sure we'd be struck by lightning. She'd always want us to come inside and stay away from windows. But I liked being out on our porch, hearing the rain drumming on the roof."

Was terrified, I thought. Past tense. As if I was never going to see her again. As if she had ceased to exist somehow, with me here on Terra.

I think Palta saw something in my eyes as I talked about home, because suddenly she slid into my arms and kissed me, there in the colonnade. The kiss felt wonderful; she felt wonderful. For a brief moment I didn't want to be anywhere else but right there, in Palta's arms.

A laughing couple hurried past us, arms around each other, paying attention only to each other. A mangy dog slunk by on the street. Everything was dark; everything was wet.

The kiss ended, but Palta stayed in my arms.

"Maybe Affron will have another plan," Palta said.

"I don't think we can trust Affron to come up with a plan," I replied. "I don't think we can trust him to do anything."

A wagon with a canvas top rattled past and then stopped. Two men got out and came into the colonnade. A lightning bolt lit up the sky. I saw a pile of rubbish, an unpainted door. The men had long beards and colorful robes. Palta pulled in closer to me as the men approached.

"Pulchellus puella," one of the men murmured as they came nearer. *Very pretty girl.* Another lightning flash. He smiled and bowed. He was missing several teeth.

The other man muttered something to him in a foreign language.

The first man shrugged. "Me paenitet," he said to us. *I'm sorry.*

And then he grabbed Palta while the other man pulled me back, punched me in the face, and knocked me down. I hit my head hard against the cobblestones, and the man kicked me in the groin.

Palta screamed and kept screaming. I didn't see what happened next. By the time I had staggered to my feet, the wagon was disappearing in the distance, and Palta was gone.

CHAPTER 15

I raced after the wagon. It didn't occur to me not to. It didn't occur to me that if the men spotted me they might stop and grab me and throw me into the wagon along with Palta. Or simply beat me to death. I had to rescue her. What else—who else?—was left for me on Terra?

I was limping from the pain in my groin. My eye throbbed. The back of my head throbbed. I tripped and whacked my knee on another cobblestone. I could barely see in the rain and the darkness.

The wagon turned. I was losing ground. I couldn't hear Palta screaming anymore. Had they gagged her? Had they killed her? Who were they? Where were they going?

I went down the street where the wagon had gone, just in time to see it turn again. I hobbled after it. I tried to think. Maybe catching up to the wagon was the wrong idea. I wasn't going to be able to out-fight those guys. But I couldn't lose sight of them. I had to find out where they were taking Palta. Maybe I could surprise them while they were asleep. Or maybe I could go back there with the others and save her.

If the others were still back at the house. If they still had the gant.

So I had a sliver of hope.

The wagon slowed down once it got to a more crowded section of the city, where people were out on the streets, even in the rain. We passed through a poor castellum with lots of taverns and shabby insulae. I could hear singing and laughter from inside the taverns.

I limped along, trying to keep far enough behind the wagon that I wouldn't be spotted. The men probably thought they had left me unconscious in the colonnade. I felt a bit dizzy, along with the pain. Back in my world, my mother would have had me at the emergency room by now, checking me out for a concussion. Did people even think about concussions on Terra?

The wagon turned, and turned again, and I found myself in an area of the city Palta and I had never visited in our explorations—the waterfront. The river was far wider here than it was back where the fisherman had let us out of his boat. Vast numbers of ships were at anchor out on the river or pulled up alongside huge docks. At a few of them men were busy loading or unloading cargo. The place stank of fish. Facing the river, the street was lined with huge windowless warehouses. I remembered Decius talking about grain imports and how important they were to Roma. The grain was brought up the river from a harbor a few miles away. This was where the imported grain was stored, maybe.

Were the men going to put Palta on a ship and send her off someplace?

She hated the water.

I kept back a little farther now. Eventually the wagon came to a stop by a small, shabby building off the main street. It was dark except for the glow of a lamp on the first floor. One of the men got out, walked up a short flight of steps, and pounded on a door. It opened after a minute, and he went inside. Before long a larger set of doors swung open to the left of the steps. Someone was holding a lamp. I saw a large open room, big enough for the wagon and the horses. Crates were piled up along the walls. The wagon went inside, and the doors swung shut. And that was all. It was like the wagon had never been there.

I waited. I saw lamplight appear in another window on the second floor. The light on the first floor went out. Nothing more happened. I made my way closer to the building. It was an old, run-down wooden place, three stories high; it had been painted once, but most of the paint had faded or flaked away. I thought I could make out the word NAVIS or NAVES painted on its side. Ship? Ships? The building looked badly built, like a big wind would knock it over. I walked around it. On the other side I spotted a small door with garbage piled up beside it.

The rain had let up a bit. I listened for sounds from inside. I didn't hear anything. But I knew that Palta was in there. I wanted to burst inside, rescue her, and kill the men who had kidnapped her.

But that wouldn't work, of course. I was just a kid, and this wasn't some video game. I needed help. I needed a weapon. I had to go back to Parioli.

But what if that took too long? What if she wasn't here when I got back? What if they put her on a ship and sailed away and I never saw her again? Could I just leave her behind and hope I could return before it was too late? And what if Affron and the rest weren't at the house? Maybe they had been arrested; maybe they were dead.

And anyway, I wasn't sure I knew the way to Parioli from here.

Palta would have known.

I had to try. I walked as fast as I could, limping and still groggy. I had never been alone at night in the city, but I was too upset and in too much pain to be scared. I ignored everyone I passed. This wasn't my world. They could all go to hell. All I wanted was to rescue Palta.

After a long while I found myself at the Forum, mostly empty at night except for a few soldiers guarding the buildings, and from there I knew the way to Parioli.

When I finally arrived at the house, with every part of my body throbbing with pain, the door was locked. I couldn't see any light inside. Was anyone there? I pounded on the door. "Let me in!" I shouted.

Carmody opened the door a minute later. "Larry, be quiet," he said. "Where have you been? Where's Palta?"

"She's been kidnapped. We have to rescue her." I rushed past him into the house. Valleia was walking towards me from the atrium.

"Kidnapped," I repeated. "We went to the Games, and afterwards two men attacked us and took her off in a wagon. They went to a building by the waterfront. They beat me up when they grabbed her. They probably thought I was unconscious, but I managed to follow them. We need to rescue her and bring her back."

Valleia put a hand on my arm. "Come sit down, Larry," she said. "You look awful."

"I don't want to sit down. We have to go. Maybe they're putting her on a ship right now. Palta can't stand the water."

Valleia pulled me into the atrium. Affron was sitting there. His eyes were closed, but he didn't look asleep. He looked like he was somewhere else.

Carmody brought me a cup of wine. I took a sip, but I wouldn't sit down. "What's going on?" I demanded. "Nothing happened to Tirelius."

"Affron couldn't do it," Valleia said quietly.

"You mean, he wasn't able to? Or he changed his mind?"

"Does it matter?"

"I don't know. I guess not. But right now we have to go and get Palta."

"Larry, I'm sorry, but we can't."

"Why not?" I had an idea. "We rescue Palta, and then we—what's the word?—we commandeer a ship, like we did outside Urbis. Make them take us somewhere we'll be safe."

"It's not that simple, Larry," Valleia replied. "Affron won't move; he won't speak. It was all we could do to get him back to Parioli. Unless we can get through to him, we're stuck here."

"But Decius will be looking for us. We can't stay here."

"Don't you think we know that, Larry?" Carmody said.

I looked again at Affron. Yes, something was wrong with

him. What? But it didn't matter. "Carmody and I can go," I suggested to Valleia. "You can stay here with Affron. Just give us the gant."

Valleia sighed and shook her head. "I'm sorry, Larry. We need the gant to protect Affron against Decius and his soldiers, if they show up."

"But Palta—"

"Palta is gone, Larry. She's probably already on a ship sailing to Barbarica somewhere. The slavers are active during the games, when foreigners visit the city and go to places where they shouldn't go."

"We have to try!" I insisted. "Palta is—is—"

She's part of our family. I wanted to say this, but I didn't. Because obviously Valleia didn't think she was.

"Valleia," Carmody said, "perhaps we could—"

"Do what you want," she responded. She looked tired and angry. "But you can't take the gant. We told Larry and Palta to stay in the house, but they didn't. And this is the result. I'm very sorry about what happened to the girl, but you can't take the gant and leave Affron here defenseless."

"Fine," I said. I turned to Carmody. "Will you come with me?"

He looked at me, looked at Valleia. "Without the gant?" he asked.

"I just need some help," I said. I felt like I was close to crying. "I can't do this by myself."

He turned back to me and slowly shook his head. "It'd be suicide, Larry. You saw two men capture Palta, but there are bound to be more at the place where they took her. Valleia is right. We can't rescue Palta, and we'd just endanger everyone else, especially Affron. I'm sorry."

"But you're a *soldier*!" I shouted at him.

"Soldiers don't go into battles they know they can't win," he replied softly.

He looked at Valleia again, and I knew that Carmody wasn't going to leave her. He was in love.

Nobody loved Palta—except, maybe, me.

I wanted to argue, but I knew it would be useless. I went

and knelt before Affron. His face looked empty, as if he was in a trance. What had happened to him? What had gone wrong inside his brain? Had the *speckness* overpowered him, the way it had overpowered the pawnbroker and Decius and the soldiers? Or was it something more?

"Please, Affron," I said. "Come back to us. I need your help. Palta needs your help."

But he didn't come back.

Finally I got to my feet. I finished the cup of wine Carmody had given me and went off to my room. Valleia and Carmody both tried to say comforting things to me, but I ignored them. I wasn't interested in being comforted. I lay on my bed in the darkness, wide awake. I didn't want to sleep. My robe was still wet, and my injuries hurt more when I was lying down, but I didn't care. My mind was filled with more than the usual regrets and worries, but I tried to stay focused.

I waited, and I thought.

It seemed like a long time, but finally I heard movement and footsteps and murmuring voices. I listened. I heard toilet sounds, and more whispering, and eventually silence. The thunder had stopped, the rain had stopped, the city and the house were quiet.

I kept listening.

I remembered early on Christmas mornings when I was a kid—Matthew and me lying in bed and listening for some sign that our parents were awake, because we weren't allowed to go downstairs and open our presents until they got up. Matthew was younger and more impatient than I was, and this was just torture for him. "It's okay," I'd whisper to him. "They have to get up eventually."

And now I was thinking: *They have to fall asleep eventually.*

I had to make sure they were asleep. If I moved too soon, I wouldn't be able to rescue Palta, and she would be doomed.

But what if Valleia and Carmody were taking turns staying awake, guarding Affron, watching out for Decius and his men? Maybe they didn't think they needed to, with the gant.

I kept listening for signs that people were asleep. Regular breathing, light snoring, silence.

Finally I decided I couldn't wait any longer, or I would probably fall asleep myself. I stood up in the darkness. I listened. I moved carefully out into the atrium and listened some more. I inched forward into the room that Valleia and Carmody shared.

A bit of starlight shone in on the room through its single window. I looked down at the bed and let my eyes adjust to the darkness.

Carmody lay next to Valleia, on his side facing her, his arm stretched out across her naked back.

I looked for the gant's blue glow, but I didn't see it. Valleia's robe was draped over a chair. I leaned over and felt it up and down. The gant wasn't in it. It wasn't on the chair. It wasn't on the table next to the bed. Did the table have a drawer? I felt for one; nothing. I went over to the small chest in the corner. I knelt down in front of it, opened it slowly and looked inside. No glow. I felt around inside. I felt clothes, maybe a blanket. No gant.

And that was all the furniture in the room. I looked under the bed. No blue glow; nothing. Maybe Valleia kept the gant under her pillow, or under the mattress. But that didn't make any sense—pillows and mattresses on Terra were thin; the gant would have made them too uncomfortable. And she couldn't waste time looking for it if Decius and his men broke into the house. Still, I tried sliding my hand around on the mattress between the two sleeping bodies. I tried sliding it under the pillows.

Valleia stirred then and muttered something, and I pulled my hand away quickly. She didn't wake up. But it didn't matter whether she was awake or asleep. The gant wasn't there.

Maybe she had suspected what I might try to do and hidden it somewhere else in the house. But of course that made no sense. And anyway, if she had hidden it, I'd never find it.

I backed out of Valleia's room, feeling completely defeated.

My brain was woozy. I was exhausted; I couldn't think. I should have been in the emergency room, with my mother fussing over me. I shouldn't have been in this awful world, trying to save a girl from being sold into slavery in Barbarica.

I turned. I stood in the atrium. I had to make a decision. Go, or stay? And then I saw a movement. A shape. A person.

It was Affron, sitting cross-legged on the floor, making those strange motions in the air. Like he was trying to find something that wasn't there.

I took a step forward. He lowered his hands.

He spoke without turning around to look at me. "It seems," he said, "that the plan was flawed. I am not the person I thought I was. My powers are still...unshaped."

I didn't know what to say. "I'm sure you tried," I replied. "But right now—"

"Palta," he said.

"We need to save her. It might already be too late. But we can all go to the waterfront and..."

Affron turned to face me. "You must save her by yourself," he said.

"How can I? Valleia hid the gant or something. I can't free Palta without it."

Affron reached into his pocket and pulled out the weapon, glowing with its own blue light. He held it out to me.

I went over and took it. This was the first time I had touched it. It was heavier than I had expected, and warmer—not like cold metal. Like something that was almost alive. "But why?" I said. "Why just me? Why can't we all be together and hire a ship and go to Barbarica?"

Affron shook his head. "It's time, Larry."

"Time for what?"

"Time for you to grow up."

My sister Cassie said stuff like that to me sometimes: *When are you going to grow up?* But I knew that Affron didn't mean it as an insult. "Why do I have to grow up right now?" I asked.

"Because you are more than you think you are, and a burden comes with that. Alas. Now go, and bona fortuna."

I didn't understand, but maybe that was because I needed to grow up. "Thank you," I whispered.

He inclined his head to me, and then he turned away.

I put the gant in the pocket of my robe, and I headed out into the night to save Palta.

CHAPTER 16

I started walking. Parioli was silent; the streets near our house were deserted. My knee was sore, my eye and groin hurt, my mind was still fuzzy. But I had the gant, and I knew where I was going.

I reached the main road and walked as fast as I could along it. Before long I saw a half-dozen soldiers marching towards me along the road, one torch-bearer in front of them and another behind. I quickly ducked into an alley and tried to think. Had they been sent by the Decius to capture Affron and the rest of us? Should I race back to the house and warn the others?

I thought for an agonizing minute, and then I ran down the alley and away from the soldiers, away from Parioli.

Maybe they were just a night patrol. And I didn't have any time to waste.

But I decided I had to make sure I knew how to use the gant.

I stopped into another alley and took it out of my pocket. I looked at its faint blue glow; I felt its warmth in my hand. I heard movement in the alley, and I saw a large rat feasting on a pile of garbage. The rat stopped and looked at me. I slowly raised the gant and aimed it. The rat didn't move. I tried squeezing the gant's handle.

Nothing happened.

My heart raced. That couldn't be right. I couldn't have gotten this far—I couldn't have the gant in my hand and not be able to use it. I squeezed again. Nothing. What if its battery or whatever had run out? But it *looked* like it still had power; it felt like it. What if my hand was the wrong shape or something? What if only certain people could use it? The rat turned back to his garbage. Maybe my hand needed to be in a different position. I tried moving my thumb to the top of the handle; I noticed a little notch there. I pushed down on the notch with my thumb while squeezing the handle with my fingers.

I felt something—a release, a momentary lightening. I saw a flash of white light.

The rat disappeared.

And most of the garbage disappeared as well, leaving behind nothing but fine ash and that odd, bitter odor in the air.

The gant felt a little hotter, but it quickly cooled down.

I had fired a rifle in Carmody's world—to kill a young blue-jacketed soldier from New Portugal, and later to kill wild turkeys. It was nothing like this. Firing a rifle had felt *physical*—the roar of the bullet, the recoil. Firing a gant was more like playing a video game with the sound turned off. It was like a fantasy; you squeezed it, you felt a sense of something powerful leaving the weapon—and you—and then the thing you aimed at disappeared.

It was far scarier than a rifle.

But knowing that I could shoot the gant made me feel safe as I headed back to the waterfront. If I ran into any more soldiers, they wouldn't capture me without a fight.

But I didn't see any more soldiers. I saw a beggar lying asleep in a tangle of ragged blankets in the shadow of a building. I saw a drunk throw up on the street and then stagger away, muttering to himself. I saw a couple having sex in an alley. I saw a black cat walking along a ledge. I saw a dog with wet fur trotting down the center of a street as if he owned it. I saw wet trash everywhere.

I tried to focus on what I was going to do when I reached the building where Palta was being kept.

Don't let yourself be surrounded. The gant would take care of anyone in front of me, but it couldn't protect me from people sneaking up from behind. If I only had to deal with the two men I had seen in the colonnade, I figured I'd be all right. But there would be more than two, as Carmody had pointed out. The whole building might be full of people. I have seen movies where at some point one guy takes on a whole crew of pirates or orcs or whatever, and those scenes have always seemed stupid to me. The pirates never have any strategy, they just come at the guy one by one or two by two, so he can take care of them all without getting a scratch himself. In real life that wouldn't happen. Someone would do something clever, something I'd never think of because I'd never done anything like this before. And even though I possessed the most powerful weapon people here had ever seen or could conceive of, they might still be able to defeat me.

Or maybe they'd all be asleep.

Or maybe they'd all be gone. And that would be the worst outcome—an empty building, a ship already headed for Barbarica, Palta lost forever.

I got closer to the waterfront. I smelled a strong fishy smell; I could make out the ships at anchor. There was no activity, no sound. The taverns and ships and warehouses were in darkness except for occasional dim lamplight. And then at last I could see the building, with the flaking paint and NAVIS or NAVES spelled out on the side. A lamp still shone in one of the second-floor windows. I stopped walking. I thought some more.

I would have to kill them all. I could show no mercy. They would show no mercy to me, or Palta, or anyone else. I would have to shoot the gant again and again and again until they were all dead. I had to hope the gant kept on working, that it didn't need to be recharged or reloaded. I had to keep my mind as clear as I could, and I had to get Palta back.

I thought again of the person I had killed in Carmody's world—a boy, not much older than me. He just happened to be fighting for the other side. I killed him because I had to, because he would have killed me if I hadn't killed him first. I still had nightmares about him. I realized that I would have nightmares about what I was about to do, if I survived. But I had to do it.

I took the gant out of the pocket. I walked toward the building and up the steps to the door that one of the men had pounded on. I tried the latch; it was locked. I took a deep breath. I aimed the gant at the latch, and I squeezed the handle. A brief flash of light, and the latch disappeared, along with most of the door and part of the door jamb. I stepped through the hole in the door and inside.

I paused to let my eyes adjust to the darkness. I saw a staircase ahead of me, doors to my left and right. I listened for voices, for sleep sounds, for sobs or cries of pain, but I couldn't hear anything.

I tried the door on the left. It was unlocked. I opened it. I could see movement in the blue glow of the gant. I heard the snickering of horses. I smelled hay; it made me want to sneeze. This was where they had brought the wagon. Was somebody in here with the horses? I couldn't spot anyone. I could search, but I didn't want to make any noise. I decided to move on. I shut that door and opened the door on the right.

In the gant's blue glow I could make out a table with papers on it, a pile of clothing on the floor, a narrow bed in the far corner. I smelled sweat and stale wine. I heard breathing.

I made my way carefully through the room to the bed. A bald man was sprawled on it, asleep. He wasn't one of the kidnappers. Was he the guy who had let them in? It didn't matter. I raised the gant, aimed, and squeezed the handle while pressing the notch. Another burst of light, and the man was gone.

I expected this to be silent, but it wasn't—I had also vaporized part of the bed, and what was left of it came crashing to the floor.

I stood there, my heart pounding, waiting for someone to call out, to come rushing down the stairs. Nothing.

So now I had killed again.

I couldn't stop to think about that. I moved slowly out of the room and up the stairs, still using the gant as a kind of flashlight. I didn't want to trip. I didn't want to make any more noise.

I paused at the top of the stairs. I saw a short hallway, again with doors on either side. Dim light shone through cracks in one of the doors on the left.

I could smell piss and sweat and fish.

I needed to sneeze. I felt dizzy. My pulse was racing. I tried to calm down.

I walked up to the door with the light under it. I pulled up the latch and opened the door.

In front of me was a large, dimly lit room. Half a dozen girls were lying on the floor. Palta was one of them. The other girls looked to be her age or a little older. On a bed in the corner, next to a flickering lamp, a man was sleeping.

All the girls were bound and gagged. One of them was moaning a little, but she—and the other girls—seemed to be asleep. I went into the room and looked down at Palta. She was breathing. Her robe was torn; her face was smeared with dirt. I needed to take care of her, but I had to do something else first.

I went over to the bed and looked down at the man. He was the one who had punched me and kicked me in the groin. He was short and ugly. He was still wearing the colorful robe he had been wearing in the colonnade, but now it had ridden up over his hairy legs. He was muttering in his sleep. I spotted a metal bar on the table next to the lamp, and I found myself wanting to slam the bar down on his head, over and over. I wanted to make him suffer, instead of just snuffing him out of existence. But I couldn't risk it.

I squatted down this time so that I could shoot him from the side and avoid hitting the bed. I aimed the gant at his head and fired. The head disappeared, but the lower part of the body remained, gushing blood onto the bed and floor.

I threw up into the blood.

I stood up unsteadily. I hoped I wasn't going to pass out. I went over to Palta and knelt beside her, keeping the gant pointed at the door. I bent over and whispered to her. "I'm here," I said.

She opened her eyes and saw me, and her eyes filled with tears of joy.

I worked her gag off. "I knew you'd come," she whispered.

That didn't seem entirely plausible, but I was glad she said it. "You're safe now," I said. "Well, pretty safe."

She looked around. "Are you alone?" she asked. "Are the others with you?"

"It's just me. I'll explain later. I killed a guy downstairs, and that man who was sleeping over on the bed. How many others are there?"

"Two, I think. The other man who took me, and fat woman. *A* fat woman. She brought us food and then left. I don't know where they are."

"All right. I've got to kill them before we do anything else." I thought for a second. "I want you to scream," I said.

Palta looked puzzled. "Scream?"

"If they're in the building, they'll think something's wrong and come to check. Then I'll take care of them."

"Can you untie me first?"

"Sure." I struggled with the knots in the thick rope, but eventually I got her untied. We stood up, and she hugged me. She was shaking. "Are you okay?" I asked.

She just held me for a moment without speaking. Finally she said, "Yes. I'll be all right. Are you ready?"

I went over and stood by the door, far enough away from it to be out of range of a knife or a fist. "Ready," I said.

Palta screamed. It was a very loud scream. The other girls stirred. After a moment I heard a door open upstairs. "Quid?" a man shouted. *What?* Then: "Clagge?" The other guy's name?

I gestured to Palta to scream again. She did. She was an excellent screamer.

I heard a door slam and footsteps coming down the stairs. "Clagge, quid agitur?" the man called out. *Clagge, what's going on?* He spoke Latin with a foreign accent.

The footsteps came closer. And then the man stuck his head inside the door. He was wearing nothing but a short gray tunic. He was holding a knife in one hand and a lamp in the other. "Ubi est—" he started to say. *Where is--.* And then he saw me. His eyes widened. He raised his knife.

I squeezed the handle of the gant and snuffed him out of existence.

I could hear the girls murmur and gasp, even behind their gags.

"Untie them," I said to Palta. "And put a blanket or something over the guy on the bed. I'll go look for the woman."

"Be careful, Larry," she whispered.

I nodded and left the room. I looked in the room across the hall. It was large and filled with random stuff—I could make out pottery and baskets stacked up on tables. I walked down the hall and checked the other rooms on the floor. More random stuff. Fine. I made my way back in the darkness and climbed the stairs to the third floor. At the top I stopped and listened.

"Vente?" a frightened female voice called out softly. "Clagge?"

The voice came from a room to my left. The door was open. I walked over to it. The room was small; gray pre-dawn light filtered in through a shutter.

A woman was sitting on the edge of a bed. She was fat and middle-aged, and the gray light didn't do her any favors. She was naked from the waist up, and her large breasts drooped down over her belly. On the table next to her was a wine jug and an overturned cup.

I moved into the room. I saw shelves with more jugs on them, robes on hooks, a fresco of a ship on the ocean.

The woman stared at me, stared at the gant. She seemed to dimly understand what was going to happen, even if she didn't know what the gant was for. She started to cry and held her hands out to me. She started talking fast—disconnected babble that I couldn't understand.

She's no danger, I thought. The men had been the danger. I could tie her up, leave her behind while I rescued the girls.

I heard sounds from downstairs—the freed girls talking, laughing, crying.

She was a kidnapper. She would have sold those girls into slavery and used the money to buy more wine. What did I care about her?

I couldn't wait. I aimed the gant at the woman and killed her, the fat body disappearing along with most of the bed. Then I left the room and searched the rest of the third floor. I didn't find anyone else. More rooms, more junk. One of the rooms had a window that looked out on the river. The river looked peaceful. I supposed the building itself seemed peaceful, if you were gazing at it from the outside. What could be going on inside this dismal, run-down place?

I walked slowly back downstairs and went into the room, where the girls were all untied and standing up, hugging each other and crying. Palta looked at me, and I nodded. "They're all dead," I said. She said something to the girls, who looked at me, and at the gant.

I put the gant into my pocket. "Vos liberi ad ire," I said to them. *You're free to go.*

And then I slumped to the floor and started crying like a baby.

I suppose it was partly from relief—I had done it. I had gotten the gant. I had come here and killed all the bad guys. I had saved Palta.

But it was something more. It was the woman upstairs. It was death. A million million universes, but this was the one that this particular version of the woman had inhabited. And now she was gone in an instant. I didn't really have to kill her. But that's what I had done.

I felt Palta next to me, holding me. The girls were crowding around me, thanking me. Their robes were dirty; their hair was disheveled; their faces were cut and bruised. But they were happy. "We all have to go," I said finally in Latin. "We can't stay here. Soon it will be daytime. You'll be safe if you leave."

They thanked me some more. They wanted to know my name, but I wouldn't tell them. They wanted to know about the gant, but I wouldn't say anything about it. And so finally they left.

All except one.

She had long blond hair that was tied up in two braids. Her robe had rich embroidery on the shoulders and back. I couldn't make out her face because she was lying face down on the floor, with her arms extended towards me, the way Palta had prostrated herself in front of Affron in the jail cell.

"You need to go," I repeated. "Get up."

"I owe you my life," she said in accented Latin.

"You don't owe me anything," I replied. "Go home."

"You saved my life," she said. "Now my life belongs to you."

I stood up and wiped my face on my sleeve; I could smell the puke on it from when I'd thrown up. Palta got up with me. "I don't want your life," I said. "We're leaving. You should leave too."

Before we left, Palta peed in the corner of the room. She didn't looking for a toilet. I think she enjoyed peeing on that floor. Then we went out of the room and downstairs. Palta held onto my arm. The girl followed us. I turned and looked at her. Her face wasn't exactly pretty, but it was strong and distinctive, with bright blue eyes, a thin nose, and a square chin. "Go home," I repeated.

She bowed deeply, but she didn't obey me.

We left the building. The sun still wasn't up, but the day was already beginning to get hot, and Roma was coming to life. I felt completely exhausted all of a sudden. I hoped I'd be able to make it back to Parioli. We started walking away from the river, away from the nightmare.

"How did you find me?" Palta asked.

I told her what happened, from the time she had been kidnapped to the moment I took off her gag. If she was upset that none of the others would help rescue her, she didn't say so. "I hope Affron is all right," she said.

"I hope so too."

"One of the men said they were going to put us on ship and take us away," she said. "The ship. A ship."

"That's what Valleia said would happen."

"He said we would be happy there—wherever we were going. But then he laughed."

"I'm glad he's dead."

Palta nodded. "It's good that you killed them, Larry. I will never forget what you did for me."

All I could say in response was: "I had to save you."

She squeezed my arm. On the street, vendors were setting up their stands. I realized I was hungry, and I bought some bread for Palta and me. I noticed the girl was still trailing behind us.

"Go home," I called out to her.

"This is the way I go home," she replied.

I didn't know what to do about her. I gave her some of the bread, which she accepted gratefully.

We walked on. "What do you think is happening to Affron?" Palta asked.

"I don't know. I don't think *he* knows."

"He shouldn't have to suffer like this."

"Yes. But we're all suffering, aren't we?"

"Do you think Valleia will be angry with you?"

"Probably. But she has bigger problems than me. At least she'll get the gant back."

"What will we do? What will happen next?"

"I have no idea. I think we'll probably have to hire a ship and leave Roma. If Affron can make it."

We fell silent as we entered Parioli. The streets were still quiet there, although the shops were opening, and a few people were outside, probably heading for the baths.

Finally we turned onto our street, and then we stopped
dead. Palta's fingers dug into my arm.

Three soldiers stood in front of our house, talking to
Decius.

CHAPTER 17

W e turned and ran.

Had the soldiers seen us?

It hurt to run. Finally I tripped on a cobblestone, stumbled, and stopped. Palta stopped too. I tried to think. "We should go back," I said, panting. "I can kill those soldiers with the gant. And Decius. We can save Affron and the rest, if they're still in the house."

"It's too late," Palta replied. "Why are those soldiers just standing out there? I think they're waiting for us. I think they've already killed the others."

I recalled the soldiers marching down the street as I made my way to the waterfront to rescue Palta. I should have gone back to the house and warned everyone. "But we don't know that," I pointed out.

And then the girl with the blond braids came up to us. "Those soldiers," she said. "They are gone."

We looked at her. "Are you sure?" Palta asked.

The girl shrugged. "Of course. You are in trouble, I think. Can I help?"

We didn't respond. Instead we walked back to our street and peered down it from the corner. The street was empty.

"There was a carriage," the girl said from behind us. "The soldiers marched off, and the one in the white robe—he got in the carriage and left. He must be an important man, I think."

"We should check inside," I said to Palta.

She nodded.

We walked slowly down the street to the house. The door was unlocked. I took out the gant, and we entered.

The house was empty. I looked for signs of a struggle—broken furniture, overturned chairs, blood on the floor. I didn't see any. What had happened? I wondered if Affron had tried to use his magic—had it deserted him again? I wondered if Carmody had tried to fight—that's what Carmody would have done. But the soldiers would have overpowered him.

"Maybe they escaped," I suggested.

Palta shook her head. "The soldiers have them," she said. "They are probably back in Urbis already. They shouldn't have stayed in the house."

I supposed she was right.

Except Valleia and Carmody thought they had the gant to protect them. But Affron had given it to me.

The sun was shining now. Birds were chirping in the small trees in the peristyle.

I looked at Palta. Tears streaked her face. I put my arm around her.

We went back outside and stood in the sunlit street. What were we supposed to do now? We could never return to this house; that was clear. Decius and the priests would still be looking for us, even if they had captured the others, if only because we had the gant. And that meant we had to continue to hide—maybe for the rest of our lives.

The girl with blond braids was still there, standing by a tree. "Can I help?" she repeated. "I am staying not very far from here. My home is your home. My life is your life."

Palta wiped her face with the dirty sleeve of her robe. "Yes," she said. "We need help. We need a place to stay. Can we go with you?"

The girl's face lit up with a smile. "Of course," she replied. "That is very good. Let's go."

She led the way back to the main road. We looked around for soldiers but didn't spot any. The girl continued to look happy, like we had done her a favor by allowing her to help us. "My name is Siglind," she said. "I am visiting Roma for the first time, to see the Games. But I do not like the place. Too hot, too dirty, too dangerous. Now I am in trouble for letting myself be—what is the word?—stolen. But I think perhaps not as much trouble as you."

"Where are you from?" I asked.

"From Gallia. Have you ever been there?"

"No, we haven't." Gallia—I remembered the name from talking to Affron. Gallia had started the revolt against the priests. I thought of King Harald's army being destroyed as the priests used the gants for the first time.

"Ah. It is very beautiful in Gallia," Siglind said. "Not crowded and filthy, like Roma. And no bad men who steal young girls."

"It sounds wonderful."

Siglind nodded happily. "I can't wait to return. And where are you from?"

"From Barbarica," I lied. "We are servants of people who came here for the Games, like you. But as you saw, they have been...taken away."

"Yes, I saw. Why were they taken away?"

"We don't know," Palta replied.

Siglind considered this, and then dropped the subject. "And what are your names?"

We told her.

"Larry and Palta," she repeated. "They are funny names. But I suppose that's how they name children in Barbarica. Siglind is also a funny name, if you aren't from Gallia. It is not far to where I am staying, anyway. We can take a bath, eat breakfast, and rest—you both look very tired. I'm tired too. And I was very scared—like you, Palta. But your brave friend saved me."

"He is very brave," Palta agreed.

"He is a hero."

The praise made me feel a little better.

In a few minutes we turned, and suddenly we were on the most beautiful street I had seen in Roma. It was more a park than a street, with a large fountain in the middle and trees everywhere. The houses were far larger than the one we had rented, with high brick walls in front and iron gates.

"Here we are," Siglind said, stopping in front of one of them.

Two soldiers were guarding the gates. I noticed that they were dressed slightly differently from other soldiers I'd seen in Urbis and Roma—their cloaks had a blue fringe, and their breastplates had the figure of a lion on them.

Both soldiers dropped to their knees when they saw Siglind. She said something to them in a language I didn't understand. They got up, bowed, and opened the gate. We walked through it. One of the soldiers ran ahead of us into the three-story building that faced us at the end of a long path. In moments the soldier reappeared accompanied by a black-haired, white-robed man. Behind them a thin, elderly woman in a dark robe and a white headdress struggled to keep up.

"Now for the yelling," Siglind murmured.

The black-haired man walked quickly down the path. He gave Palta and me a quick glance, and then dropped to one knee in front of Siglind. Then he got up and started talking fast and angrily—again, in a foreign language—waving his hands in the air and pointing back towards the building. The old woman joined him, and she started talking at the same time, crying and beating her breast.

Siglind said something in return, talking just as fast. She pointed to us. She crossed her hands over her breast. She pointed up to the sky. Finally she, too, started to cry, and she prostrated herself on the path in front of the two of them, her body heaving with sobs.

And this caused the old woman to howl and the man to get down on both knees and apparently beg Siglind to get up.

Finally she did. The old woman embraced her. The man bent over and kissed her feet. Then he crawled over and kissed my feet, then Palta's feet. Finally he stood up and bowed to us. "You are our honored guests," he said to us in good Latin. "My name is Venerix, and I welcome you to the embassy of Gallia."

The old woman still stared at us suspiciously, and she didn't speak. "This is Lafreia," Siglind explained to us. "I have failed her, my father, and my homeland by not obeying her just commands. She doesn't trust you, but she will come to love you because you saved my life. Won't you, Lafreia?"

Lafreia inclined her head maybe a fraction of an inch. She didn't seem impressed by us, with our torn and dirty robes.

Siglind smiled. "Now the yelling is done," she said to us. "It was not so bad. We all take a bath, and the servants wash your clothes, and then we eat and talk. Yes?"

Venerix bowed some more and led us inside.

We walked through a large entrance hall with marble floors, white columns, and a grand staircase flanked by ten-foot-high painted statues of a man and woman wearing armor. There was a mosaic of a lion on the floor. Everyone who saw Siglind stopped what they were doing and bowed deeply until we had passed.

"What is embassy?" Palta whispered to me in English.

"It's, um, a building where people who represent a foreign country live. In the capital city of another country."

Palta didn't look like she quite got the idea. And I didn't quite get it myself. Gallia was a province in the Roman empire, I assumed. Maybe provinces had embassies to each other, or to Urbis. And who exactly was Siglind? She certainly seemed important.

Beyond the entrance hall we entered what looked more like a residence, only much bigger than our house in Parioli. Two upper floors surrounded the huge atrium, with balconies looking out over flowers and trees and a central fountain.

"Let us go to the tepidarium," Siglind said. "Wash the Roman dirt from our bodies."

She led us down a flight of stairs into a large, steamy, brick-lined room with a pool in the middle; it was almost as big as the public bath I had gone to in Urbis. She motioned to a couple of shirtless men at the far end of the pool, and they immediately started dumping hot water into the pool from enormous cauldrons. Then she took off her sandals and robe, handed them to one of several women who were standing there, and walked down into the pool. "Come, then," she called out to us.

So Palta disrobed and followed Siglind into the pool.

"You too, Larry," Siglind said to me. "The women will take care of your clothes."

"I have my weapon," I replied. "No one can touch my weapon."

"Oh, yes," Siglind said. "Your weapon is a thing of magic. We must talk about it." She said something to the women, who nodded.

So I took the gant out and set it on a table and then removed my clothes and joined Siglind and Palta in the pool.

It felt unbelievably wonderful after all that had happened. The warm water was just what my aching body needed. Siglind was older and had larger breasts than Palta, and it was very hard not to stare at them, but I was too tired to be aroused by her nakedness. Siglind closed her eyes and ducked her head under the water, then came back up and motioned to the men to put in more buckets of hot water. "It is good, isn't it?" she said to us.

We agreed.

"Last night was like a bad dream," she continued. "I went off exploring by myself, away from Lafreia and my guards. I was told not to do this, but still I did it—I am like that, I'm afraid. And I ended up being taken by those bad men. I was very stupid and very frightened. Venerix sent men out to search for me when I didn't come back, of course. He stayed up all night worrying. He was about to ask the Romans for help. That would have been highly embarrassing, but what could he do? Now all is well.

Venerix and Lafreia are too happy that I am safe to stay angry with me. If I hadn't come back, they would have been thrown in prison, or worse."

I decided I needed to clear something up. "You seem to be very important here, Siglind. Who are you?"

"Ah, I have not said. My father is Carolus, king of Gallia. He let me come to Roma for the Games, although he thought it was a stupid and dangerous idea. He was right, as usual."

"So you are a—a—" I tried to think of the Latin word.

"*Regis filia*, yes. A princess. It is a good thing for you when a princess owes you her life, Larry. Although men have all the power in Gallia. My father keeps threatening to marry me off to someone. I suppose he will someday."

"And you're living here in the embassy while you're in Roma?" I asked.

She nodded. "Yes. It is very nice, isn't it? But Roma itself—ah, I cannot wait to leave it."

"Where is Gallia?" Palta asked.

Siglind waved her hand. "You do not know? Gallia is north, over the mountains. It is so lovely. And the people are proud and strong. Tell me about your homeland. My father would never let me go to any part of Barbarica."

Palta looked at me. "That's a long story," I said.

"We have plenty of time," Siglind responded. "But as you wish. Now we shall eat." She motioned to the women, who came to the edge of the pool with towels for us. We dried ourselves, and then the women handed us white robes. Mine was too large for me, but it was soft and clean and smelled way better than the one I had been wearing. I put the gant in one of its pockets. Then Siglind led us upstairs to a large dining room lined with frescoes of fierce warriors slaying their enemies. She gave some orders, and in moments we were served delicious bread and cheese and figs along with sausages and big slices of beef—more meat than I'd eaten since I'd been on Terra.

"Now tell me how I can help you, Palta and Larry," Siglind said as we ate. "You are in great trouble, of course.

I saw how quickly you turned away when you saw the soldiers in front of your house. I am thinking perhaps you—or your masters—stole that magical weapon. I am thinking it belongs to the priests, and you did not bring it from your homeland. But you don't need to tell me this. Here is what I want to say. My father will be very interested in this weapon. I would like you to show it to him."

Did Siglind understand that it was this weapon—or ones like it, anyway—that had been used to destroy her ancestors during King Harald's revolt? I figured maybe she did. Palta and I looked at each other; I didn't know how to respond.

So Siglind kept talking. "You know," she said, "if you are in trouble in Roma, the best thing for you to do is to leave the city. It is no good here anyway. In addition to being hot and dirty, the people smell bad. If you come to Gallia, you will be safe. We love to fight, but we are just, and we do not harm our friends. You will be our honored guests, and that will be very fine. Palta, eat some beef. Is it not good?"

Palta tried a bite and forced a smile. "It is good," she said. I wondered if she had ever eaten beef back on Gaia.

"So what do you think?" Siglind went on. "Come to Gallia with me?"

I tried to think. But I was exhausted, my body hurt all over, and the bath and the food were making me even sleepier. Palta and I were on our own now; we couldn't afford to make a mistake. "You are very kind," I replied. "But we will have to discuss this. Can we rest first and talk later?"

"Of course! We have excellent beds here—too soft for Gallic warriors, but still very nice. Rest, and we will talk some more."

She summoned servants, and we were escorted upstairs to beautiful rooms overlooking the atrium. The beds were as soft as Siglind had promised, and they were surrounded by thin curtains that billowed gently in the warm morning air.

We went into Palta's room and sat on the edge of her bed. "Gallia is far away," she pointed out. "And we know nothing about it."

"But how can we stay in Roma?" I asked. "We have no money, no friends, and everyone is looking for us. How do we survive? How do we get back to the portal?"

Palta tugged at her earlobe and said, "I don't know. I miss Affron."

I sighed. "We're safe here for now, I guess. Let's get some sleep, and then we'll figure it out."

"Yes, of course." She squeezed my hand.

I went to my room and lay down. I wasn't at all sure we would figure it out. I had saved Palta, but now I had less chance of getting home than ever. And maybe less chance of surviving. I took the gant out of the pocket of my robe and placed it next to me on the bed. And then I closed my eyes and fell fast asleep.

It seemed like no time had passed when I felt someone shaking me. I opened my eyes and saw Siglind looking down at me, holding an oil lamp. Behind her the room was in darkness. "Ah, Larry, I'm sorry to awaken you," she said. "But we must talk. There is danger."

I sat up. "What danger?" I asked.

"You didn't tell me that every soldier in Roma is looking for you and Palta. I think you really should not have that weapon. We must save you, before it's too late."

CHAPTER 18

W e roused Palta, and Siglind brought us downstairs to
a large torch-lit room where Venerix sat at a table
covered with papers. He stood and bowed when we arrived,
but now he didn't look like he wanted to kiss our feet.

We sat opposite him.

"Speak," Siglind ordered Venerix.

He bowed again and sat back down. "The Princess
Siglind mentioned your names to me," he said to us. "I
have encountered those names—Larry and Palta—before.
The priests of Via have ordered your arrest. Posters seeking
information about you and three others, including two
viators, have been distributed throughout Roma for some
time now. I presume that you know this."

He paused, waiting for us to respond. I just shrugged.

"I certainly know about the viator Affron," he went on.
"One could not walk through the city in the past few weeks
without hearing about him or seeing his name scrawled on
walls. But I don't know who you are or why the priests want
you. And now I find that you are here, in our embassy."

"Get to the point!" Siglind demanded.

I saw annoyance flicker on Venerix's face. *He's angry*, I
realized.

"The Princess Siglind did not mention exactly how you
managed to save her from those slavers," he went on. "I

wish she had. Trust me, news like this has a way of spreading quickly, even in a city as large as Roma. Another of the girls you rescued last night told her parents the complete story—about a young man who arrived and made the slavers disappear using a magical device that could only have belonged to the priests. The parents recalled the posters. Their daughter's descriptions matched that of the young man and woman on the posters. They brought this information to the Roman authorities, who have apparently redoubled their efforts to find you as a result. Governor Decius is not happy about you."

"Do you know what happened to Affron?" Palta asked.

Venerix shook his head. "He is dead, I assume, or soon will be. My understanding is that he and Decius were in league against Tirelius, and now they are enemies for some reason. Decius does not let his enemies survive. But I do not care about him. I just know that you two are our guests here, and if the priests discover that we are harboring you, this will be profoundly dangerous for all of Gallia. Gallia's loyalty to Urbis is always being called into question. The priests will suspect the worst if they find out."

Siglind nodded. "That is all very well," she said, "but I have told Venerix that if he tries to turn you in to the priests I will cut off his testicles and make him eat them for dessert."

Venerix bowed to her. "The Princess Siglind has been kind enough to make her wishes clear to me."

Siglind laughed. "Venerix is a wonderful ambassador," she said to us. "But you see the problem. You cannot stay here in our lovely embassy—too many people will notice you. If the priests discover that we are hiding you, they are the ones who will cut off Venerix's testicles."

"If the priests discover that we are hiding these two, my testicles will be the least of our problems," Venerix murmured.

Palta and I looked at each other. "We will leave the embassy if you want, of course," I said. "We have no wish to put you in danger." I didn't want to say that, but I figured I had to.

"No no no!" Siglind exclaimed. "You must come with me back to Gallia!"

"Even that will be a problem," Venerix pointed out. "Just getting you out of the city may not be easy. The reach of Decius is long, and the reach of the priests is even longer. There are priests in Gallia, too—the king's chief minister among them—and the king must heed their desires."

"My father does what he pleases, not what the priests tell him to do," Siglind said angrily.

"Of course, my lady," Venerix responded. I got the sense that he was just being polite, though.

Siglind made a face, as if what she really wanted to do was cut off the testicles of some priests. "Larry and Palta will be safe in Gallia," she asserted. "My life is owed them, and my father will make sure the debt is paid."

"As you say," Venerix replied. "But first we must get them to Gallia."

Siglind didn't seem worried by this. "You will think of something."

Venerix inclined his head to her. "I am honored by the trust you place in me," he said.

"We must leave in the morning," she announced to us. "Early. Every moment you are here, more servants will see you. They will have a chance to whisper to each other. Perhaps one of them will mention something to the fruit-seller, or to the Roman boyfriend who does dirty things to her behind the tavern. You must leave with me."

My eye was throbbing. Had it been only a day since the guy had punched me in the colonnade—since I had killed him and everyone else who had kidnapped Palta? It was hard to think, but the answer seemed clear: We had no choice. We had to leave Roma. Palta nodded to me. "We are very grateful for the offer," I said. "And we're sorry for the trouble we're causing everyone."

"No trouble at all!" Siglind exclaimed. "You will love Gallia! And then, perhaps, we can find a way to get you to your homes in Barbarica."

We got up to leave, but then Venerix said, "Can you show it to me—the weapon?"

I hesitated, and then took out the gant and put it on the table. He stared at it. He touched the barrel, and then quickly took his hand away, as if the thing had burned him. "It is from the priests, yes?"

I nodded.

"I won't ask how you got it or why you have it," he said. "I don't want to know. I am very glad that you could use it to save Princess Siglind. But I will tell you that this is a weapon of evil. Do you know the story of King Harald?"

"I have heard some of it," I replied.

"My grandfather was in King Harald's army. King Harald did not want to destroy the priests of Via. He had no wish to rule their empire. He just wanted the priests to respond to the pleas of his people for justice. We in Gallia are different from Romans, and we needed to be treated differently. And what did the priests do? They ignored those pleas; instead they rained death on Harald's army from the walls of Urbis. Worse than death, because there were no bodies left to bury, to treat with reverence and honor. It was as if those brave men had never existed. It was a sorry day for Terra when that happened."

Siglind reached out and patted Venerix's hand. "We will avenge those deaths someday," she said.

"Yes, my lady. But in the meantime I must do my job and keep you—and Gallia—safe."

"Ah, you are a good and wise man, Venerix. We leave tomorrow morning, and that will make your life so much easier."

Venerix inclined his head to her once again. "Easier, my lady," he said, "but much less interesting."

I put the gant back in my pocket, and Siglind brought us back upstairs to our bedrooms. "All will be well," she told us. "Venerix will not let us down."

"We are very grateful," I replied.

And then Palta and I were alone once again. "I don't want to go," Palta said.

"I know. But we don't have any choice, do we?"

She didn't answer. "Terra is not the world I had hoped it would be when Affron brought me here," she said.

"I know," I said again. We sat in silence for a while, and then Palta went off to her room.

I had a hard time getting to sleep. My body's clock was out of whack, I suppose, and people were making a lot of noise—getting ready for the princess's departure, I figured. But mostly I was thinking about home, and how this would be one more step further away from it. And then I had a twinge of *speckness*, as I thought of Affron and Valleia and Carmody, and all the other people I would never see again, on this world and every other one.

Had Affron and the others already been hanged on that scaffold in front of the temple of Via? Was there a world in which they had survived? Was there a world in which I would make it home to my family and tell my story to Kevin?

The twinge passed, and finally I drifted off to sleep. When I awoke much later, Palta was there beside me.

Siglind roused us early in the gray pre-dawn light. It was going to be another hot day. The embassy was in an uproar, as wagons were loaded and soldiers were mustering and Venerix was giving orders to everyone. The three of us went down to the dining room and ate breakfast. "I am so excited!" Siglind said to us. "I am sorry that you are not going home. There is no feeling like it."

Palta and I didn't reply.

"They will tell us when they are ready for you," Siglind went on. "The fewer people who see you, the better, of course. Venerix knows what to do. At first I hated him, with all his rules. But if I had followed his rules, I would not have gotten into trouble. And yet, if I had not gotten into trouble, I would not have met you."

"We are very grateful for his help—and yours," Palta said.

"His idea is to pack you up like clothing in a chest—I hope it won't be too uncomfortable. He is worried that the

Roman soldiers will spot you if you are just sitting in one of our wagons. We will be inspected at the city walls. They may question everyone—I don't know. I am a princess— they shouldn't do such things to my people."

I didn't like the idea of being stuffed into a box, but I supposed the plan made sense.

Finally Venerix appeared in the dining room. He bowed to us. "We are ready, my lady," he said.

Palta and I stood up.

"I am sorry to have to do this," he said to us. "But you understand the danger."

"We understand," I replied. "Hiding us is a good idea."

We left the dining room and went into the atrium. Two beige-colored robes were draped over chairs; Palta and I put them on, and I transferred the gant to the pocket of my new robe.

Beside the chairs were two large chests with lions painted on them—one for Palta, one for me. Siglind gave each of us a hug. "Oh, my friends," she said, "we will keep you safe!"

We shook hands with Venerix. Then we got into the chests, and he shut the lids.

The chests were large, but not quite large enough for me to be comfortable in mine. There was plenty of air— someone had cut holes in the lids—but I had to pull up my knees and bend my head, and I knew I was going to get claustrophobic after a while. And hot.

I heard Venerix give what sounded like an order, and then a couple of people picked up my chest and carried it, with me swaying inside. What if I threw up from the motion? What if I needed to pee?

I could sense when we were outside, and then the chest was shoved somewhere. I heard a door shut. I heard men and women talking in a foreign language, the sounds of horses shuffling and snorting. People moved past me. More doors slammed. I started to sweat. And then Siglind was whispering through one of the air holes. "It will be over soon, Larry," she said. "Are you all right?"

"Yes," I lied.

"You are very brave. I must leave you now."

Another door shut. Someone yelled a command, and then we were in motion.

I heard the sounds of the city as the horses clopped along: people talking and arguing, music playing, a herald announcing who had won the races at the Games yesterday. Was he going to say anything about Palta and me? *Be on the lookout for a young man and woman...*

Before long we started to move faster. Heading north, towards Gallia. Had I been to this part of the city? I had probably seen very little of Roma, despite the time I had lived in it. Would I ever see it again? I had no desire to. Like Siglind, I thought it was dirty and loud and crowded, even in the nice neighborhoods. But I had gotten used to it, just as I had gotten used to Carmody's world, with its chamber pots and drikana, that awful disease. It was just another way of living.

Meanwhile, I was dripping with sweat. My left arm had gone to sleep. My groin ached from where it had been kicked. I felt awful.

And then we slowed and stopped.

"Salve!" a man's voice called out. I heard footsteps. "Returning to Gallia?" the voice asked, closer now.

I couldn't make out the response.

More footsteps, very close now. What if I sneezed? What if the guy could smell my sweat? What if he decided to open a chest just to show he was the boss?

I held my breath. The footsteps moved away.

"Have a safe voyage!" the voice called out. Someone replied, and then the carriage started moving again, even faster now, and I felt every bump as we sped along.

Were we out of the city now? Or would there be more checkpoints to pass through? We kept going. I felt like I was becoming dehydrated from all my sweating. What if I passed out? Maybe it would be better if I passed out, so I wouldn't have to endure any more of the motion and the heat. Either I'd come to, or I wouldn't. If I didn't, would that be so bad?

Finally the carriage stopped again. I heard footsteps, and then people were lifting the chest up and placing it onto the ground. The lid opened, and I was staring up at Siglind. She reached down and pulled me up out of the chest. "Larry, you look terrible!"

"I just…um…just need to, um…" I realized that I didn't know the Latin word for "pee."

"Yes, of course. We must hurry, though. We are still near Roma."

We were on a wide road bordered by trees, and beyond the trees were fields. The road went off into the distance in both directions. I stretched and walked over to the trees. Palta was already squatting down behind one. Her robe was soaked with sweat, like mine. I peed against a tree.

"That was awful," I said.

She nodded, but she didn't look as bad as I felt. Perhaps she was used to this sort of thing on Gaia. We walked back in silence. The chests were gone from the roadway. In front of us I saw half a dozen Gallian soldiers on horseback. Behind us were carts filled with servants and baggage, as well as a string of pack-mules. In the carriage, Siglind smiled at us.

"Come into the carriage with me," she said. "You are safe. We will not be stopped now."

"Won't your people wonder about us getting out of those trunks?"

Siglind waved her hand dismissively. "I will make up some story if they ask. We have left Roma behind. The danger is gone."

I wasn't going to argue. The carriage was ornate, with the familiar lion crest on the doors. We climbed inside. Lafreia was sitting there, wearing a gloomy black robe despite the heat. She glanced at us with distaste, but Siglind ignored her and poured some water from a jug for us, and we drank it down greedily. Then the carriage started up, and we were underway again. The carriage seats were cushioned, but still we jounced and swayed and felt every bump on the road. The road was long and straight; alongside it I saw a lot of what looked like tombs. Was this where Romans buried their dead? I also saw inns and cattle and flocks of sheep and distant villages.

"I would rather ride a horse," Siglind was saying, "but my father insists on the carriage."

"I've never ridden a horse," I said.

Siglind looked shocked. "That is awful. Riding is one of the great pleasures of life. Do you not have horses where you live in Barbarica?"

"Something like that."

She shook her head. "There is much I want to know about your life, Larry."

"I'll tell you someday. Not now."

Siglind didn't object. She was happy to do the talking, and Palta and I were happy to listen. She talked incessantly about Gallia and its great soldiers, its glorious history. And she talked about her father, King Carolus, and what a great and wise ruler he was.

But after a while I began to get the sense that the reality didn't quite match up with her descriptions. Gallia might have been an important kingdom once upon a time, and King Harald's revolt might have been a big deal, but now it was just another province controlled by the priests. It seemed like her father didn't really have all that much power—he just did what the priests told him to do. And Gallia's soldiers might have been fierce warriors, but nowadays they didn't have anyone to fight; Siglind talked about them protecting the borders against invasion from Barbarica, but she admitted that those borders had been quiet since the Great Revolt. "When war comes, we will be ready!" she insisted.

But would there ever be another war? "Who is going to fight the priests, after the way they defeated King Harald?" I asked.

"The day will come," Siglind replied. "And on that day, we will crush our enemies beneath our feet."

It wasn't clear to me if she was talking about crushing the barbarians or the priests. I could feel the slight warmth of the gant in my pocket. Gallian soldiers could defeat barbarians, I thought; it would be a fair fight, at least. But the priests couldn't be defeated except by other people with gants. Or maybe by Affron. And now Affron was gone. If the Gallians wanted to avenge their defeat in the Great Revolt, they weren't going to do it with swords and spears.

For all her talk about the glory of Gallia, Siglind was also very pious when it came to Via. To her, Via was just the way in which the gods interacted with people on Terra. "I love the gods," she said. "They have done much good for Terra. We owe them everything. It is the priests I despise. I do not know why the gods continue to show them favor. Why can't they move Via to Gallia? We would do much better with it than the priests."

I looked at Palta, who shrugged and said nothing. There was no sense talking to Siglind about where we really came from, or what Via really was. She wouldn't believe us.

We stopped to eat lunch at one point. I noticed the servants staring at Palta and me, but they didn't speak to us. I wondered what kind of story Siglind would make up to explain why we had left Roma hiding in chests.

At any rate, most of the conversation was in Siglind's language, which they called *Gallic*. I remembered Affron telling me that Gallia was the same as France in my world, more or less. I had been taking French in school, but I couldn't follow any of what these people were saying. I was pretty proud of how much Latin I had picked up on Terra, but I thought that learning yet another language might be beyond me.

Eventually we got back in the carriage and headed north again. "How long will it take till we reach Gallia?" Palta asked.

"Ah, far too long," Siglind replied. "Seven days, if the weather is good. And then two more days till we reach the royal castle."

When the sun went down, we camped by the side of the road. Women servants made a fire and cooked food; the men set up a tent for Siglind and Lafreia, but we all ate together under the stars. The food tasted wonderful, and the cool, clear air felt great after the city and the long ride. "At last I can breathe!" Siglind said.

The soldiers set up sentries, and a servant gave us each a thin blanket. Palta and I lay down away from everyone else. The stars were miraculously bright, and I felt pretty good, despite my injuries.

"This is not so bad," Palta murmured.

"No," I agreed. But we were still in danger. And what would happen when we got to Gallia? Siglind had mentioned helping us go home to Barbarica. But there was no home for us there. There was no home for us anywhere in this world.

We went to sleep finally, and at dawn ate breakfast with the others. Then we climbed into the carriage with Siglind and Lafreia, and the journey continued.

The weather got a little cooler as we continued north. Siglind became less chatty as she ran out of things to say. In Carmody's world I had gotten used to how long journeys took in a wagon or on foot, of course, but there I had only traveled from Glanbury to Boston; now we were going much further. The road was occasionally busy as it went past a village or small town, but mostly we had it to ourselves, traveling mile after mile through empty countryside.

On the fifth day we headed up into mountains; I had never seen anything so spectacular. The servants unpacked heavy cloaks and handed them out to everyone. Before dark we stopped at a large inn and took over most of it. Palta and I slept in a long, narrow room with all the servants. There was one small smoky fireplace that failed to keep us warm; I shivered all night. In the morning I was happy to be on the road again, with the sunlight to warm us and the scenery to entertain us. "It will not be long," Siglind said as the carriage climbed ever higher into the mountains. "I cannot wait."

Another day in the mountains, through a pass, and then the rode took a long, winding path down on the other side.

Another day's journey through farmlands and forest, and finally across a bridge that spanned a wide river.

"Home!" Siglind shouted when we reached the other side. The carriage stopped. She hugged Lafreia, Palta, and me. And then she got out, knelt down, and kissed the earth of Gallia.

PART IV

Gallia

CHAPTER 19

The journey continued, but everyone seemed happier now that we were in Gallia; even Lafreia smiled once or twice. The landscape was much the same—fields and forests, isolated farmhouses, an occasional small town in the distance—but the people we passed were dressed differently: the men usually wore loose pants, and their hair was long; women often had their hair in braids like Siglind's, and their robes were far more colorful than those that Roman women wore.

And people recognized our carriage, with the lion crests on its doors. Many stopped what they were doing and knelt as we passed. Siglind approved. "They love us," she said. "My father is a great man."

Now that we were in Gallia, Siglind's conversation became more personal. For the first time she told us that she had an older brother, Feslund, who was heir to her father's throne. Feslund didn't take her seriously enough because she was a woman, and she deeply resented that. She loved her mother, Queen Gretyx, but she thought Gretyx took too much interest in Feslund and not enough in her—the queen just wanted Siglind to behave better so that she could be married off to someone suitable. I got the sense that Siglind had no use for anyone who had a claim on her father's affections. She didn't want to get married, since it meant that she would be parted from the king. But sometimes she talked as if she couldn't wait to have a husband, so she would no longer be treated like a child and ignored by the important people.

I also got the sense sometimes that she had forgotten the problem Palta and I were presenting the king. She had convinced herself that her father would be delighted with her—and us—for bringing one of the priests' weapons to him. "We will give him the greatest weapon that Terra has ever seen," she said.

"But Venerix said—" I began to reply.

"Oh, Venerix worries too much," she said. "My father will make great use of this weapon. You'll see."

That seemed unlikely to me. If I understood the situation in Gallia correctly, Venerix was right to be worried: we, and the gant, were a danger to the province, and if the king had any brains he would realize this.

It occurred to me how difficult it was to always be judging people, especially from worlds so different from my own. Siglind seemed smart sometimes, and then she seemed awfully naïve. She was nice to us, but how could I be sure she really meant it? Lieutenant Carmody had seemed nice back when Kevin and I were in his world, and then he had plotted to keep us from ever returning home. It wasn't that he was evil; he was just thinking about more than my happiness—his career, the war his country was fighting, its success after the war. We really couldn't rely on anyone.

I talked about this with Palta, on our last night on the road. "On Gaia, we trusted other members of our tribe," she said. "And even they would let us down sometimes. In the end there is no one but yourself."

That seemed like an awful way to live.

The next day we saw vineyards and orchards, and shepherds tending flocks of sheep on the slopes of the green hills. We crossed lots of small streams, and then the road went through a big city. People weren't kneeling there, but many waved and cheered as we passed. Siglind was practically jumping out of her skin. "Lugdunum!" she exclaimed. "Our capital!"

We passed quickly through Lugdunum—it was far smaller than Roma—and out into open land once more. On a hill in the distance we saw a castle surrounded by high walls. I had never seen a real castle before.

And then the carriage came to a stop. "What is happening?" Siglind demanded. She leaned out the window and yelled at the driver. "Go on! Faster!"

But the driver didn't respond, and the carriage didn't move. We all got out. Up ahead, a rider was talking to the soldiers guarding us. When he saw Siglind, he rode past them and up to her.

He got off his horse. He was tall and bearded, with long brown hair; he wore a blue cape over a white robe. Like Siglind, he wasn't particularly good-looking, but he seemed self-assured and graceful. *Feslund,* I thought.

He looked at Palta and me, and then said something in Gallic to Siglind.

Immediately they started arguing, gesturing at us and the sky and the distant walled town. I thought they might start hitting each other. Lafreia tried to restrain Siglind, holding her from behind and muttering in her ear. Eventually Siglind burst into tears; Feslund didn't seem moved. Finally he turned back to Palta and me. "You will come with me," he said to us in Latin.

"You cannot do this!" Siglind shouted to him.

Feslund ignored her. "You will come now," he said.

"Oh my friends, it will be all right!" Siglind said to us. "I will talk to my father and explain. We will not let you down."

"What's going on?" I asked her.

"Venerix sent a messenger ahead of us to warn my father about you. Venerix is not so good a friend as I thought. My father orders that you be kept outside the castle until he decides what to do with you. In the meantime, no one is to see or speak to you. It is not right! You should be honored! They should hold a feast for you!"

"Where are we going?" Palta asked.

"A house in the countryside—it will be very nice, I suppose. I will see to that. But it won't be where you belong."

"Come," Feslund said to us. "You will take horses from these soldiers and follow me."

"We can't ride," I replied.

He looked like he didn't believe me, and then he shrugged. "Very well. We'll take a wagon."

"Thank you for all you've done for us," I said to Siglind.

"Oh, my friends," she said again, and she hugged us both. "All will be well," she insisted. "I just need to talk to my father."

Feslund ordered the servants out of their wagon. They didn't look happy about it. We got into the wagon and headed off behind Feslund and one of the soldiers.

"We should have expected this," Palta said to me in English.

"Maybe. But we couldn't have done anything else."

"When Feslund was talking to Siglind, he called us danger to Gallia. A danger. He told Siglind she was a fool to bring us here."

"You understood what he was saying?" I asked.

Palta shrugged. "I've heard enough Gallic by now," she said. "It's not hard to follow, if you know Latin."

I shook my head in astonishment. "Did he say what they were going to do to us?"

"Their father is off hunting. We need to be kept out of sight until Carolus gets back and can make up his mind."

"Does Feslund know about the gant?"

"He didn't say anything about it to Siglind. But wouldn't Venerix have brought it up in the message he sent?"

We fell silent and pondered what was going to happen to us.

Feslund led us onto a path off the main road, through a small village, to a small stone house within sight of the castle. Chickens scrambled out of our way as we rode up to it. A donkey stared curiously at us in the front yard. An old

man and woman bustled of the house and bowed deeply to
Feslund. We got out of the wagon and followed them
inside. The house was darker and not as open as the Roman
houses I'd been in; it felt closer to the houses in Carmody's
world—a big kitchen with an open hearth and a fire always
burning; no atrium, no peristyle. It smelled earthy; it made
me want to sneeze.

Feslund gave orders in Gallic to the couple and the
soldier who had accompanied us. Then he gestured to Palta
and me to follow him back outside. "You will stay in this
place," he said in Latin. "I will send another guard—this
fellow is no good. Do not speak to anyone. Do not go
anywhere. The old couple here will take care of you, but I
have ordered them not to speak to you any more than is
necessary. And do not try to escape—you will not succeed.
Understood?"

We nodded.

"And the weapon—give me the weapon."

Palta and I looked at each other. So Venerix had
mentioned the gant in his message. "What should I do?" I
asked Palta in English.

"I don't know," she replied.

"None of your foreign speech," Feslund said in Latin.
"Give me the weapon now."

I slowly took the gant out of my pocket and aimed it at
Feslund. "No," I said. "First we have to talk to your father."

Feslund stared at the gant, and then he laughed. "You are
refusing me?" he asked.

"Yes," I replied. "You know what this weapon can do, I
think. It is what killed King Harald and his army. Your
sword is no match for it."

"You are a child," he pointed out. "I can run you through
with my sword in an instant."

"This weapon would destroy you before you could get
your sword out of its scabbard."

Finally he shrugged. "Try to escape if you like. You will
fail, even with your weapon. Kill me, and you will have all
of Gallia tracking you down, in addition to the priests and

the Roman army. Your capture will be swift, and your deaths will be unpleasant."

"We don't want to escape," I replied. "We just want to talk to King Carolus."

"Why?" Feslund asked.

"Just tell him. He owes it to us—I saved your sister's life."

"Yes, she made that point to me several times." Feslund shrugged again. "Very well. But you cannot speak to him now—he's hunting, which he likes to do much more than he likes ruling this country. Keep your weapon. I will give him your message."

Ignoring the gant that I was still pointing at him, he mounted his horse and rode away.

"What are you doing?" Palta asked in English. "What happens when we talk to the king?"

"I don't know," I said. "But we can't give up the gant. It's all we have. And if we don't talk to King Carolus, maybe he'll just decide to send us back to Urbis, no matter how much Siglind begs him not to."

"But how will we change his mind? Do we just ask for his mercy?"

"I don't know," I responded. "It depends on what he's like, I guess."

"Maybe we'd be better off if we killed the guard and escaped."

I shuddered at how casually we could talk about killing someone. "Where would we go once we escaped?" I replied. "Barbarica? We have no idea where that is. Feslund is right. The gant isn't going to be enough to keep us safe. How long does one last before it runs out of power, anyway?"

She shrugged. "I have no idea. I did not see one often on Gaia—they were too valuable. When they are used up, the blue glow disappears."

I took a quick look at the gant. It was still glowing—but was the glow dimmer than when I had first seen it back in Urbis? I couldn't tell. Was there a way to turn it off to save the battery or whatever? Didn't look like it. I put the gant back in my pocket. "Anyway, we can escape if we have to. I think we're better off trying to get the king on our side."

Palta nodded. "You're right," she said. "But I don't think it will be easy."

We went back inside. The old man and woman were standing in the big kitchen, looking frightened. The man was bald and bearded; he wore loose black pants and a dirty white tunic. The woman wore a long skirt, and her white hair was covered with a scarf. Palta spoke to them in Gallic, and they began to relax. The woman started to bustle around the kitchen; the man showed us to a small room with a couple of narrow beds jammed into it. The mattresses looked thin and lumpy, but they would be an improvement over sleeping on the ground.

Later in the afternoon another soldier rode up to the house. He was tall and handsome, with a scraggly beard and long brown hair worn in a pony tail. He dismissed the other soldier and bowed to us. "My name is Arminius," he said in Latin. "I'll be staying here with you."

"You'll be guarding us, you mean," Palta replied.

Arminius shrugged. "I don't expect anyone will harm you. And I don't expect you will harm anyone. So really, I'm just here to keep you company. What's for dinner? Do I smell roast chicken?"

I wondered if he knew about the gant. If he did, he didn't mention it. The old woman served us the chicken after a while, and we talked with Arminius as we sat at a small wooden table in the kitchen—no one seemed to have told him not to speak to us, or maybe he was just ignoring that order. I liked him a lot. It was hard to tell how much he knew about our situation, but he clearly was an old friend of Feslund's, and he understood the prince's strengths and weaknesses. "He is loyal to his friends and suspicious of foreigners. So he is suspicious of you."

"We don't mean him—or anyone—any harm," I said. "We just want to talk to the king."

"We will sort it all out soon enough," he replied. "This is Gallia. Emotions always run strong. People make mistakes and are forgiven."

That was encouraging—but it wasn't clear how it applied to Palta and me.

We all went to bed early. The house didn't have a toilet, so I was back to using a chamber pot. My bed was uncomfortable, and I couldn't sleep. Neither could Palta, it turned out.

"We aren't going to make it back to Via, Larry," she said out of the darkness. "The king will never agree to that."

I didn't respond. I didn't know what to say.

"Perhaps we can ask him to let us go to Barbarica in exchange for the gant," she went on. "We can disappear in one of those lands that the priests don't control."

"But Tirelius wants to take over Barbarica with his gants," I pointed out. "And without Affron there's no one to stop him."

"We can go far away," she said. "We can change our names. It is a big world."

I felt tears pressing against my eyelids. It was a big world, and none of it was home. "I suppose so," I said. "We have to go somewhere."

We fell silent, and after a while her regular breathing told me that she was asleep. Much later, when I finally got to sleep, I dreamed of home, and I woke up in despair when I saw the chamber pot in the corner of the room.

We aren't going to make it back to Via.

The old couple gave us different clothes—loose-fitting pants and shirts like the old man wore. I had gotten used to robes by now, but it felt good to wear pants again. Palta, too, felt more comfortable. "This is like what we wore on Gaia," she said to me. "Only ours were not so good."

I would have loved a bath, but the house didn't seem to have one. Instead we just splashed cold water on our faces from a bucket in the kitchen.

After breakfast Arminius announced that he was going to give us riding lessons. "Prince Feslund told me that neither of you can ride a horse. We must take care of that."

And so he did. Of course, Palta was much better at it than I was. The first time Arminius got her up on his chestnut-colored horse, she looked like she belonged there; and the horse seemed to know it. Almost from the beginning she could get the horse to do exactly what she wanted—speed up, slow down, turn, stop. Arminius was delighted.

He was not delighted with me—and neither was the horse, who seemed to sense that I didn't know what I was doing and so felt no need to do anything himself. I was always afraid of falling off, even when Arminius was simply leading the horse slowly in a circle. It was embarrassing.

Also, the insides of my thighs felt like they were on fire after a while—I was using muscles I had never used before.

"It will come to you," Arminius said after a while. But he seemed happy to call a halt to the lesson.

And that's mainly what we did for the next few days. I improved a little, and the pain in my thighs started to fade; Palta looked like she was born to ride. At meals Arminius would tell us stories of his life. He had recently returned from the east, on the border with what sounded like Russia. He had been the captain of a troop of Gallian soldiers there protecting the empire against a barbarian invasion. Just like Siglind said, it wasn't very exciting. "We had to be ready for battle, but the battle never came," Arminius said. "The barbarians knew better."

"Did it bother you that you never got to fight?" I asked.

He shrugged. "There was no glory in it, but perhaps some of us rate glory too highly."

"What about defending the priests' empire? How did you feel about that?"

"We don't have much choice, you see," he replied. "Gallia has been part of the Roman empire for centuries now. It is the world we live in. I could imagine a better world, but it doesn't exist."

Perhaps such a world does exist, I thought. But that wasn't worth bringing up.

Meanwhile I became more and more nervous, as the days went by and we didn't hear from King Carolus. How long did hunts take? Was he back and just didn't want to see us? What if Feslund had changed his mind and decided not to relay our request to him?

And there was this: Palta was convinced that we had to trade the gant for freedom in Barbarica. What other choice did we have? But the more I thought about it, the less I liked that idea. We had another choice, didn't we? One that she wouldn't like. What should I do about that? Should I talk to her about it? I found that I couldn't bring myself to do it. I was a coward, really.

And if I was a coward with Palta, what would it be like when I was standing in front of a king?

So we practiced riding, and we ate good food, and we talked to Arminius. And then one night after we had gone to sleep I opened my eyes to see Arminius standing over us in our small cubiculum, holding a lamp. "Well, then," he said. "Wake up, you two! It seems that you have been summoned. Let's go for a ride."

CHAPTER 20

Outside it was chilly and windy. A wagon was waiting for us; its driver sat, half-asleep, on the bench in front next to a lamp hanging from a pole. Arminius pushed him aside and took the reins, and Palta and I got in behind them. We set out, making our way back through the village to the main road by lamp light and a quarter moon.

I glanced at Palta. She looked a little scared. I was scared too.

There was no one else on the road. The castle walls loomed in the distance, flags flying from the parapets. White smoke rose from chimneys above them. I thought I heard an owl hooting.

The gates were open when we arrived. The guards saluted Arminius and let us through without a word. Now we were on a cobblestone path lined with torches. The castle itself was straight ahead, a massive stone building that looked like it could house a thousand people. Arminius drove the wagon around the castle and turned into a large courtyard lined with stables. He brought the wagon to a stop in front of a large door and handed the reins back to the sleepy driver. "Come along," he said to us. "Time to meet royalty."

He led us inside the castle.

We walked along a smoky torch-lined passageway, then
up a narrow staircase and down a hallway lined with
gorgeous tapestries of wild animals being hunted by men
with bows and arrows. Arminius stopped in front of a large
wooden door. "Call them 'my lord' and 'my lady,'" he
advised us. "Bow when you meet them, and don't offer to
shake hands. Stand until they offer you a seat. And
whatever you do, don't underestimate Queen Gretyx.
Clear?"

We nodded.

Arminius knocked loudly on the door.

"Enter!" a muffled voice called from inside.

He opened the door, and we all went in.

The room was smaller than I had expected. I noticed
thick carpets on the floor and more hunting tapestries on
the walls. King Carolus was sitting in a large wooden chair
with a book in his lap. Next to him was a table with cups
and a black-and-green two-handled jug on it, and behind
him was a bookshelf; I had never seen a bookshelf in
Roma. The queen was standing by a large fireplace in
which a few logs were burning low.

Like most Gallians, the king had long hair and a beard—
black streaked with gray. He was wearing a dark robe. His
eyes were gray, and I thought they looked at us with
kindness.

Queen Gretyx, on the other hand, had the gaze of a
viator—her striking green eyes seemed to be staring into
our souls. She was a tall woman with a mass of curly
brown hair that framed a thin face. Her bright green robe
was embroidered with gold, and she wore a large gold
necklace. She was motionless—except for those eyes.

Arminius introduced Palta and me, and then went back
and stood by the door. We walked forward a couple of
steps and bowed.

"Well then," the king said in Latin. "You are the ones
who saved my troublesome daughter. For that you have my
eternal gratitude."

I bowed again. "Thank you, my lord."

"But what are we to do with you?" he went on. "It seems that the priests of Via want very badly for you to be returned to them."

This worried me. Did the priests know we were in Gallia? "My lord, I hope you will have mercy on us."

"Perhaps, perhaps, but—"

The queen suddenly spoke. "You have the weapon?" she asked me.

"Yes, my lady," I said.

She gestured to Arminius. "Take it from him."

Before I had a chance to react Arminius had grabbed me from behind and pulled the gant from my pocket. He handed it to the queen and returned to his post by the door. He patted my shoulder as he walked by me, as if to say he was just doing his job.

The queen hefted the gant and aimed it at the bookshelf, but didn't try to use it. Instead she handed it to Carolus, who looked like he didn't want to touch it. He put it on the table next to him. "You stole this from the priests," he said to us.

"My lord, a viator gave it to me," I said.

"And that viator stole it from the priests."

"I don't know that this is true," I said. And actually, it wasn't true, if Gratius had in fact gone to Gaia to get it.

This seemed to annoy the king. "Of course it's true," he snapped. "Who else has such things? Who are you? Who is this girl? You don't speak Latin like a Roman."

Palta answered before I could. "We are just servants of the viator Affronius. From Barbarica."

"I have heard of Affron," the queen said. "But what is he to us? You are the problem. You are a danger to the kingdom."

"There are rumors about you, I'm told," Carolus added. "A boy and a girl wanted by the priests, brought here to Gallia by my foolish daughter. Before long my chief minister will hear them. He may already have heard about you, for all I know. That is not good. He himself is a viator, and his first allegiance is to the priests. He will not be pleased to discover that we are harboring you. Siglind should not have brought you here, and Venerix should not have allowed her to do so."

"My lord, we have no wish to cause you trouble," Palta said. "Simply allow us to return to our home in Barbarica. You will be able to return the weapon to the priests, if that's what you want to do."

"And tell them I found the weapon but let you two escape? How does that help me? No, you must be return to Urbis and face whatever punishment the priests think you deserve."

So much for Palta's plan. "My lord," I said, "will you grant me a few more minutes of your time? I have an idea."

"An idea?" he replied. "Why should I listen to your ideas? Do not propose to sell this thing to us, or some such nonsense. I am not interested in it. I do not even want to look at it. Weapons like this have caused too much pain to my family and my kingdom."

"Not to mention, we are already in possession of it," Gretyx pointed out.

"Of course," I said. "I want to suggest something you can do with the weapon."

He gestured for me to continue.

"In private, my lord," I said.

The king shrugged, and then gestured to Arminius to leave. "Stay outside the door," he said.

"Yes, my lord," Arminius replied, and he went out, closing the door behind him.

Palta was staring at me. What was I up to? Well, she couldn't blame me. Her idea hadn't worked.

"Well?" Carolus demanded. His eyes may have been kindly, but he now looked annoyed. He was tired of us and the problem we had created for him.

"My lord, we know how you can defeat the priests and take power in Terra."

"What? Nonsense. You are children."

"Perhaps. But we escaped from Urbis along with Affron and another viator. We used a secret passage that the priests are unaware of. We can get back into the city using the same passage. Once inside Urbis…You see this weapon—it is called a *gant*. There are many more gants like this in Urbis, in an armamentarium. They are the weapons that were used to destroy the army of King Harald. The priests are holding onto them in case there is another revolt—and, if Tirelius has his way, they will use them to conquer Barbarica and extend their power over all of Terra. We know the location of this armamentarium. We know that the soldiers who guard it are not trusted to have these gants. We believe that, with our help, soldiers from Gallia can sneak into Urbis and take control of the armamentarium, using this gant. And once your soldiers have the weapons stored there, nothing can stop them from defeating the priests."

I paused. Everyone was silent. I could hear the crackling of the fire. I could hear my heart pounding.

"This is absurd," King Carolus said finally. "You expect me to risk my kingdom for this…this childish fantasy?"

"It is not a fantasy, my lord. You know we escaped from Urbis. You know what this weapon can do. You know how unpopular the priests are—perhaps you heard about the protests and riots before the Roman Games. I am offering you a chance to avenge your grandfather's death. A chance to become a legendary ruler, instead of someone who has to follow orders from your chief minister. Yes, you will risk losing your kingdom and your life. But if you don't do this, you will spend the rest of your life doing whatever the priests tell you, and wondering why you never took the one chance you had of defeating them."

The king seemed nonplussed at what I said. When he responded, he talked about something different. "These weapons—these *gants*—were given to the priests by the gods," he pointed out. "It would be sacrilege to use them against the gods."

I wanted to tell him that this wasn't true. Gods had nothing to do with the gants. But I knew he wouldn't believe me. In Carmody's world—a world like mine had

been back in the eighteenth century—Kevin and I had his
calculator watch to show people, and they had no way to
explain it; they had nothing like it, and they had no religion
to point to: their God didn't send them watches or weapons.
Here, the priests had turned the truth about the portal into
myth and mystery over the centuries. People believed what
they were told to believe. Even kings and queens.

So I said: "This is what the priests want you to think. But
the priests are just men and women. And the gants are just
weapons, like swords and spears. I used this one to save
your daughter's life. Why can't you use them to save Terra
and avenge King Harald?"

"You are setting a trap for us," the king said. "You bring
our soldiers to Urbis, and then turn them over to the priests.
It will give the priests an excuse to destroy us."

"Why would we do that, my lord?" I asked. "We bear
you no ill will. Princess Siglind rescued us from the priests.
We will be forever grateful to her. We just want to find a
way to stay alive. If you won't let us go to Barbarica, let us
help you destroy Tirelius."

The room was silent. Palta looked at me. Was she angry?
I couldn't tell.

"I want to use this weapon," the queen said suddenly.

"My dear, no!" Carolus protested. "It is not right!"

But she ignored him. She went over to the table and
picked up the gant. "What do I do?" she asked me.

"Do you see the notch on top?" I asked. "Put your thumb
in it. Squeeze down on it while you squeeze the handle."

"Show me."

I went over and helped her position her hand. "You'll
need to aim at something you don't mind destroying," I
said. "The gant is powerful beyond anything you have
experienced."

She aimed at a large pot filled with flowers that sat on the
floor in front of the bookshelves. "I don't understand how
this can work," she said.

"I don't understand it either. Just do what I told you.
There will be a slight sound and a flash of light."

Gretyx held the gant out in front of her for a long moment, and I thought she was going to lose her nerve. But suddenly we saw that flash of white light, and the pot disappeared, along with some of the books behind it.

A bitter odor filled the room.

She and Carolus looked at each other. "That is…remarkable," she said finally.

The king seemed very upset. "It is not right," he repeated.

Gretyx put the gant down on the table and went back and stood next to the fireplace. "I didn't realize it would destroy those books, too," she said. "That is really too bad."

And then she started to interrogate me. "How many of these gants are in the armamentarium you spoke of?" she asked.

"I don't know an exact number. I assume that there are many—there must have been many to destroy King Harold's army. Enough to conquer Urbis; enough to conquer Barbarica. Affron was considering this very plan—to sneak into Urbis and take over the armamentarium."

"Why did he reject it, then?"

"Because it will involve many deaths—soldiers, priests, perhaps others as well. He couldn't bring himself to cause that much death."

"Very noble of him," the queen remarked. "And he was sure the guards aren't armed with these weapons?"

"That's what he said."

"And the priests don't have more of these weapons elsewhere?"

"I don't know for sure. But they are very careful with them. Look at how much they want to capture Palta and me. So I don't think many people have them."

"How did you get this gant? Did Affron give it to you?"

"Yes, he did. He gave it to me so that I could save Palta—as you know, she had been kidnapped by the same people who took Princess Siglind. The priests apparently captured Affron while I was doing that, and the princess took us in."

"Why won't the priests have extra guards at Urbis, just to prevent this sort of attack?" Gretyx asked. "They know you have this thing."

"Why would they think we want to return to Urbis?" I responded. "I'm sure they expect us to get as far away from there as possible."

King Carolus suddenly stood up. "Enough!" he ordered. "This is impossible, and I won't allow it."

Queen Gretyx seemed surprised by the interruption. "My lord," she said, "I think we should at least—"

"We will not. Arminius!" he called out.

The door opened immediately and Arminius entered.

"Take these two back to where you are keeping them. The weapon stays here."

Arminius bowed. "Yes, my lord." I saw his eyes move to the hole in the bookshelves.

"There will be no more discussion about any of this," Carolus went on. "Do you understand?"

Palta and I bowed. Before we left, I took a look at Gretyx. She was staring calmly at me, as if she were weighing how much she could trust me. And then she looked back at the fire.

CHAPTER 21

W e were silent on the wagon ride back to the stone house.

We stayed silent as we walked into our cubiculum.

And then Palta lay down on her bed and burst into tears.

"I'm sorry I didn't talk to you about my idea before we went to the castle," I said. "But when the king said he wouldn't let us go to Barbarica, it seemed like this was the only other option."

She shook her head. "That doesn't matter, Larry," she said. "What matters is that the king will never agree to the plan. We are doomed."

"I think there's still a chance. Queen Gretyx was interested."

"And what power does she have?"

"I don't know," I admitted. "But why was she asking so many questions, if she doesn't have any power?"

Palta shook her head. "Even if everything works out— even if they agree to your plan and take over Urbis—what does that mean for me? You will go home in Via, and I will be all alone here."

I had thought of that. "You wouldn't have to stay here," I pointed out. "You could come with me back to my world. My world is safe—safer than Gaia, at any rate. People get along with each other, mostly. You could be happy there."

"I don't belong in your world," Palta said. "I think perhaps I don't belong in any world."

"On my world, at least you'd have a friend," I said.

"Ah, Larry, that is very kind." But she didn't say she would come.

Finally we went to sleep. When we woke up the next morning, nothing seemed to have changed. Arminius was still with us, and he didn't say anything about our visit to the castle. Only: "We may as well have fun while we can." So we went back to our riding lessons as if nothing had happened.

Days went by. What was going on? Was Gretyx trying to convince the king to take the risk and attack Urbis? Maybe Carolus was wavering. Maybe they were talking to Feslund. Would he be in favor of trying to conquer Urbis? I was pretty sure he would be.

Then one morning Siglind rode up on a beautiful black horse. She looked upset as she dismounted.

Arminius tried to head her off. "My lady," he said as he bowed to her, "I believe you're not supposed to—"

She ignored him and came up to Palta and me. "Let us go away from Arminius," she said. "He is a fine fellow, but what I have to say is not for his ears."

We walked around to the other side of the house.

"This is not good," she declared. "My father tells me nothing, but I am worried. Preparations are being made for a journey. I fear the worst—that they are sending you back to the priests."

My heart sank.

"You must escape from Gallia and find your way home," she went on. "Leave tonight. Stay off the main road and head north. If anyone stops you, use your weapon to kill them. You will be on the frontier in seven days' time. You will be able to find your way into Frisia, outside the control of the priests."

"We don't have the weapon," Palta said. "Your father has it."

Siglind raised her hand to her mouth. "Ah, me," she whispered.

"We can't just walk out of Gallia," I said. "We're sure to be caught."

"Yes," she agreed. "It is too dangerous without the weapon." Then she brightened. "I will go talk to my father. I will throw myself at his feet and beg for your lives. He will not deny my request. I should have done this already."

"Thank you," I said. "You are very kind."

"I owe you much more than this. Don't despair. I will make everything right."

We walked back around the house. Arminius was waiting for us, holding Siglind's horse. She nodded to him, mounted the horse, and rode off.

Arminius sighed. "Princess Siglind is a proud young woman," he said. "But she has no power. I hope you understand that."

"At least she wants to help us," Palta said. And she walked back into the house. I followed her. There didn't seem to be much to say.

And the next morning Arminius wasn't there. The old man and woman told us they had no idea where he had gone. He had ridden off before they got up.

We ate breakfast. And we waited.

In the early afternoon he rode up to the house. But now he was dressed in his soldier's gear, wearing a breastplate and a cloak with a lion on it; he had a sword sheathed in a scabbard by his side. Behind him came the same wagon driven by the same sleepy guy who had been with us when we went to the castle. Now he was wearing a straw hat to protect his face from the sun.

Arminius got down from his horse, looking grim. "Well then," he said. "Bad news. We're headed to Urbis. Right now."

Palta and I looked at each other, and I felt my eyes well up with tears.

Palta spoke to Arminius. "Did Siglind—?"

"Plea for your lives?" he responded. "I am told that she did. Alas, it only seemed to convince the king that he had to hand you over to the priests without any further delay. Come, into the wagon with you."

We did as we were told. "I'm afraid I have to tie you up," he went on. "People seem to think you might run away."

He had a coil of rope with him. He cut off a couple of pieces and tied our hands behind our backs—not very tightly. Even so, I could tell that it would be difficult not falling over when the wagon went over bumps. Would we be tied up all the way to Urbis?

"You'll be traveling with the chief minister," Arminius informed us. "His name is Lexulus. Be on your best behavior with him, or he can make your lives very difficult."

"What's going to happen to us in Urbis?" Palta asked.

Arminius shrugged. "You know better than I. Evidently you have offended the priests. I'd like to think they will show some mercy, but I cannot say. The priests have not always been known for their mercy."

"Are you coming with us to Urbis?"

"Apparently so."

He led us through the village and back to the main road, where more soldiers were waiting, along with a couple of wagons and a carriage like the one Siglind had ridden in. When we arrived, the carriage door opened, and a man stepped out.

It must have been Lexulus. He was thin, tall, and beardless; he looked Roman. And he was wearing the purple robe of a viator. He came over to the wagon and stared at us. He seemed surprised. "You are young," he murmured.

We didn't respond.

"You have made terrible mistakes," he went on. "But you would be well-advised to make no further mistakes. On our journey you will not speak to anyone about what you know, or what you think you know—you will only cause trouble for those you speak to, as well as yourselves. You have caused enough trouble already. Do you understand?"

We nodded.

Lexulus continued to stare at us for a moment, and then he turned and walked back to the carriage. He signaled to Arminius, and then stepped up into the carriage and closed the door. Arminius got us organized—soldiers in front, soldiers behind, carriage and wagons in the middle, and we headed south. Back towards Urbis.

We passed through the same lovely countryside we had passed on our way to Lugdunum—trees and wildflowers by the side of the road, flocks of sheep on the hillside, vines and grain growing outside the small villages. I was sad to think I would never see this countryside again.

I had no doubt that we would be executed when we got to Urbis. I wondered what life would have been like if we could have escaped to Frisia, or someplace in Barbarica. Would it have been so bad? I recalled Carmody's world— that, too, hadn't been so bad, after we had managed to survive Kevin's sickness and the war. Ultimately we had found a home, a family to love us and care of us. Could that have happened here?

"I'm sorry," I said to Palta. "I shouldn't have brought up the idea of attacking Urbis. Maybe if we kept trying to convince the king to let us go to—"

"You saved my life," she interrupted. "You have nothing to be sorry for."

We fell silent. The wagon rattled on, hour after hour. I could see the mountains in the distance. I tried to remember my geography. Were they the Alps? Didn't matter. We would make our way through the mountains, then south, into the heat of Roma. Day after day, each day getting closer to our deaths. Maybe it would be cooler there by now. I had no idea what the date was. At home, I probably should have been starting high school.

"Lexulus must have the gant," Palta said at one point. "He'd bring it back to Urbis along with us. If we could get hold of it, we could escape."

"And how would we do that?" I asked.

She didn't respond.

It made sense that Lexulus would bring the gant back to Urbis, but so what? He had the gant; we didn't. And he didn't look stupid or careless.

Arminius halted our progress early in the evening, and we made camp by the side of the road. Servants set up a tent for Lexulus; he went inside, and a soldier stood guard by the entrance. Another soldier untied our hands and stood next to Palta and me while we sat on the ground and ate cheese and fruit. When we were done, he tied our hands again.

Arminius came by at one point and checked on us. "Are you comfortable?" he asked.

"Of course not," I replied. "Can't you untie us? We're not going anywhere. You know we aren't."

"It's not my decision, I'm afraid. Be grateful your feet aren't tied as well. Our job is to get you back to Urbis, and Lexulus doesn't want to take any risks."

Having said that, he knelt down, untied the robes, and tied our hands in front of us instead of in back. Which was much more comfortable. "Thank you," I said.

He didn't reply. Instead, he silently stood up and wandered off. A servant came by and handed us each a blanket. Stars came out. Crickets chirped. The horses snickered. Palta snuggled up beside me, and eventually she seemed to fall asleep. But I couldn't sleep. My arms ached; I was upset; I wanted to go home. At home, having your hands tied was something that happened on TV, not in real life.

I don't think I ever really got to sleep that night. If I did, it was that weird kind of waking sleep where your dreams seem to merge with reality, and you're not sure which is which. I saw shadows; I felt movement. Someone was whispering. I thought it was my kid brother Matthew, lying in the other bed in our room. Why wouldn't Matthew just shut up and let me sleep?

And then someone screamed, and I was wide awake.

I struggled to sit up. I heard the clash of metal against metal. More screaming. Horses whinnying. I saw soldiers grappling with each other ten feet away from me. No one was paying any attention to us.

"Stay down," Palta whispered to me. "Let's go."

We started to crawl away from the camp, into the darkness of a meadow by the side of the road.

I don't know how far we got. I just know that the noise suddenly stopped. We paused, trying to figure out what was going on.

And then I smelled it: the bitter odor that I now associated with the silent, total obliteration of human life.

Lexulus must have been using the gant.

"Don't get up," Palta whispered. We kept crawling. But it already seemed hopeless to me. How far could we get on our hands and knees?

"Ah, there you are."

The voice came from behind us. It was Lexulus.

We stopped and turned around.

He was fifteen feet away from us. I could see the gant glowing blue by his side. "You two are far more trouble than you are worth," he said. "No sense bringing you back to Urbis, it seems."

I tried to think of something to say to him, come up with some reason why he shouldn't destroy us. But it all seemed hopeless.

I saw him raise the gun. I waited for the end.

But the end didn't come. As he aimed the gant a darkness exploded on his breast, and he toppled over on his face.

A long spear stuck out of his back.

Arminius strode out of the darkness. He bent over and took the gant out of the chief minister's hand; then he checked to make sure that Lexulus was dead. Finally he straightened up and looked at us. "I think perhaps he was right," he said. "You are both a lot of trouble. But this is certainly an interesting weapon."

CHAPTER 22

A rminius took out his sword and sliced through the ropes that bound our hands. We stood up and rubbed our wrists gratefully. Then he turned and led us back to the camp site.

It was horrifying: bodies were strewn everywhere—soldiers with gaping wounds in their chests, servants with their throats slit. I had no idea how many other people Lexulus had killed with the gant.

On the side of the road a few other soldiers stood by their horses, staring at us and looking terrified. And Prince Feslund was leaning against Lexulus's carriage, his bloody sword by his side.

Arminius brought us over to Feslund and handed him the gant.

Feslund looked at it, and then he looked at Palta and me. "The chief minister had a terrible aim, or I might have disappeared with the others," he said.

We didn't respond.

"Anyway, your wish has been granted—we will attack Urbis."

He looked at Arminius after he said this, as if to make sure the other man agreed. But Arminius simply said, "Let's not mention this to the men just yet. They aren't ready for it."

"I leave that up to you, of course," Feslund replied.

My heart lifted. But still, I was worried. "This isn't what your father wanted," I pointed out.

"My father is a frightened old man," Feslund replied. "It was a mistake talking to him. You should have brought your idea directly with me."

"If I might suggest, my lord," Arminius said, "we need to clean this mess up and get going."

Feslund ignored him. Instead, he waved the gant at me. "What do you call this thing?" he asked.

I told him.

"Gant," he repeated. "What a strange word. Show me how to use it."

I went over to him and demonstrated how to hold the gant, the way I had with Queen Gretyx. Feslund caught on immediately. He began shooting at the corpses and making them disappear. He laughed with delight. "This is how you clean up a mess!" he said. "Much easier than burying these bodies."

"You shouldn't keep doing that," Palta said to him.

"And why not?"

"The weapon—the gant—will not last forever. If you want to conquer Urbis, you must not use up its power."

Feslund seemed puzzled by this. "What do you mean, 'use up its power'?" he demanded.

"It will no longer work," she explained. "It will be like a fire that has burned out. I don't know how long this will take, but it will happen."

The idea still seemed to bother him. Perhaps he was thinking: how does this girl know? Or perhaps: if the device was given to us by the gods, why would it 'burn out'? Why should magic have limits?

Finally he looked at Arminius. "What do we do?" he asked. "We cannot leave this mess here. No one must know what's happened. Word of this must not reach Urbis—or my father. My mother may be able to keep him in check, but there are limits even to her power."

Arminius shrugged. "We can bury the bodies. But it will be difficult to hide the wagons and the carriage."

So Feslund used the gant to destroy the vehicles while Arminius set the remaining soldiers to work burying the bodies and cleaning up the scene of the fight.

"Were you working for Feslund all along?" I asked Arminius.

"I had some idea that this would happen," he admitted.

"Do you understand what it's all about?"

"I understand enough—although I'll need to understand more before I'm convinced this won't be a complete disaster for Gallia. But there will be time enough to figure this out—now we need to help the men here. We have to be back on the road quickly. Are you ready to use your riding skills?"

What riding skills? I wanted to reply.

"We're riding to Urbis?" Palta asked.

"Actually, no," Arminius said. "We can't take the land route—too many people would spot us on the road. We need to ride to Massalia and from there sail to Urbis across the great sea."

"Sail?" Palta repeated.

I could sense the fear in her voice; perhaps Arminius could too. "Don't worry," he said. "It is getting to be late in the season, but the winds should still be favorable and the sea calm. We will lose time compared to a hard ride overland, but that will be all right, unless Carolus discovers our plan and Gretyx can't stop him from sending a messenger ahead to warn the priests."

Palta grabbed hold of my hand and squeezed it. She was shaking; I thought she might fall over. "Is there no other way?" she asked. "I—I do not like ships."

"None of us likes ships," Arminius replied. "We are soldiers. We fight on land. But we have no other choice but to go by water—it's the only way to reach Urbis in secret."

Palta didn't respond. I'm not sure she was able to respond.

Why was she so afraid of water?

I decided to change the subject. "Won't the king wonder where Feslund has gone?"

"Eventually, perhaps," Arminius said. "But for now he thinks Feslund is on a hunt with his bodyguards." He gestured at the soldiers. "Hunting is something that the royal family does frequently—perhaps because they have nothing more important to do."

"But the queen knows the truth."

"Ah, Feslund would not take a step without her approval. It was her idea to let Lexulus start out for Urbis, and then ambush him on the road. Now that the ambush has happened, we are committed. If we fail—well, that is not worth thinking about."

"And Siglind? Does she know about the plan?"

"No. And I would not want to be in the same room when Siglind finds out that her father has sent you to Urbis. But come, let's help out. Everyone will have a heavy heart. We have lost many friends here tonight. Gallians should not be fighting Gallians."

So we all set to work—except for Feslund, who stood on the road looking at the gant.

Its blue glow had dimmed—I was sure of it.

It took us an hour or more, but finally we finished burying the dead and cleaning up the road to Arminius's satisfaction. Then we all stood by the graves where the soldiers and servants were buried. "May the gods have mercy on them—and on us," Arminius murmured.

Then he nodded to Feslund. "Now we ride to Massalia," Feslund said to the men. "All will be explained in good time. I know that this has been difficult, but know that you did Gallia a great service tonight, and you will be doing it an even greater service in the future."

"We must ride through the night," Arminius said to Palta and me. "Can you do it?"

Palta nodded.

"I don't know," I replied honestly.

"You'll be fine," he replied.

Palta and I mounted a couple of spare horses, and we all headed back the way we had come. My horse was named Flinty, and he was pretty manageable, for which I was very grateful. Even so, I couldn't make him go as fast as the others wanted to go, which meant that I was always holding everyone up. Feslund yelled back at me at one point, but Arminius murmured something to him, and after that he shut up.

Palta stayed next to me. "You're doing very well," she said.

"I'm awful. But I guess I could be worse. Anyway, I'm sorry about having to sail to Urbis. That never occurred to me."

She was silent for a while. And then she simply said, "It will be all right."

Eventually we reached a crossroads and went left, leaving the main road, which was called the Via Aureliana, and heading west, instead of north to Lugdunum. We kept going for another couple of hours until Arminius called a halt. I was deeply relieved to get off my horse—and I was sort of proud of how well I had done, even if I had slowed everyone down. We set up camp by the side of the road, and Palta and I lay down on the ground. I was exhausted, and my thighs were aching from the ride.

And beyond that, I was only now beginning to realize the horror of what had happened. How many people had been killed in Feslund's raid? How many more would have to die in Urbis?

Palta seemed to sense what I was feeling. "It will be all right," she repeated. "We're doing what we need to do."

And then she snuggled up against me. I got to sleep finally, but I didn't sleep well, and eventually I woke up enough to understand why. Palta was moaning softly, and her hand was digging into my arm so hard it almost hurt.

I turned over and shook her awake. She opened her eyes, and I saw terror in them. "Are you okay?" I whispered.

"Why did they shoot at us?" she asked, her voice shaking.

"Why didn't they just let us go? We couldn't have harmed them."

"Who? Who are you talking about?"

She shook her head. "I can't...." And then she seemed to calm down a bit. "It was a nightmare," she explained. "About something that happened on Gaia. I'm sorry."

"What happened? Don't be sorry. Tell me." She had told me so little about Gaia, compared to what I had told her about my world.

But this time was different. This time, lying in a field in Gallia among the sleeping soldiers, she finally had something to say.

"I was so young," she began. "I don't know how old—I don't even know how old I am now. There was no one to tell me, after..."

"After what?"

She shook her head and began again. "On Gaia, the gants ruined everything. The world collapsed. I don't where they came from, who invented them, how many there were. But they made death so easy, so...clean. You couldn't protect yourself from them. So we all ended up in these tribes, these small communities, and we had as little contact with anyone else as possible. I was with my father and some other people—fifteen or twenty, I think."

"No mother?"

"My mother was dead. Papa never talked about her. I remember our tribe had a farm, so we had food to eat, and I felt safe. I didn't know any better. We also had a gant. We were very careful with that gant—it was like a sacred thing. No one told me what it was for, or anything about it; I just knew it was very important. Now I realize it was our only protection against outsiders who wanted to take what we had.

"And one day I saw everyone become worried. I didn't understand why. I asked Papa, and he didn't want to say, but finally I overheard other people talking. Bad people were coming, they said. And our gant had gone dead. Without the gant we were helpless, they said. The bad people were going to capture us, or kill us.

"Do you understand, Larry? The blue glow was gone. Like a fire that has burned out."

"What happened then?" I asked.

"I don't remember all that happened. Many meetings, much talk. And finally one night my father woke me and said, 'We must leave, child. Right now. The bad people are almost here.'

"He put a jacket on me and gave me the little doll that I loved and we hurried out of the farmhouse. I didn't hear or see anything. How did he know the bad people were coming? I think now the others had decided to stay and surrender to the bad people, and my father disagreed with this. So he wanted to save me. But I don't know—perhaps someone had turned against us. Perhaps the others had left, and we were the only ones left behind. It was all very confusing to me.

"We ran across the fields and into the woods. Dawn was coming. I heard shouts behind us. My father picked me up and carried me. He was a strong man. I felt safe in his arms. 'We must cross the river,' he said. 'They will not follow us to the other side.' I had never been to the river before. I don't think I knew what a river was.

"We made it to the river. I could not take my eyes off it—the water, endlessly flowing in the dawn. I thought it was beautiful. But there were still shouts behind us, and my father was looking for something on the bank. Finally he found it—a boat, hidden in the reeds. He put me in the boat and pushed off with an oar. He was sweating. We made it out to the middle of the river. 'Keep down, child,' he said. 'Whatever you do, keep down.'

"And those were the last words he spoke. Because then my father disappeared. Someone must have shot at him from the bank, but I didn't know that—I just knew that my father was there, and then he was gone. When you are that close to someone who is destroyed by the gant, you feel a sort of trembling in the air. And you know the white powder that comes afterwards? Some of it fell on me. I could feel my father's dust on my face."

"I'm so sorry," I said.

"Why did they have to do that, Larry?" Palta asked. "Why didn't they just let us go? We couldn't have hurt them. We just wanted to go away."

"I don't know."

"I think I know, although I didn't understand until much later. They didn't want my father. They wanted me. They wanted girls—girls who would grow up and become women."

I shivered. "What happened next?" I asked.

"I didn't know what to do. I didn't understand what had happened. Where was Papa? Maybe I could have used the oar, but the oar had disappeared, too. And the gant had made a hole in the side of the boat. Water was pouring in; the boat was sinking. Now it was just me, with the water rising up over me, and the bad people coming after me. And I ended up in the river. Perhaps I threw myself in. Perhaps I was hoping I'd drown—but I don't think I understood what it meant to drown. I went beneath the surface, and it was so cold and dark. It wasn't beautiful anymore; it was death, clutching at me, pulling me down into its depths."

She fell silent.

"But you didn't die," I said.

"I don't know why," she replied. "It seemed to go on forever, the darkness and the cold, and I couldn't breathe and I couldn't think and I missed my Papa and I was afraid of the bad men. And then I don't know what happened, but I opened my eyes and I was lying in mud by the side of the river, and my clothes were ripped and wet, and the sun was shining down on me. I was still holding on to my little doll. I was alive, but I didn't want to be."

She fell silent again. I put my arm around her and held her close. "That's a good reason to be afraid of water," I said.

"But it's not good to be afraid without a reason," she murmured. "You have to be strong. The river saved my life, after all. The bad men didn't find me—maybe they thought I'd drowned, or maybe the river carried me too far away for them to bother chasing me. Instead, I was rescued by a fisherman who brought me to his home and cleaned me up and let me live with him. Pretty soon it became too dangerous for him to be on his own without a gant, and we left his home and joined a tribe in the city. It was better, then. It was never really all right until Affron came and took me away from Gaia, but it was better."

Palta closed her eyes, and after a while I could feel her fall asleep. I listened to her gentle breathing. I couldn't sleep, though. Dawn approached, when we'd have to be on the road again—towards a sea voyage, and more danger.

Much more danger.

CHAPTER 23

In a few hours we set out. Palta didn't say anything more about what she had told me in the night; we just rode our horses through a glorious Gallian day. I seemed to work my way through my soreness, to the point where I was actually enjoying the ride. Feslund was in great spirits. Arminius, on the other hand, was quiet and serious.

We rode all day, with a brief stop to eat and to feed and rest the horses. The people we passed on the road looked at us with puzzlement and maybe a little fear. A few of them recognized Feslund and bowed to him or knelt; he waved back at them and laughed.

At twilight we camped. The soldiers caught rabbits and roasted them over a fire, and we all sat around the fire afterwards eating the meat and drinking water from a stream. The soldiers spoke mostly Gallic, but occasionally lapsed into Latin that I could understand with a little difficulty. They were friendly and happy to be on a mission instead of hunting, although they were baffled by the mission's purpose. They were worried about having killed the chief minister. They had no idea who Palta and I were or why we were so important. And the gant terrified them. They knew what had happened to King Harald and his army, and that this must have been the kind of weapon the priests had used against them. And they found that troubling.

"I do not like it," a short, stocky soldier named Priscus said. "This weapon doesn't belong to us. It has been stolen from the gods."

Feslund was quick to stop that sort of thinking. "It hasn't been stolen from the gods—we have taken it by right from the priests. Do you think that only the priests speak for the gods?"

Priscus didn't seem able to answer that question. But he also didn't seem convinced. Probably he and the other soldiers had been taught that, yes, in fact, only the priests spoke for the gods.

I began to worry about how the soldiers would react when they were finally told what their mission was. I remembered that this was why Decius had rejected this very plan—he couldn't be sure his soldiers would go along with it. I had thought it would be easier to convince Gallian soldiers; perhaps I had been wrong.

After supper Arminius and Feslund took Palta and me aside and quizzed us about the plan. Or, rather, Arminius did the quizzing, and Feslund mostly listened. We went over everything—all that Queen Gretyx had asked me about and more. Some things Palta and I had answers for, like how to get into Urbis, and the locations of the important buildings; some things other people would have to figure out, like where to land and the route to take from there to Urbis. And others were simply unknown: How many soldiers guarded the armamentarium? How could we be sure they didn't have these magical weapons? How could we be sure no one else did?

Arminius seemed skeptical. "It is risk piled on top of risk," he said.

"But can we succeed?" Feslund demanded.

"Perhaps."

"Perhaps? That isn't good enough. We must be certain!"

Arminius shrugged. "The only certainty is that many people will die. Including Gallians. And we will need many more men than the few we have with us now."

"I will send someone ahead to Massalia," Feslund said. "We will get men from the garrison, and tell the commander to have ships ready for us."

"That would be wise."

Feslund seemed annoyed at Arminius's lack of enthusiasm. "If you were me, wouldn't you do this?" he persisted. "Wouldn't you try to avenge King Harald and wrest control of the empire from the priests?"

"We took the first step when I buried my spear in the back of Lexulus," Arminius replied. "Now we have no choice but to continue. We are all doomed otherwise."

That was the most Feslund could get out of him.

There was one part of what I was proposing that Arminius didn't understand. "Why do we need to take over the temple of Via during the attack?" he asked. "What concern is that of ours?"

I couldn't tell him the truth, of course, which was that if we didn't secure the portal, the priests could use it to obtain more weapons from Gaia. But he wouldn't understand.

I did my best to explain. "Via is the way that the priests talk to the gods," I explained. "We need to make sure we control Via. Otherwise, there's no telling what the priests may be able to do."

"What if the gods are upset with us for taking over Via?" he asked.

"Why should they be upset?" Feslund interrupted. "Perhaps it is the will of the gods that we do this—that is why they have sent these two children to us. We must do it, my friend. As you said, we have no other choice."

"Then we will do it," Arminius said with a sigh. "And let us pray that the gods approve."

The next day we continued on to Massalia. Feslund was the only one in high spirits; everyone else seemed tense. Including me. This had all been my idea, and now that it was really happening, I was becoming increasingly worried about it. I had only been thinking about finding a way home—I hadn't been thinking about the other people who would be affected by what I wanted to do.

The way home was not going to be easy.

One of the soldiers was missing as we set out. "We have sent Escondo on ahead to Massalia," Arminius explained to the soldiers. "We need more soldiers. We need ships. We cannot waste any time."

"Can you tell us where we're going?" one of the soldiers asked.

Arminius shook his head. "Soon," was all he said.

"Are we going to Urbis?" another asked. "I'm told that Lexulus was taking the two children back to Urbis."

Arminius ignored the question, and he mounted his horse and set out.

We rode through the most beautiful landscape I could imagine—even more picturesque than along the Via Aureliana. And the weather was perfect—none of the oppressive heat that we had endured on that first journey. The farmers in the fields waved to us; the people in the small villages we passed through bowed to us. At night we lay down next to a campfire and gazed up at a clear sky smeared with stars. I learned the names of the soldiers and a little bit about their personalities—Priscus, quiet, devout, and competent; Sulliger, easygoing and happy just to be on a journey with his fellow soldiers; Vetorix, a thin young soldier with a scar on his cheek...

And, of course, Arminius, who somehow was our leader, even though Feslund was the prince, the one with the ultimate power. Feslund seemed to know that nothing should happen if Arminius didn't approve. He would be angry if he wanted to keep riding and Arminius said it was time to camp for the night; but he would always give in and do what Arminius suggested.

"I do not trust Feslund at all," Palta said to me one night. "If we succeed, it will be because of Arminius."

I didn't disagree.

And finally we smelled salt air and saw seagulls overhead. "Massalia is not far," Sulliger said to us. "I was born near here. It is the best, most exciting city in the world!"

We arrived at twilight, but the shops were still open and the narrow streets were crowded and noisy. We made our way through the city to a stone building overlooking a harbor filled with ships, where we all dismounted. "This is the garrison," a friendly soldier named Cymbian said to us. "I was stationed here once."

Arminius and Feslund went inside while the rest of us sprawled on the ground and waited. I noticed that Palta couldn't tear her eyes away from the harbor. It looked calm and pretty to me, but she was clearly terrified. I took her hand and squeezed it. "You'll be fine," I said.

She nodded silently.

In a few minutes Arminius and Feslund came out, followed by Escondo and a gray-haired soldier named Ploterus, who was evidently the commander of the garrison.

"We depart at first light," Feslund announced to us. "We have no time to waste. Come inside and eat, and then we will get ready."

We got to our feet and headed inside the building. As we did, stable boys came to take care of our horses. I had grown fond of Flinty, and as the boy led it away I realized with a pang that I would probably never see my horse again.

The garrison smelled of sweat and salt. The soldiers there greeted us and led us to the dining hall at the back of the building. Everyone seemed excited. I think our soldiers were happy to get reinforcements, and the soldiers from the garrison were happy to get the chance to fight, even if no one was sure where we were headed or who we were going to fight. As usual, everyone glanced curiously at Palta and me.

We were served a meal of cold ham, hard biscuits, and some sort of oatmeal. Then the soldiers set to work getting their gear ready and stowing it in wagons to be brought down to the two ships that would be taking us across the great sea to Urbis. After that, everyone went to sleep on uncomfortable cots in the barracks—everyone except Palta,

that is, who was given her own room because she was
female. She didn't look happy to be separated from me, but
she didn't object.

I had slept in a barracks in Carmody's world, after the
battle where I had killed that soldier from New Portugal. I
felt tired and scared now, as I had then. Back then, at least,
the battle had been over and our side had won. Here, the
battle was approaching, and it was not at all clear that our
side would win.

The soldiers grunted and snored while I tossed and
turned, unable to settle down. My mind buzzed with
questions. How long would we be at sea? Would Palta be
okay? Where would we land, and how would we get from
there to Urbis? If—when—we got into the temple, how
exactly would I get back home? Would Gratius still be in
Urbis? He would help me—wouldn't he?

And what about Palta? Would she come with me back to
my world? And if not, where would she go, what would
she do?

And how could I leave her behind?

It was a long night.

We arose before dawn and had a final meal before
leaving. I sat next to Palta, who didn't touch her food. "Did
you sleep?" I asked her.

She shook her head.

"I didn't either."

"I suppose there'll be time to sleep on the ship," she said.

"Lots of time to do nothing."

We walked outside. The weather was chilly, and the
winds were calm. I wondered if the soldiers had packed
any clothes for us; if it got any colder, I'd need a jacket or a
cape. I didn't see Arminius, Feslund, or Escondo. Priscus
got us organized and marched us down to the harbor. The
soldiers were quiet, still waking up. The city was already
coming to life, and people stopped what they were doing to
watch us go by on the cobblestone streets.

Feslund and the others were waiting for us on a wharf in
the harbor. "The ships are outfitted and ready to go,"

Arminius explained to the soldiers in Latin. "Two rowboats will take us out to them, and then we leave. We will give you more instructions when we are on board."

Palta squeezed my hand hard when she saw the rowboats. Did they remind her of the boat in which she and her father tried to escape on that river in Gaia?

It was at this point that we heard the sound of a horse galloping towards us. The crowd that had gathered in front of the wharf parted to let it pass. And then some of them started to kneel. The rider dismounted at the edge of the wharf and strode out to us.

It was Siglind, her hair tied back, wearing simple pants and a shirt.

"Hello, my friends," she said to Palta and me. And to Feslund she said, "Did you think you would be able to leave me behind, brother?"

And then they started arguing in Gallic.

CHAPTER 24

A rminius ordered the soldiers to move to the far end of the wharf, but he let Palta and me stay where we were, so we overheard the argument.

I looked at Palta for a translation. "She went back to see us, and we were gone," Palta said. "She asked her father where we were, but he wouldn't answer. So she was worried. Arminius was gone. Feslund and his bodyguard were gone. And then she found out that Lexulus was gone. She talked to her mother, and Gretyx told her not to worry. She hinted that big things would soon be happening, and all would change for the better. Gretyx seemed very pleased with herself."

"But how did Siglind end up here?" I asked.

"That's what Feslund wants to know." Then Palta paused to listen to more of the argument. "Siglind figured it out," she said. "She guessed that Lexulus was bringing us back to Urbis with the gant. And that Feslund and his men were going to attack Lexulus and his bodyguards before they left Gallia. But that couldn't be all. Gretyx wouldn't have been so happy if they were just freeing the two of us. Siglind decided that Feslund and her mother were planning to attack Urbis using the gant. And the only way to do this was to take the sea route from Massalia. She decided that this plan was crazy, but she had to be part of it. So she rode

night and day to get here. And now that she sees that
Arminius is with us, she is not so sure that the plan is
crazy."

Now Feslund was gesturing angrily at Siglind and
pointing off into the distance. "He is telling her to go
home," Palta said. "He tells her that this is no place for a
girl. Siglind tells him that she is the equal of any of these
soldiers, she deserves to be part of this expedition. And so
on."

And then Arminius stepped in and spoke softly, in Latin.
"This is not good," he said. "Now both of the king's
children are missing from Lugdunum. Carolus might have
believed that Feslund was off on a hunt, but with Siglind
gone as well, the king will understand what is happening. It
is likely that he will send a messenger to Urbis to warn the
priests. He has probably done so already. He will think that
this is the only way he can save his kingdom."

"He will not do such a thing," Feslund replied. "He will
know that this would mean sacrificing his children. My
mother will stop him."

"My lord, he may think that he has no choice. A
messenger riding hard and changing horses frequently will
get to Urbis far more quickly than Lexulus with his soldiers
and servants and prisoners. So we must consider what this
means for us."

"Are you suggesting that we give up?" Feslund
demanded. "Gallians never give up!"

"If the messenger arrives before we do," Arminius
responded, "if the priests know we are coming, then we are
doomed."

"Then we must go all the faster!"

Arminius shrugged. "We can only get there as fast as the
winds will take us," he pointed out. Right at the moment, I
noticed, there was no wind.

"Of course we must go!" Siglind added. But she looked
worried.

"What will happen if we don't go?" I asked. "We've
killed Lexulus and stolen back the gant. We're all doomed

in that case as well. Including the king and queen."

"Yes," Arminius agreed softly. "We have gone too far to turn back."

"Then let us proceed!" Feslund said. He gestured to the soldiers. "Into the boats!" he called out.

And that seemed to settle it. We were still going to Urbis, and Siglind was coming with us.

"Aren't you worried that you're disobeying your father?" I asked Siglind.

She sighed. "My father is a great man, Larry, but he has lived his life under the thumb of the priests. That makes him cautious sometimes when he should be bold. I am sure he will forgive me when he sees the glory we achieve for Gallia."

"You are very brave," Palta said.

"A Gallian princess has no choice but to be brave. Come, let us find a place for us in the boat."

Palta hesitated, and then climbed awkwardly into the rowboat; Siglind and I followed.

"We Gallians are great mariners," Siglind said, noticing the fear on Palta's face. "The journey will be swift and safe."

"Pala has never traveled on the sea before," I said by way of explanation. I didn't think Palta was able to speak.

"Far worse dangers await us than this," Siglind replied. I agreed with that, but it wasn't much consolation to Palta. When we reached our ship, we were pulled up on board and joined the rest of the soldiers. The sailors, bearded and deeply tanned, stared openly at Palta and Siglind. Had young women never sailed on their ship before? They didn't seem to recognize that Siglind was a princess. She ignored them.

We were on the smaller ship along with Arminius, Priscus, and some of the other soldiers. Feslund and the rest were on a larger ship nearby. Both had a big square sail on a mast in the middle and a smaller sail on another mast in the front; they didn't look much like the sailboats I was familiar with.

Most of the men stayed on deck as the voyage got under way, but Palta and I climbed down a rickety set of stairs into the hold, which stank of stale olive oil. Palta found a small open spot amid our gear and lay down, closing her eyes and curling up into a ball. I put my hand on her shoulder to let her know I was there. The ship rocked gently in the sea; this didn't bother me, but it made Palta whimper softly.

After a while I could feel the ship start to move, and the rocking subsided. I thought this might make Palta feel better, but it didn't seem to. My sister Cassie got seasick easily, but Mom gave her some pill before we went on a whale watch or a ferry ride, and that kind of took care of it. But there were no pills on Terra. And of course Palta's problem went far deeper than Carrie's.

Eventually Siglind joined us. "We're under way," she said softly, squatting down next to Palta.

"How long till we get there?" I asked.

"With a favorable wind we should arrive in three days or so. It's a good time of year to sail, but one can never count on favorable winds. One can never count on anything when sailing."

Palta groaned.

"I am sorry, my friend," Siglind said. "We will do all we can to make you comfortable."

She found a blanket to put over Palta, and a thin pillow that she slid under her head. Then the two of us stayed with her, holding her until she seemed to fall asleep.

"Poor darling," Siglind whispered.

"She had a bad experience in the water once," I said.

"Then we will take good care of her."

We sat in silence for a while, and when I looked over at Siglind, I noticed that there were tears on her cheeks. "What's the matter?" I asked.

She hurriedly wiped the tears away. "Nothing, nothing," she replied. And then: "Ah, Larry, life is hard, even when you are a princess. I have longed for glory, and here it is, within my grasp, but..."

She fell silent. But I thought I understood. "Even if we take Urbis from the priests," I said, "Feslund will ignore you, and your father will be angry at you."

She didn't respond for a long time, but then she seemed to recover her usual good spirits and said, "But what if we can make Gallia the powerful nation it once was? That will be worth anything!"

"I hope we succeed," I said.

"Of course we will succeed!"

It was a long day. The soldiers came down eventually and settled themselves in the hold, where they played dice and sang songs. We had a lunch of biscuits, cheese, and weak beer; Palta ate nothing. Siglind and I had to help her get up on deck so she could throw up over the side, then clean her and half-carry her back down.

Arminius looked worried when he saw her. "Is she going to be all right?" he asked me when we got her settled once again.

"She's stronger than she looks," I replied.

"When we land, we will face a long march by night to reach Urbis," he said. "And we cannot delay to give her time to recover."

"She'll be ready."

He just shook his head. One more thing for him to worry about.

Finally night fell, and I lay awake next to Palta, still unable to sleep, listening to the creaking of the ship and the snoring of the men.

It is really happening, I thought. We are going to attack Urbis.

And it was all far worse than I had imagined it would be.

In the morning, Arminius finally gathered the soldiers together and told them the purpose of our mission. They were astonished and—some of them—terrified. "We cannot do such a thing," Priscus complained. "The gods will not allow it."

"The gods have given us this extraordinary weapon," Arminius responded. "This *gant*. It is a sign of their favor.

We would dishonor them if we failed to use it."

"There are not enough of us," Cymbian pointed out. "We cannot take a whole city with a few dozen men."

"We just need to take one building in the city—the armamentarium. Then, with enough of these gants, we can conquer the whole world."

"We will succeed," Siglind added, "and the glory will be ours forever!"

We discussed the plan further, and none of the soldiers complained any more in public, but I think that was only because they trusted Arminius. Afterwards I saw some of them muttering to each other out of earshot of Siglind and Arminius. They weren't happy.

I wondered if Feslund was having better luck with the men on the other ship. Would he use the gant to demonstrate its power to the men who hadn't seen it in action? I recalled how dim its blue glow had seemed, the last time I had seen it. We needed that gant to still be working when we reached Urbis.

And the next day the storm arrived.

It came slowly, with the wind picking up and gray clouds covering the sky. And then the rain began, light at first and then a torrent. Lightning flashed and crackled. The wind became stronger. The sailors ordered everyone into the hold. The ship pitched up and down through the high waves; water starting leaking in. Almost everyone was seasick; the hold stank of vomit. Palta buried her face in my chest and shivered uncontrollably. Even Siglind looked frightened. "Oh, Larry, this is bad," she said over the howling of the wind.

"The gods are angry at us," Priscus muttered.

In the midst of it all, clutching Palta and more scared than I'd ever been in my life, I thought wildly: *Maybe he's right.*

A board gave way a little, and water started leaking into the hold. We frantically tried to jam the board back into place, but then another board gave way, and another. Some of us started bailing, passing buckets of water from hand to hand up the steps to the deck. But before long we realized this was useless—we weren't going to be able to keep ahead of the water now pouring in on all sides. "Everyone on deck!" Arminius shouted.

We scrambled up the steps. I half-dragged Palta, who could barely walk. Waves poured over the deck. The ship pitched this way and that. We wrapped our arms and legs around the railing. Lightning struck the mast at the front of the ship, which cracked and fell into the sea. I heard the captain shout an order, but no one seemed to do anything. Then the main mast cracked. "It is too late!" I heard a sailor cry.

And then the ship pitched over onto its side, and all of us were flung into the raging sea.

CHAPTER 25

I held onto Palta as the waves crashed over us. I'm a pretty good swimmer, but swimming didn't matter now; it was all I could do to keep Palta's head above water and not surrender to the storm and the pitiless sea that seemed determined to drag us down into its depths. I swallowed a mouthful of water and spat it back out. I saw a soldier flailing as he tried to get hold of a piece of the mast. Another wave hit us, and when we came up again the soldier was gone. Then a wooden barrel hit me on the side of the head. The pain made me cry out, but I think that barrel saved my life, because somehow I managed to clutch a rope handle on its side, and I held onto it with one hand and Palta with the other as we rode the huge waves.

"Are you all right?" I asked Palta.

"Don't let go of me, Larry," she gasped. "Please don't let go."

"I won't. We'll be all right. Feslund's ship will rescue us."

But what if it didn't find us? What if it had sunk, too? And what if I did let go? What if another wave tore Palta from my grasp? My arms were already starting to ache.

Every time a wave crested I looked around. I couldn't see anyone else, just debris from our ship. What if Siglind had drowned? Or Arminius? What if everyone was dead except the two of us, alone in the middle of the sea? Then surely we too would die before long.

I managed to pull Palta over so that she could grasp the handle along with me. And we held on until the wind and rain let up and the waves subsided. I thought I saw a figure bobbing in the distance—was it Arminius? But I was too tired to call out to him, and then he slipped out of sight.

Palta started to cry.

"We'll be fine," I said to her. "We just have to wait to be rescued."

She didn't reply. And I thought I knew what she was thinking: maybe this would be the worst way to die—in the water, holding on for your life as the hope of rescue slowly fades, realizing that this will be where it all ends, and it's just a matter of time till you give up and slide beneath the surface, unable to resist any longer.

We waited. The sun finally broke through the clouds, but the water was cold, and we were shivering. What would happen if the sun went down and we still weren't rescued? How long could we survive? *Hypothermia*—wasn't that the name for what would happen to us, even if we didn't drown? Maybe we'd get delirious and lose consciousness.

Maybe I'd see my family one last time, in my delirium.

We spotted more debris—boards and barrels and soggy clothes. But no people.

"I'm sorry," I said to Palta.

"You have saved my life twice now," she replied. "Don't be sorry."

I remembered kissing her in that colonnade after the Roman Games. What a sweet feeling that had been—up until the moment that she had been snatched away from me. Terra was a very cruel world, I decided.

Time passed. The sun was low in the sky. We waited, numb and shivering. The side of my head throbbed from where the barrel had struck it. My arms throbbed with the effort of holding onto the barrel. *This can't last much longer,* I thought.

"Look!" Palta said, pointing off to our left.

As usual, she could see things before I could. But in a few seconds I could make it out—in the distance, a ship. Was it a hallucination? But we both saw it, right?

Was it coming towards us?

It was!

We waved frantically at the ship and shouted as it approached. And finally we heard shouts in return, and we knew that we had been saved.

The ship pulled up close to us, and I saw Feslund leaning over the railing. "The gods be praised," he said. "I thought you were lost."

A sailor threw us a line. We grabbed it, and he pulled us to the ship. We managed to climb the rope ladder on the side and then fell onto the deck exhausted. Other sailors wrapped blankets around us and gave us cups of wine, which we gulped down gratefully.

"Have you seen anyone else?" Feslund asked us.

My teeth were chattering, and I found that I could barely speak. "No," I managed to say. "Are we the only ones you've rescued?"

He didn't bother to answer me. Instead, he muttered something to himself and shouted an order.

"Siglind?" Palta asked. "Did you find Siglind?"

"No Siglind," he replied. "No Arminius. Just Cymbian and a couple of sailors. I should throw the sailors back. We have no need of more sailors."

"Are you going to keep looking?"

"Of course we're going to keep looking," he snapped. He turned away and went back to the railing.

The warmth of the wine was working its way through me, making it hard to think. Siglind and Arminius? That couldn't be true. The two people who had been kind to us in Gallia.

Palta leaned against me, quietly weeping.

We couldn't take Urbis without Arminius to lead us, I thought. And even if he survived, there might not be enough soldiers left to lead.

Eventually we went down into the hold and changed into dry clothes provided by a sailor. Cymbian was there. He simply nodded to us, too weary to speak. After a while we decided to go back up.

The ship continued to look for survivors. A sailor had climbed the mast and was searching the sea with a telescope. They have telescopes in this world, I thought without interest. In a few minutes the sailor gave a shout, though, and not long after that sailors hauled Priscus aboard. He lay down next to us, and again they gave him blankets and wine. He could barely speak, except to curse himself for offending the gods. "Should have had nothing to do with this," he said. "This is what happens."

Then there was no one for a long time, as the sun sank below the horizon and I was starting to give up hope. Finally the sailor shouted again. And, a few minutes later, Siglind came over the side, to cheers from the sailors and soldiers. Feslund hugged her, and she joined us underneath blankets on the deck. "Oh, my friends," she said, and then she started weeping uncontrollably.

"Did you see anyone else?" Feslund asked, repeating the question he had asked us.

But she couldn't respond. It seemed like she would never stop shivering. Finally she managed to speak.

"I saw him—Arminius," she said. "I was holding onto a plank, and he was swimming towards a soldier—I don't know his name. The soldier was waving his arms and calling out for help. But the waves came crashing over him. Arminius reached the man, and he tried to hold onto him, to keep him afloat. But I could see the man clutching him, dragging him down. Then another wave came, and another, and I almost lost my grip on the plank. And when I had a chance, I looked around, and I couldn't see them. Oh, my brother—what if Arminius has drowned?"

"We will keep looking," Feslund muttered.

He went back to the rail, and Siglind started weeping again.

Darkness fell, and the stars came out. Someone gave us bread and salted meat to eat. I must have fallen asleep finally, because I opened my eyes to find Feslund shaking me by the shoulders. "Into the hold," he said. "I have something to say."

He went down the steps into the hold, and everyone on deck followed him. A couple of flickering lamps shone on the soldiers sitting on crates or sprawled on the floor. There were about twenty of them—all of us that were left, I realized. Some looked somber; some looked scared. Feslund stood in front of them.

"We cannot spend any more time searching for survivors," he said in Latin. "They cannot be found, and we cannot delay. I have told the captain to resume his course towards Urbis."

The soldiers were silent for a moment, but I saw them looking at each other. Finally Escondo spoke. "My lord, many of our friends are still missing. Arminius is missing."

"I am sorry," Feslund replied. "They are very likely dead. We have wasted too much time here. If we don't leave now, news of our expedition will reach the priests, and we will be doomed."

"It is the will of the gods," someone called out, and several others muttered their agreement.

"It has nothing to do with the gods," Feslund retorted. "The storm was just bad luck."

"Bad luck or not, there are too few of us now," Vetorix said. "We cannot hope to take Urbis with twenty men and a couple of girls."

"Nonsense," Feslund said. "We have this weapon—the gant. We are Gallians. We will take Urbis. We will rule Terra. We will avenge King Harald."

I think maybe Feslund expected this to rouse the soldiers, but it didn't. No one cheered. No one agreed with him. No one vowed to avenge King Harald. There was no reaction at all. The soldiers wouldn't even meet his gaze. He stared at them uncertainly for a moment, and then he stormed back up the steps to the deck.

"Arminius would talk some sense into him," Escondo muttered.

"We could be back in Massalia in three days," Sulliger said. "Have the soil of Gallia beneath our feet."

"He is leading us to certain death," a burly soldier I didn't know added. "I don't mind dying, but I'd like my death to mean something."

Suddenly Siglind stood up and began speaking quickly and loudly in Gallic, pointing at soldiers and gesturing to the sky, or maybe just to Feslund up on deck. The soldiers shifted uncomfortably.

I looked at Palta. "She says they must do their duty," Palta murmured. "She says it will be hard, but when has that stopped Gallian soldiers? They must have faith. Yes, the odds are against them, but that will only make their glory greater when they succeed. Our lives are short, and we must spend them doing something important, something that matters. And what could be more important than this? I will come with you. I will die with you, if need be. And if you don't choose to come with me, I will go by myself."

Siglind stopped talking and sat down finally, crossing her arms and looking around at the men. There was silence for a few moments, and then Priscus walked over and knelt before her. He was followed by Sulliger, and Vetorix, and Escondo…and finally every one of the soldiers was on his knees, pledging their loyalty to her. Tears ran down her face. "Pour Gallia," she whispered. *For Gallia.*

And that was how the decision was made.

Feslund stayed on deck while the rest of us found blankets and pillows and slept in the hold. "I wonder if the gant got wet during the storm," Palta whispered to me.

"Will that make it stop working?"

"I don't know. But it's one more thing to worry about. And Larry?"

"Yes?"

"The water—it doesn't bother me so much now. It has tried twice to destroy me, and I am still alive. Why should I be so afraid of it?"

I squeezed her hand. "That makes me very happy," I said.

And I slept well, despite all that had happened, despite all the threats we faced.

The next day dawned cloudless, and the wind was favorable. Feslund was in good spirits, especially once he found out that he would not have to force the soldiers to obey him. It was clear that he wasn't going to give Siglind any credit for their changed attitude, though. He simply assumed that his message had finally gotten through to them. "We should reach land by sunset," he said. "There is no time to waste. We must complete our preparations. We attack tonight."

Tonight? How could we do it tonight? Many of us were in terrible shape. I was still weak from the ordeal we had undergone the day before, and my head still hurt from when the barrel had struck it. I knew that Palta was in even worse shape than me. Couldn't we take a day to regain our strength? But Feslund wasn't going to delay.

My worries increased as Feslund laid out the details of the plan. The captain knew of a small cove five miles or so from Urbis. The ship would take us there, and sailors would row us ashore. We would travel the rest of the way by foot, under cover of darkness.

I recalled the terrain outside of Urbis—hilly and wooded until you reached the plain in front of it. Good for concealment, but what if we got lost? "How will we find Urbis in the dark?" I asked.

"We will find it," Feslund replied, waving his hand in the air as if this was a trivial problem.

"I think I'll know the way," Vetorix said. "My family has relatives near Urbis. I spent a summer at their farm once."

"You see?" Feslund asked, as if all our problems would be solved that easily.

"Will you be all right?" I asked Palta later.

She shrugged. "I have no choice."

They gave Palta and me a sword and a breastplate. I hadn't expected that. Their regular swords were far too heavy for us to carry on a five-mile trek, so we got short swords—really just long daggers; I felt like a hobbit.

"If we have to use our swords, we're doomed," Priscus muttered.

I was pretty sure he was right.

We waited on deck as the sun sank low in the sky. Just after it set we saw land in the distance.

If we didn't find the cove before the sunlight disappeared, would we have to put down our anchor and wait till the next day? We needed to know where we were. We needed a place for the ship to be safe and out of sight.

And then the clouds rolled in, and the rain started.

Rain would be another problem.

Feslund went over to the ship's captain, a gray-haired man with skin like leather. "Where is the cove?" he demanded. "You said you knew how to find it. Are we lost?"

"We will find it, my lord," the captain replied. "Be patient."

But Feslund was not a patient man. He paced the deck. He glared at the soldiers. He made a fist with his left hand and pounded it into his right palm.

"We need Arminius," Siglind murmured.

But we didn't have Arminius.

We got closer to land. There were trees near the shore, and hills beyond. Where was Roma from here? Where was the river we had sailed down with the fisherman? Palta would probably understand the geography. But it didn't matter; all that mattered was finding our way to Urbis, and Via.

Finally the captain gestured to a break in the trees. "There," he said.

We steered towards the inlet, gliding slowly through the water. The shore was dark—no lamplight, no torches. After a couple of minutes the captain raised a hand. The sailors dropped the anchor. The night was quiet, except for the pinging of the raindrops on the water and the deck.

The sailors quickly lowered the boat and rowed the first group of soldiers to shore.

Palta and I were on the final trip. Being in the boat didn't seem to bother her. Siglind was on the shore to help us get out. Then we stood on the sand and watched the boat row silently back to the ship.

"At last it begins," Siglind murmured.

PART V

Urbis

CHAPTER 26

F eslund was deep in discussion with Priscus, Escondo, and Vetorix. Finally he broke off the conversation and addressed us all in a low voice.

"Vetorix will lead us," he said. "We must be silent; we must be vigilant; we must stay together. It is early yet—people may be outside, even in the rain. If we make good progress, we will delay entering the city till later at night. Understood?"

We understood.

We checked our equipment and started off—single-file, in silence. Vetorix and Feslund were in front; Siglind was right behind them; Palta and I were in the middle. My heart was thumping with tension as we headed off through patchy woods. We crossed a narrow, rutted cart-path and then made our way through fields planted high with grain. In the distance we saw a village—a dozen or so cottages, with lights shining in the windows of a few of them. We detoured around the village and kept going. Now the woods were thicker.

Palta seemed to be doing okay. We weren't going fast. Five miles would take us a couple of hours, maybe more if we had to take a lot of detours. The rain had let up a bit, which was a help.

And then we heard a voice. "Quis estis?" *Who are you?*

A man was peeing in the woods off to our left. His voice was unsteady; he sounded drunk. Why was he there, at night, in the middle of the woods? We never found out. He saw the glint of our swords, perhaps, and started to run. A couple of soldiers took off after him. I lost sight of them, but soon I heard a grunt and a strangled cry, and then silence.

A few moments later the soldiers returned; their swords were dark with blood. I shivered. We set off again.

And then it started to rain harder. Before long we were trudging through a cold, drenching downpour.

I was so sick of water.

After a while we started heading uphill. Had we reached the hills surrounding Urbis? I thought we had been marching for an hour or so, but I could have been wrong.

It seemed to take forever to get to the top of the hill—but I couldn't see the city from the top. Instead, there was just the black outline of another, larger hill. My heart sank. Feslund called a halt, and we rested while Vetorix and another soldier went off to scout this new hill. The rest of us sank down into the mud and leaves. The trees gave us little protection from the rain.

Palta looked exhausted now. She closed her eyes, leaned back against a tree, and let the rain fall onto her head and down her face.

"The rain is good," Feslund said to us. "The more it rains, the harder it will be for the soldiers patrolling the walls to spot us."

No one replied.

Finally Vetorix and the other soldier returned. Feslund stood up, and they spoke quietly to him. "One more hill," he announced, "and then you will see the walls of Urbis!"

If he had expected a cheer from us, he didn't get one, although I was pretty relieved. We all stood up, got back in line, and started walking again.

The next hill was awful. We couldn't find a path, so we ended up scrambling over rocks in the darkness, often tripping and sliding down into the person behind us. Once Palta fell and didn't get up.

"Can you make it?" I asked. "Maybe we can carry you." I remembered the way we had half-dragged, half-carried Affron away from Urbis.

She struggled to her feet. "I can make it," she said. But she looked like she was about to collapse. And then, finally, we reached the top. Feslund raised a hand, and we stopped. Through the trees and the driving rain we could make out the long dark walls of Urbis, dotted with torchlight. Beyond those walls, sitting on a hill at the center of the city, I thought I could make out the temple.

Haec Est Via.

Finally.

The soldiers gazed at the city in silence. Were they excited? Terrified? Or simply exhausted?

Standing next to me, Siglind murmured, "Now we become immortal."

"We rest here," Feslund said after a while. "And then we take this city for Gallia."

We sprawled on the ground again and ate some soggy bread and cheese. Palta leaned against me, and I put my arm around her; she was shivering, and so was I. Now, I thought, it was up to her. I would never be able to find the entrance to the Egorinthine tunnel, the one we had used to escape from Urbis, but I knew that she would have no trouble—even in the dark and the rain. She wouldn't let us down.

She closed her eyes; I closed mine. We fell asleep in the rain.

…until Priscus shook us awake sometime later. "Let's go," he said. "You two, the prince, and me."

We struggled to our feet. Feslund was waiting for us. "First the four of us," he said, "then everyone. Bring us to the entrance to the tunnel."

We made our way down the hill. The rain wasn't quite as strong as it had been. I kept looking at the walls of Urbis to see if I could spot any sentries. If I could see them, they could see us. But I couldn't make out anyone in the darkness.

We were to the left of the main gates. Was that where the tunnel was? When we got near the bottom, Palta started going laterally, further to the left, staying behind trees so we couldn't be spotted. After about twenty minutes she stopped and pointed out onto the plain. "It's there," she said.

"Where?" Feslund demanded. "I don't see anything."

"It's hidden. The priests probably filled in the opening if they discovered that we had used it."

"Well, the weapon will take care of that, won't it?"

"That is the plan," she responded.

"What if they filled in the entire tunnel?"

"They wouldn't bother doing that. It's far too long."

We had explained this to Feslund already. It was clear that he was nervous.

We crouched down and made our way to the spot where Palta said the tunnel ended. It didn't look like much of anything—but I could make out a circle of concrete under a small layer of dirt.

I looked up; I still didn't spot anyone on the parapets.

"We should stand with our backs to the walls to block the light from the gant," Palta said.

We lined up behind the circle of concrete, and Feslund took the gant out from an inner pocket. It was wrapped in a cloth, which he carefully removed.

It shone a very dim blue.

My heart sank.

I looked at Palta. She sighed. "Try it," she said.

Feslund raised the gant and shot at the concrete. Some of it disappeared, but not enough. He tried again. About six inches were gone now. He tried once more; a couple more inches turned to ash. "It's not working!" he said. "How far down does this concrete go?"

"About the height of three men to the floor of the tunnel, I expect," Palta said. And then she added, "Save what's left of the gant's power."

Feslund looked at her in disbelief and despair. "Then what do we do?"

Palta shrugged. "We will have to find another way into Urbis."

CHAPTER 27

"What do you mean?" Feslund demanded. "What other way is there?"

"There is a postern," she replied. "We could get in through it. But we have to get out of sight and talk about it. This will be far more dangerous than using the tunnel."

Feslund and Priscus both seemed to understand what a *postern* was; I didn't. "Wouldn't the postern be guarded?" Priscus asked.

"It wasn't when I found it," Palta responded. "But come—we can't talk here."

We retreated back to the hill. A postern, it turned out, was a small concealed gate in the walls around a castle or city. The castle at Lugdunum had one; and so did the walls of Urbis. The gant could probably cut through the hinges or the lock of a gate, Palta pointed out, even if it didn't have the power to cut through twenty feet or so of concrete. But the risk was far greater. We would have to go right up to the wall; and if we managed to get through into Urbis without being noticed, we'd then have to make our way through the city in the open, instead of through an unused tunnel.

And, of course, we would have to fight the guards at the armamentarium with only our swords.

But we didn't seem to have another choice. "We will do it," Feslund said. "We cannot turn back. Lead the way."

"My lord," Priscus said, "isn't it clear that the gods—"

"Do not speak to me again of the gods," Feslund snapped. "Right now, I am your only god. Now let's go."

Priscus looked stunned, but he didn't reply. Once again we moved through the trees until Palta stopped us. "It's straight ahead," she said. "Hidden by those bushes."

Across the plain, I could make out dark bushes by the wall. And above them, at the top of the wall, I saw a sentry walk by. A torch flickered twenty yards away from him. He went past the torch and kept walking.

"Let's go," Feslund said.

I heard thunder in the distance. Rain might help, I thought.

We crept across the open plain to the wall just as the rain started pouring down again. We made our way into the soggy bushes and soon found the gate—a heavy wooden door, really. It was locked. We had a brief discussion, and then Feslund aimed the gant at the lock and shot. The lock glowed white and disappeared, along with a couple of bricks from the wall. We tried opening the door, but it wouldn't budge. So he blasted another hole next to the first one, and then another, until finally enough space opened up for a person to wriggle through.

We can't keep doing this, I thought. We were going to have more doors to get through, more ways we would need to use the gant. And eventually it would stop working.

We ended up in a narrow, musty passage. We shuffled along the passage until we reached the inner door, and Feslund used the gant again to blast a hole in it. Anyone nearby would have seen the flash of white light, I thought. Was anyone nearby?

Feslund looked through the hole. "Trees," he said. "Bushes. No people, no guards. That's good." He turned to Priscus. "Go back and get the men," he ordered. "We've wasted too much time."

"Yes, my lord." Priscus went back along the passage and crawled out through the hole in the outer door.

"Now we enter Urbis," Feslund said. He carefully wrapped up the gant and put it away. Then he crawled through the hole in the inner door and landed in the mud. Palta and I followed him. Feslund didn't seem to mind the mud or the rain. He looked satisfied, for the moment.

I was exhausted. My legs felt rubbery; my back ached. I couldn't imagine how Palta must have felt.

The two of us sat down and leaned back against the wall. Feslund stood up, waiting impatiently for his men. "We cannot delay," he muttered. "How far to the armamentarium?"

"An hour's walk," she said. "But we will need to circle around some castella. And the rain will slow us down."

"We cannot delay," he muttered again, as if saying that would make everything happen faster.

We waited. How long till dawn? I wondered. What if we made it this far, only to run out of time?

Finally the soldiers arrived, crawling through the opening in the inner door one after the other.

"Any problems?" Feslund asked Priscus.

"No, my lord. Everyone is here and ready."

"Good, good. We follow the girl now. Be vigilant—this is not the route we expected to take. We will be out in the open and easy to spot. Let's go."

And so we set off behind Palta through outer Urbis. She set a fast pace; I could barely keep up. No one spoke, but still we made a lot of noise, as our swords jangled and our boots stomped; I hadn't noticed this when we had been outside the city. We walked mainly through woods and meadows, staying away from the main road, but occasionally we couldn't help passing close to a castellum or an outlying building of some sort. But we saw few lights and no people.

And it continued to rain.

Finally we were in inner Urbis. The temple of Via loomed above us. Now we had a harder time avoiding houses and buildings. Occasionally Feslund called a halt and discussed the route with Palta. The men looked tired and sullen. The journey had taken too long. It felt like it would never end.

And then, finally, Palta pointed. "The armamentarium," she whispered.

We crouched down to observe it.

It sat by itself in the corner of a park, as if the priests didn't want to call attention to it. It was small, black, and windowless, and surrounded by a tall iron fence. We saw no movement, no sign of guards. Feslund sent a couple of men to circle around the fence. They came back a couple of minutes later; they hadn't seen anyone. There were two doors—a large main entrance, and a smaller side entrance.

One of the men tried the gate in the middle of the fence; it was locked.

So now what? With a fully powered gant we would have had no problem getting through the gate and into the building. But how many times could we risk using it?

Feslund took Priscus and Escondo aside and discussed the situation.

"We cannot make a mistake now," Siglind whispered to me.

Finally Feslund and the others returned. He went up to the gate, took out the gant, shot the lock, and pushed the gate open. It happened so quickly that we didn't quite know what was happening. He came back to us. "Priscus will take five men and guard the front entrance," he said. "The rest of us will go in the side door, swords drawn— Escondo and I in front, the princess, the girl, and the boy in the rear. We don't know how many soldiers are guarding this place or where they are. We cannot let any of them leave the building alive. We are told that they don't have these weapons from the gods, but we can't be sure. We need to kill every one of them before they have a chance to use whatever weapons they have. When we're done on the first floor, Escondo will stay behind with three men to guard the side door, and I will lead the rest upstairs. Understood?"

The soldiers nodded. I wasn't going to object to being in the rear, although I could tell that Siglind was annoyed. We took out our swords, crept through the gate, and assumed our positions. Feslund raised the gant, but the other soldiers were in front of me and I couldn't see what happened next. They stirred uncomfortably, though, and I knew that the gant hadn't done its job.

There was a long pause. "Move back," Feslund said. "The lock is weakened. We will break the door down. And then the battle will be joined."

We took a few steps back, and then Feslund and a burly soldier launched themselves at the door. It gave way with a loud crack, and we rushed into the armamentarium.

We were in a large entrance hall decorated with the usual mosaics and statues, and lit by a single flickering oil lamp. A sleepy guard sitting at a table was struggling to get to his feet. Feslund reached him before he could draw his sword and plunged his own sword into the guard's chest. Somewhere a dog started barking. Our other soldiers fanned out across the hall and into the rooms off it. I followed Escondo's men. We entered a large cubiculum lit only by the lamp in the hall. In the dim light I saw four men rising from their cots and reaching for their swords.

I had my short sword out and ready, but I knew I was no match for anyone in this room, so I hung back while Escondo's men did their job. Each picked out a target and attacked. Two Roman guards were run through before they could get to their swords. The other two were able to raise their swords and defend themselves, but they were outnumbered and quickly backed up in the face of the attack. One tripped over a bed, and Escondo buried his sword in the man's belly. The final guard fought furiously, but within a couple of minutes he too sank to the floor, his white robe soaked with blood.

Escondo checked to make sure all the guards were dead, and then he left the room without a word. My heart was thumping; I noticed I had blood on the sleeve of my loose white shirt—how had that happened? I felt awful.

"All dead," Escondo reported to Feslund, who was standing out in the hall with his men. The dog was still barking.

"No one else on this floor," Feslund replied. "Send two men through that door—I think it goes down to the basement. You and another man guard the side door. No one gets out."

Sulliger had found a lamp and lit it. Feslund took it from him and headed up a narrow staircase hidden behind the entrance hall. Palta and I followed, along with about ten soldiers.

On the second floor we found the dog, large and black and chained to the wall. He wouldn't stop barking. "Someone kill the thing," Feslund ordered.

Vetorix bend down and slit its throat. I felt sick when I saw the blood spurting out of the poor dog's throat. Palta gripped my arm.

Beyond the dog was a short hallway and a large iron door. Feslund walked down the hall to the door and tried the knob; the door was locked. He took out the gant; it had lost all its blue glow. He tried it on the lock. Nothing happened; the gant, finally, was dead. "Not good," he muttered. He put the weapon away and led us up one more flight of stairs. We found nothing but a dusty storage area. No soldiers, no weapons.

We went back down to the first floor. Feslund brought most of the men guarding the doors inside. "The weapons are in a locked room on the second floor," he informed everyone. "But the gant has no power left, and the door is too thick to break down. There must be a key here somewhere. Find it."

The soldiers spread out. The most obvious place to find a key was with the dead guards. Vetorix searched the body of the guard still lying by the table in the hallway. Escondo and his men took a lamp and went back to the cubiculum where they had killed the other guards. I went with them, but I couldn't bring myself to go inside.

The men rummaged around a bit, and then one of them shouted something in Gallic. He came back out holding a single key on a black iron ring. Feslund grabbed it from him and raced upstairs. He returned a few moments later, his face clouded with anger and frustration. "It doesn't fit," he said. "There must be another key."

"Maybe it opens a strong box," Sulliger suggested, "and the real key is inside the box."

"Then find the strong box," Feslund snapped.

And what if the key wasn't even here? I thought. Wasn't that just as likely? What if Tirelius kept the key, or some general back at the soldiers' barracks?

We were so close. One stupid door stood between us and the gants. Between me and the portal.

I noticed Palta sitting on the floor.

I sat down next to her. She had done everything we had asked of her—getting us into Urbis, finding the armamentarium. Now she was just staring ahead at a mosaic of the temple of Via on the opposite wall. The guard's corpse lay in front of it.

"We're running out of time," she murmured.

"I know." Surely it wouldn't be long now till dawn arrived. Till someone came upon us here, a handful of soldiers without the special weapons we thought would make us invincible. Was it too late to try to make it back out of Urbis? Didn't matter—Feslund would never allow it. He'd rather die here, and we would die with him.

The soldiers continued to look for the key, and Feslund became more and more agitated as they failed to find anything. "It has to be here!" he shouted, although he must have known that it didn't have to be here. And then he shouted at me: "I should never have trusted you. A stupid little boy who can barely ride a horse or carry a sword."

My face grew hot. Palta squeezed my hand.

And then with her other hand she pointed at the mosaic and murmured, "There."

She got to her feet and went over to the mosaic. At its bottom were tiles representing the rocks of the hill on which the portal had been found. One of the tiles was a slightly different color from the others. And in the center of the tile was a keyhole.

She motioned to Feslund, who put the key into the keyhole; it fit. He turned the key, and the tile swung out, revealing an opening behind it. Inside the opening was another key.

He took the second key and raced back upstairs. The rest of us raced up behind him.

Feslund put the key in the lock; again, it fit. He opened the door and held up the lamp.

Inside were row upon row of gants, all glowing with a bright blue light.

CHAPTER 28

No one spoke for a while. Everyone who could fit moved into the room and just stood there, staring at the weapons.

Finally Feslund strode forward and picked up a gant. He aimed at an empty wall and fired. A huge hole opened in the wall, and the familiar bitter smell wafted over us. Some of the soldiers were from the Massalia garrison and hadn't seen what a gant could do. I could hear them gasp with astonishment and disbelief.

Feslund nodded, satisfied.

"Everyone take two of these things," he said. "Then go outside. The boy and I will show you how to use them. Then we divide up and conquer Urbis. Come, we must hurry!"

The men scrambled to obey.

I grabbed my gants off a shelf along with everyone else. They felt heavier than the one I had used before. Their blue glow was reassuring; these weapons would not run out of power anytime soon.

Palta was waiting for me outside the room. "Aren't you going to take any?" I asked.

She shrugged. "I suppose. But many people will die in the next hour. I don't want to be part of the killing."

I nodded. "I'm sorry," I said. "I—"

She put a finger on my lips to make me stop talking. "It's fine," she said. "Let's get you home."

We went downstairs and out the main entrance of the armamentarium. The pouring rain had now turned into a drizzle. I showed a few soldiers how to use their gants; it wasn't hard. I was with Priscus when he fired his weapon for the first time, blowing away a tree outside the iron fence. He looked disappointed. "This is too easy," he said to me. "Where is the glory in fighting with such a thing?"

"It's not about glory, I suppose," I replied. "It's about defeating your enemy."

Priscus shrugged, as if he wasn't quite sure that this was how he viewed the matter. "We will win if the gods allow it," he said.

"Well, they have allowed us to capture these weapons, haven't they? That's a good sign."

He didn't respond.

The training was over in a matter of minutes, and then it was time to head out. Feslund left four men behind to guard the armamentarium—there were plenty of weapons left over, and we didn't want Roman soldiers getting their hands on them. "Ten of us go to the soldiers' barracks," he went on. "The girl will show us the way. The rest go to the pontifex's palace to capture or kill Tirelius and the other leaders."

"One more thing," I said.

He looked at me, annoyed. "What?"

"We need to take the temple."

"Why?"

Again, we had been over this with Feslund, but he seemed to have forgotten. "Because that's where Via is," I explained. "That's where the priests petition the gods. We don't know how that works." I did know how it worked, obviously, but I wasn't going to explain. "We don't want priests going there," I went on, "and somehow ending up with more weapons."

He pondered this and then said, "Fine. Any volunteers?"

Priscus volunteered, along with Sulliger and Vetorix. And Siglind.

"That's enough for now," Feslund said. "Too many, perhaps. We shall meet at the statue of Hieron when we are done."

Once the assignments were settled, it was time to leave. Feslund said a few final words. "What we do here today will be remembered forever," he said. "Let us make our fatherland proud of us."

The soldiers reacted enthusiastically this time. At last they could see how close they were to victory.

"Be safe," I whispered to Palta before she left with Feslund.

"Don't worry about me," she replied. She paused for a moment, and then said, "And don't leave before we can say goodbye."

"Of course I won't," I said. "Anyway, I'll need to find a viator to take me home. I hope I can find Gratius."

"You'll find him."

She squeezed my hand, and then she was gone.

My group started out towards the temple, which loomed in the distance above us. I knew the way to get there—not across the forum, which might have people in it even though dawn hadn't yet arrived. And the temple's main doors would probably be guarded. Instead, I would take a route Palta had suggested—around the forum, through the grounds of the schola, then up a long set of steps cut into the hillside at the rear of the temple.

We trudged through the darkness, holding our gants by our sides. We stopped once as we approached the main road and a wagon rattled by, a lamp swaying back and forth on a pole beside the driver. The driver didn't see us. Then we crossed the road, walking past a small castellum near the one where Hypatius had lived; it seemed so long ago now that he had brought Carmody and me to his house. Soon we had made our way to the soggy fields behind the schola.

The schola—where the best of the best recruits to the priesthood ended up. Potential viators like Affron and Valleia. What would happen to those students when this was finished? What would happen to everyone here? I realized that I had no idea what Feslund was planning to do once he had defeated the priests. Probably he had no plans. At any rate, if things worked out for me, I would never know what happened to Urbis, or Terra, or any of these people. Whatever happened, it wouldn't be my fault, I told myself, not for the first time. I hadn't asked to be brought here. And once I came here I had just wanted to go home, and they wouldn't let me. And these were the consequences. Still, the soldiers and sailors who drowned in the great sea, the man peeing in the woods, the guards at the armamentarium, the poor dog…they hadn't asked for what had happened to them, either.

But I couldn't stop to think about that.

The schola was an impressive brick building with a row of marble columns along the front. The back was plainer, though. A few carts sat haphazardly around a large wooden door. Soggy cloths were spread on the grass. Lights glowed in a couple of windows.

"People are rising," Priscus noted.

I had to find the steps up the hill. I was tired and shivering from the endless rain. I had a blister on my heel. My back ached. My head was throbbing.

I needed to get past all that and do my job.

It was near dawn now, and we had lost the invisibility that night and rain had given us. Priscus laid a hand on my shoulder and pointed off to the right, to a couple of men in the distance standing next to a tree. I thought I spotted a rake and a shovel leaning against the tree. Were they gardeners? Had they noticed us? What would they make of four men and a woman striding across their grounds, carrying strangely glowing metal objects in their hands?

"Shall we kill them?" Siglind asked.

Priscus shook his head. "Faster," he whispered.

We left the schola behind, and we reached a park—deserted, thank goodness—and then finally I spotted the worn granite steps, ascending at a steep grade up the hill to the temple towering above us.

"Here," I said.

"At last," Siglind murmured.

Priscus went first, followed by Siglind. I was in the middle, and Sulliger and Vetorix took up the rear.

Priscus strode up the steps as if he had just gotten out of bed after a great night's sleep. I had to practically sprint to keep up, and still I fell behind. He glanced back finally and slowed down a little, but he didn't look happy about it.

When we reached the top, we stopped for a moment while we caught our breath. We were at the entrance to a small, beautifully maintained garden, filled with flowers I didn't recognize. A sign said that the garden was dedicated to viators who had not returned from their travels. Did the soldiers have any idea what that meant? Birds were starting to sing in the trees. I looked behind me, and the view across Urbis was spectacular, but we were at the wrong side of the temple to see what, if anything, was happening at the soldiers' barracks. At the other end of the garden was a small cottage, and beyond that was the temple. We walked up to the cottage. Priscus tried the door; it was unlocked. He went inside, and in a minute came back out. "Looked to be the gardener and his wife," he muttered. "They are gone now." I could smell the bitter odor of the gant from inside the cottage.

We moved on to the temple. A narrow set of stairs off to the right led to an unobtrusive doorway. We went over to it. Priscus went down the stairs and tried the door. It was locked, so he shot it open, and we went inside.

We were in a cool, dark hallway lined with life-sized marble statues of noble-looking men and women wearing the purple robes of viators. Were these the ones who hadn't returned from their travels? I didn't bother to find out. It was spooky, though, having all those faces staring at us as we walked along the hallway. Other corridors branched off to the left and right. At each one we paused, listening for movement. We heard nothing. We saw no one. We kept going.

"Big place," Vetorix muttered.

The temple was indeed huge, and there were only five of us. How was this going to work, exactly? The main thing would be to keep people away from the portal; I didn't want viators racing off to Gaia. But how long would we have to do that?

Until Feslund's men had taken care of the soldiers, at least. They must have made it to the barracks by now. And the deaths would be starting.

Finally we found a narrow winding staircase made of some kind of polished wood. We went up one flight, opened a creaky iron door, and looked out at a large open area filled with clothing hung on racks. "Laundry?" Priscus murmured.

"Strange-looking," Sullinger said.

I saw denim jackets and corduroy pants and puffy shirts and odd-looking hooded garments and more. It wasn't laundry; it was clothing that viators would wear when they went to different worlds.

We didn't see anyone. We went back to the stairs and up another flight.

And that's when we heard the music start to play. I have heard big pipe organs a couple of times in my world, and this music was like that—deep and rich and full of bass, music you could feel as well as hear. The sound was one thing; the music itself was something else. As with other music I'd heard on Terra, the harmonies were slightly off, and the melody—if there was a melody—didn't go anywhere I expected it to go.

We stood by the door for a moment, just listening, and then Priscus quietly opened it a crack. After a moment he shut it.

"I saw Via," he murmured. If he was trying to sound like a hardened soldier he couldn't do it. His voice was filled with awe. "It is beautiful."

"What is happening?" Siglind demanded. "Why is music playing?"

It took him a moment to focus on her question. "It's a sunrise service, I presume."

"Are people out there?" I asked.

"I couldn't tell," Priscus replied. He seemed to be in a daze.

"Let's go upstairs," Siglind said.

We climbed another flight. I tried to remember what was upstairs in the temple—a long balcony, I thought. Anything else?

Priscus opened another door slightly, looked out again, and then silently closed it.

"What did you see?" Siglind demanded again.

"I never thought to see the real Via," he said, as if he hadn't heard her question.

"Yes, but what else? How many people?"

He didn't reply.

Siglind pushed him aside and opened the door. She took a quick look, and then closed it. "We are behind a narrow balcony," she reported. "Downstairs twenty or more people are prostrate on the floor, and a priest is standing on the altar next to Via."

We stood there silently. We need to do something. Someone needed to be in charge. I looked at Priscus; he said nothing.

"We must kill them all," Siglind said finally.

Sulliger and Vetorix looked to Priscus for confirmation. He didn't react at first, as if he hadn't heard what Siglind had said. Then he slowly shook his head. "It isn't right," he said. "Not in this place. Not in front of Via. The gods—"

"Enough of this," Siglind interrupted. "You will do as your princess commands."

He paused for a moment, and then shook his head once again. "I'm sorry, my lady. I can't. It's not right."

And so Siglind raised her gant and shot him. He disappeared before our eyes, along with a chunk of the wall behind him. Sulliger and Vetorix gasped. It took me a moment to understand what had happened. How could she do that? How could she kill Priscus?

"You two head back downstairs," she ordered them. "Larry and I will stay up here. Go out the door, and use your weapons on those people. Make sure none of them get away."

They hesitated, and then bowed and hurried back down the staircase.

"I'm sorry, Larry," Siglind said, "but there is no time for weakness in war. Let's go."

She opened the door and went out onto the balcony. I followed her, still in shock from what she had done. The organ music was even louder now.

I looked down and saw the portal. At last. And I saw the people prostrate in front of it—men and women, all wearing white robes. A couple of them were young; maybe they were from the schola. My age. A few were white-haired.

No one had spotted us; with the music so loud, no one had noticed the wall giving way from Siglind's shot.

Siglind raised her gant.

Did we really have to kill them all? What would that accomplish? I didn't want to do that. But I wasn't in charge; Siglind was. She fired her gant, and one of the worshippers disappeared. Then another. And then, finally, someone noticed what was happening, pointed, and screamed. The organ stopped. I saw Sulliger and Vetorix on the main floor; they too were firing now. People were scrambling to their feet and starting to run, but they disappeared before they got far.

The temple doors opened and guards rushed in, responding to the screams. I finally used my gant to kill one of them. Someone else—I didn't know who—destroyed the others.

And in moments the floor was empty.

The bitter odor was strong now; it was a stench in my nostrils. I felt like I couldn't breathe.

"Close the doors to the temple!" Siglind shouted to Sulliger and Vetorix.

They moved quickly to obey.

"Let's go down," she said to me.

We hurried back downstairs, out through the door and

around the altar over which the portal hovered.

The screams had stopped. The priest, the guards, the prostrate figures, the people who had been running—everyone had disappeared.

Except, not quite. Perhaps it was the distance from which we were shooting, or the angle, or something. But here and there on the marble floor, now turned to rubble in spots, were bits of clothing and body parts—a finger; a foot still in its sandal; an ear.

I hadn't expected that.

I turned away from Siglind and threw up.

She patted me on the back. "Don't worry, Larry," she said. "We did what we had to do."

I wiped my mouth on the sleeve of my robe, which was still damp from the rain. I tried to answer, but I couldn't.

The massacre couldn't have lasted more than a couple of minutes.

Where is the glory in fighting with such a thing? Priscus had said of the gant. I looked down at my weapon; I was starting to hate gants.

I went over and stood staring up at the portal, surrounded by flowers and candles. Why was it visible here and not in my world, or Carmody's? Its blueness was like the ocean, not quite solid, always shifting. It felt so...familiar.

I broke my gaze away from it and went over to the place where the brown-robed man had sat when Valleia and I had come out of the portal; he had been writing in a large book that lay open on a polished table with intricately carved legs. The table was there; the book wasn't. But behind the table was a door with a key still in its lock. I opened the door, and I saw shelf after shelf of such books—recording, it seemed, the details of every trip of every viator, back through the centuries.

Somewhere in those books was my route home. I opened one of the books at random. The writing was incomprehensible.

I left the room. Vetorix and Sulliger had come up to the altar and were staring at the portal as if they were hypnotized. "I never thought to see it," Sulliger whispered. "So beautiful."

"And now it is ours," Vetorix replied.

Siglind approached us. The two soldiers looked at her nervously.

"Enough," she said. "Vetorix, stand by the front doors. Sulliger, you search the temple for—"

She didn't finish her sentence. Because at that instant Sulliger disappeared in a flash of white light, leaving behind nothing but ashes and a bitter odor in the air.

I didn't have a chance to think, because Siglind knocked me to the floor, and we rolled under the table. I couldn't breathe. Someone, somewhere in the temple, had a gant like ours, and now we were the hunted, now we were the ones who were helpless.

"Run," Siglind said to me. "Behind the altar."

And then the table disappeared, and a smattering of gray ash fell on me.

"Go!" Siglind shouted. "Go! Go!"

I got up and ran. But I looked back for a moment, and I saw Siglind standing with her gant out, and I realized that she was covering me, trying to spot the shooter in the gray dawn light.

And then she, too, disappeared—one moment a living, breathing woman, filled with courage and determination and loyalty, and the next just a spray of ash, a bitter smell, a memory.

Instead of running behind the altar, I leaped up the altar's stairs and dived into the portal.

After a moment I looked up. As usual, I had difficulty making the inside come into focus, but I could see the shimmering outlines of lights and dials. Or was I imagining them?

And now what? Was I safe from the shooter? Maybe, but I couldn't stay here forever.

But I could just walk—or crawl—out the other side. Into another universe. And perhaps it would be home. Even if it wasn't home, maybe it would be safer than where I was right now. Or maybe it would be a desolate world destroyed by disease or a comet or the curse of some awful invention like gants.

I knew so little.

If I went to a new universe, I would probably never get home. If I went out the other side of the portal, I could never say goodbye to Palta.

I sat inside the portal, unable to decide what to do.

And something happened as I sat there. I felt my mind shift, and the shimmering lights and dials rearranged themselves somehow. They weren't real, I thought. Or, no, they were real, but a different kind of *real*...Were they really made by gods? Or were they something else?

And my mind spun with the kind of *speckness* I had felt before. So many universes, so many versions of me and everyone.

And yet here I was, trying to save my life. This life. Now.

I waited. I caught my breath. The speckness faded. And then I crawled slowly out of the portal and back into the temple.

I saw Vetorix off to my left, next to the altar. He was crouching down, aiming his gant at something, at someone.

I saw him squeeze the handle. I heard a crash. And a scream. A woman's scream.

Vetorix raced forward, towards the crash, towards the scream. And then he disappeared.

I got to my feet, gant in hand, and raced around the portal and down from the altar. I opened a door, hoping it would take me to a staircase, but I found myself in the small room where Valleia had bathed and changed after bringing me here from my world. The room was dark. I smelled soap, or perfume. The floor was a little slippery.

I took a deep breath.

Priscus. Siglind. Sulliger. Vetorix. All gone.

I was the only one left.

And someone was out there with a gant.

A woman. Was she injured?

I opened the door a crack. I couldn't see anything. Had she seen me? Probably. But her attention had been focused on Vetorix.

Now it would be focused on me.

I couldn't stay where I was; I was too exposed. Whoever was out there knew far more about the temple than I did, presumably. The door to the staircase was to my right, perhaps thirty feet away. I could go downstairs and leave the temple the way we had entered it. Or I could go upstairs. To the balcony, where I had heard the scream. I could hunt the woman down.

I made my decision. I raced towards the door to the stairway, half-running, half-sliding across the marble floor. I opened the door, then slammed it shut behind me and ran up a couple of steps in case the woman was going to shoot at the door. That didn't happen, so I took a moment to catch my breath.

Then I went upstairs. Once again, I opened the door a crack. I saw nothing. I opened the door and walked out onto the balcony, holding the gant in front of me.

Sunlight spilled through the windows. I didn't see anyone on the balcony. On the right side of the balcony, halfway along, was a large hole; beyond that the balcony tilted down, ready to collapse.

Was that the cause of the crash?

I walked slowly forward, towards the hole. I passed enormous windows, their lower halves covered by thick purple draperies. I checked behind the draperies as I went, ready to shoot. After each step I stopped and listened and looked around.

I knew how careful I had to be. But I was tired. I had been up all night, marching through the rain, searching, worrying, killing. My reflexes were a split second slower than they needed to be when I pulled the final drapery back next to the hole, and I saw the witch.

It wasn't a witch. It was an ancient woman with a craggy face and long white hair. I had glimpsed her before, tending the flowers on the altar as I walked out of the temple that first time with Valleia. I had barely noticed her then. And now...

Now there was a bloody stump where her right hand should have been. The arm was tied off above the stump with a piece of cloth.

And before I could react she had launched herself upon me, trying to wrest the gant from my grasp. Her hand shook. Her eyes were black and watery. "Diabolus!" she hissed. *Devil!*

I was terrified that I would squeeze the gant too hard trying to hold onto it and it would go off and I would be the one who disappeared. I got my left hand around her throat and squeezed. The old woman's fingers only seemed to get stronger, though, and the gant fell out of my hand. She broke away from me and lunged for it. I pushed her back and tried to grab it myself.

But it clattered through the hole in the balcony floor and down to the floor below. The woman gave a despairing cry. We were both at the edge of the hole.

She tried to push at me, but she had no leverage.

I scrambled back away from her, and I realized I had a second gant in my pocket. She stood up and started to come for me again.

And, then, somehow, I realized that I didn't need the gant. The confusion and dizziness I had felt in the portal had turned to power. I could *transmit* that dizziness, that speckness. I could make her feel the staggering immensity of the multiverse and her pitiful role in it. She didn't matter; nothing she did mattered, against the backdrop of all that was or could be.

I could transmit all this, and so I did.

Her eyes widened as she felt the power of my mind. She staggered, the way the pawnbroker had staggered before Affron. She took a step back before my onslaught, and she lost her balance and went through the hole. Her hand grasped desperately at the edge but couldn't hold on. And then she was gone. I saw her—I *felt* her—land with a horrifying thud on the marble floor below.

I took a deep breath. I was shaking. What had happened? What had I done? And then I got up and ran—back to the stairway, back downstairs, past the portal to where the old woman was lying face down and motionless on the floor, near the wreckage that had fallen from the balcony above.

First I picked up my gant.

And then I turned her over.

But she wasn't dead. She was holding another gant—her gant—in her left hand. Before I could grab it from her, before I could use the power I had discovered inside my mind, she squeezed the handle.

And nothing happened.

I took it away from her and stepped back. Her hand fell to the floor, her eyes clouded over, and her broken body lay motionless at my feet.

To be safe I shot her then, and she disappeared like all the others into the immensity of the multiverse.

And then I sat down on the temple floor and tried to understand what had just happened.

CHAPTER 29

First, I remembered a thunderstorm.

It was one of my earliest memories. I was asleep in my room, and a big thunderclap woke me up. I saw lightning crackling outside the window, I heard rain drumming on the roof, and I was terrified. I must have cried out, because my mom came into my room right away. I don't know where Cassie or Matthew were—maybe she had already comforted them. Maybe I was so little that Matthew hadn't even been born yet.

"It's just a little storm, Larry," she said to me. "It'll go away."

I must have kept crying, because she got in bed next to me. And that was always the best thing. She stroked my hair and held me close. "It won't be long," she murmured. "The storm always goes away."

And she was right. The thunderstorm raged outside for a while, and then it started to fade. And what did it matter, anyway? It couldn't hurt me, because my mom was holding me, and that meant everything was going to be all right.

I don't remember what happened next. I must have fallen asleep, because I always did.

And now I remembered what I had also remembered back in the colonnade with Palta: my mother was terrified of thunderstorms. While she had been comforting me, she was also frightened herself.

I missed my mother.

Here on Terra, she was far away; my world was far away. There was only me. And who was I? After what had just happened, I didn't really know. I could barely think.

Was I safe, or in terrible danger? If a hundred soldiers suddenly stormed the temple, could I defend myself with my pair of gants? Or, perhaps, with my mind?

I tried to understand what I had done to the old woman.

Presumably she had been the temple's caretaker—someone who spent her life in the place. And maybe the priests had trusted her with a gant to make sure that bad people could not desecrate the most sacred place on Terra.

But her gant was no match for the power I had found inside me.

Where did that power come from? Affron would know. Affron had seen something in me. A kindred spirit, perhaps.

But why me?

It made no sense.

But it felt like it made sense. In enough universes, someone could do almost anything.

I shook my head and tried to focus on this moment. Should I stay here in the temple, or leave and try to find the others? Were they still alive? How many other people in Urbis besides the old woman had gants—viators and soldiers and random people?

Finally I got to my feet and went over to the massive front doors. I didn't see any way to lock them or bar them. If people wanted to come in, the only way I could stop them was by killing them.

I realized that I was afraid to go outside. It was daylight; the element of surprise was gone. Anyone could shoot an arrow at me as I walked across the forum, or sneak up behind me and stab me in the back.

I decided to stay in the temple. Eventually I went back up to the balcony—this time going around the other side, away from the collapsed section. I stayed on the lookout for anyone else who might be hiding behind the draperies or coming up from the lower floors of the temple. But I was alone.

At the front of the temple, the balcony turned into a wide gallery filled with seats. Behind the gallery was a door. I made my way through the seats and opened the door.

I walked into a long, narrow room. Behind me was a fresco of the rising sun. Ahead of me was a single huge window looking down at all of Urbis—the forum, the palatium, the soldiers' barracks, and beyond to the castella and parks and woods of outer Urbis, all the way to the city walls in the far distance.

Smoke was rising from the barracks.

The forum was empty.

The main road leading to outer Urbis was empty.

The sun had risen over the hills outside the city. A new day had dawned.

Why was no one around? Just because it was so early? Or had news spread about the attack? Anyone who saw the smoke would realize that something bad had happened.

I realized that I was very tired. I wanted someone to come and rescue me, comfort me, tell me it was okay to fall asleep.

I couldn't allow myself to fall asleep.

But I did.

The second time I caught myself nodding off I decided I had to do something. If there was smoke at the barracks, perhaps my friends needed me.

So I forced myself to go back downstairs to the front of the temple. I pushed one of the doors open and walked out into the early morning sunlight.

The day was cool, but the clouds had disappeared. Sunlight glinted off puddles on the forum's cobblestones.

The forum was still empty. Down below, the statue of Hieron seemed to gesture up to me. This was where we were supposed to meet. No one was there.

Gant in hand, I walked down the long set of steps from the temple.

I was halfway across the forum when I saw movement off to the right. A door opened in the pontifex's residence. I raised my gant.

I saw Feslund, and I relaxed. Then I saw Palta, and my heart leaped up. A few others were with them: Mellor, Cymbian, Escondo, Ploterus.

And in the middle of them was the pontifex, Tirelius, looking tired and confused.

When Palta spotted me, she broke away from the others and rushed to embrace me.

"It's been awful," she said.

"Yes," was all I could think of to reply. "Awful."

"Where are the others?" Feslund asked when he reached us.

"All dead," I replied. "I'm sorry."

That startled him. "Even Siglind?"

"Yes. I'm so sorry," I repeated.

He grimaced. "What happened?" he demanded.

I tried to summarize, but I was too exhausted to say much. "A lot of people were inside the temple when we got there," I said. "For a sunrise service, I guess. We killed most of them, but an old woman had a gant and started firing at us. She killed Siglind and the others. Then I managed to kill her."

Everyone was silent for a moment, and then Feslund said, "Let's go into the temple."

I noticed Tirelius. He no longer looked confused. He was staring at me with cold black hatred.

We headed up the temple stairs, going slowly at first so that Tirelius could keep up; finally Ploterus and Cymbian took him by the arms and half-dragged him. Mellor and Escondo faced the forum as we ascended, scanning it for threats. Palta took hold of my hand. "Something happened in the pontifex's palace—I don't know what," she said. "Maybe someone had a gant there, too. Several of our soldiers died. We got there after we took care of the barracks."

"What happened at the barracks?" I asked. "I saw smoke."

"A fire started; I don't know how. Perhaps a lamp overturned."

"The soldiers?"

"All dead—those who were in the building, anyway. Many of them ran out in their underwear to get away from the fire, and we shot them one by one. When the others saw what was happening, they stayed inside and burned to death."

"Oh." I couldn't think of anything else to say. I looked at her. Her expression was grim, but she didn't look as devastated as I felt. She was used to war and savagery and loss, I guess. I was just a kid from a peaceful town who had never suffered anything—until the portal came along.

Finally we reached the top of the steps and entered the temple. It was just the way I had left it. I watched as the others took it in—staring in awe at Via, noticing the wreckage of the balcony, the overturned chairs, the body parts, the blood.

"It is bad not to have my sister's body," Feslund murmured. "She should be buried with great honor. She was a princess."

"She saved my life," I said.

He looked at me as if to say: *You are not worth a princess's life.* And I suppose he was right.

"Orders, my lord?" Escondo asked Feslund.

"Let me think," Feslund said. He looked around. He had a lot of problems, I knew. Even with all the weaponry in the armamentarium, how could he hope to hold Urbis with so few men? The original plan had been to send soldiers back to the ship as soon as the city was secure. The ship would bring news of the triumph to Gallia, and reinforcements would arrive within a few weeks. But if King Carolus had sent a messenger to warn the authorities, soon an army would be on its way from Roma to reinforce—or save—Urbis. And who knew how many other people in Urbis had gants? People like the old woman

I had killed, ready to give up their lives to save Via.

Feslund's victory was far from secure.

While he conferred with Escondo, Palta and I went over to Tirelius.

He was standing before the altar, looking up at the portal. His arms were crossed. His whole body was trembling slightly. From age? From emotion?

"Send me home," I said.

For a moment I thought he hadn't heard me, but then he turned slightly and faced us. "Home?" he repeated.

"In Via," I said. "You know how to do it. Every viator's journeys are logged over there," I went on, pointing to the high desk where the monk had recorded Valleia's trip to my world. "All the records are in that room. Find Affron's records. Or Valleia's. Find out the settings they used in Via. Send me back to my world."

"Why don't you ask Affron or Valleia to take you back?"

"You know as well as I do that they're dead. Now do it."

Tirelius looked at the two of us for a long moment, and then slowly shook his head. "You are foolish children," he replied. "You have destroyed a great civilization—for nothing. So you can return to your parents, or your friends, or the trivial comforts of your lives. For centuries our world has been as happy and peaceful and prosperous a place as one can find. And we have looked. We have explored countless worlds. We have seen what works in human society and what does not. We have made our choices, and they have been good ones. And now?" He waved his hand at the destruction in the temple. "This."

"I don't care about Terra," I said. "I didn't ask to be kept here, to be hunted down. Don't blame me for trying to go back to my home. Now do as I say."

I waved my gant at Tirelius. But he just shook his head again. "Has it not occurred to you that you would never be safe from us, even if we did bring you back to your home? We can always go there and grab you back, or kill you. In every universe in which you exist."

"But you don't control Via anymore," I pointed out. "Feslund does."

Tirelius shrugged. "I will not argue with you. Kill me if you like. I have no reason to live in a world ruled by that Gallian fool. And no other viator will help you—I can assure you of that. Any sympathy they might feel for you will disappear when they look at this." He waved his hand at the destruction in the temple. "They will kill you the first chance they get. And if somehow you manage to survive, you will be doomed to live your life here on Terra, pondering the consequences of your stupidity."

And then he turned back to Ploterus and Cymbian, as if he had no further interest in talking to children like us.

It occurred to me that I didn't have to threaten Tirelius; I didn't have to wave the gant at him. I imagined that he was the old woman, trying to kill me. And I was angry and terrified, and suddenly I could feel this weapon inside me...

Tirelius staggered; Ploterus caught him by the arm to keep him from falling. The pontifex shook off Ploterus and turned to stare at me with his cold eyes.

And his eyes were frightened.

I stared back at him, and then I was the one who turned away.

"We'll find another viator," Palta was saying to me. "We'll find Gratius. Gratius will take you home."

I didn't respond. Instead I sat down on the altar steps and put my head in my hands.

I wasn't going to do it; I wasn't going to destroy Tirelius. Now I knew how Affron had felt, at the pawnbroker's, at the Circus Maximus.

For some reason I tried to count up how many people I had killed in my time on Terra, but I had lost track. On Carmody's world, it had been that one kid from New Portugal in the middle of a battle, and he had haunted my dreams. Now I was on my way to becoming numb, hardened. Would I dream about the old woman? The soldiers rushing into the temple? The worshippers prostrate on the marble floor?

About Tirelius, staggering under the power of my mind?

Even if I could get home, I would never be the same now. When I returned from Carmody's world, I hadn't been the same either, I guess, but really, I had been better—more understanding, more forgiving, more mature. What had Terra done to me?

When I finally looked up, Palta was sitting next to me on the stairs. She silently reached out her hand, and I took it. I looked over at her, and I remembered how many times she had come into my bed, looking for comfort from another human being. I thought of my mother, comforting me when I was little and frightened—even though she was frightened herself.

We needed each other.

So we sat there, trying to think what to do next.

Eventually Feslund came over. "You two stay here and hold the temple," he said. "I'm going back to the armamentarium with the pontifex as a hostage. Cymbian and Ploterus are returning to the ship. Things will not be easy here until we get more men."

"We need food," Palta pointed out. "We haven't eaten since yesterday."

"Then look for it," Feslund said impatiently. "There must be something to eat in this place."

He summoned the other soldiers, who took Tirelius and left the temple. Palta and I were alone.

"You could go search for Gratius," she suggested.

"Where? He probably lives in one of those castella like Hypatius did. But which one? It's hopeless. We can't just go walking around Urbis. That would be too dangerous."

We were silent for a while. I wanted to tell her about what happened with the old woman, but I couldn't figure out what to say.

"Maybe I should go look for food," Palta said finally. "You stay here."

"Okay." I didn't feel like moving. And I wasn't hungry.

She returned a while later with some figs and a stale loaf of bread. "I found a couple of side entrances," she said as we ate. "I barricaded them as well as I could."

I nodded. "We can't barricade the front doors, though," I pointed out. "They don't lock, and they open out. If people want to come in, they'll come in."

"Would we have to kill them?"

"Maybe we can just scare them away. Show them the power of the gant, and they'll keep their distance."

"I don't think many people will come near the forum today," Palta said. "They'll know about our weapons. They'll be terrified."

That seemed likely. "But we haven't killed all the soldiers," I said. "The ones guarding the city walls are all still alive, for example. And more may be arriving any minute. They won't be so easy to scare."

"We'll have to stand watches through the night," Palta replied. "We can't let anyone take us by surprise."

That seemed reasonable. But how long would we have to do that? Would we have to sit here day after day, guarding the portal, until reinforcements finally arrived from Gallia? In the meantime, as Tirelius had pointed out, people would kill us if they had the chance.

And after the reinforcements arrived? *You will be doomed to live your life here on Terra, pondering the consequences of your stupidity.*

We sat there silently for a long time as the day passed. No one came; the temple was silent; the portal loomed behind us—taunting me, I felt sometimes. *I'm right here. Why don't you walk in and use me?*

We took turns going to the bathroom and searching for more food. I found a bottle of wine in a storage room, but we were afraid to drink too much of it in case we both fell asleep. Then I remembered the gardener's cottage, and I went there. I filled a sack with fruit, cheese, and bread. I looked around; it was a lovely little place, with flowers everywhere. *The flowers will soon wilt,* I thought. I smelled smoke. I went outside, and I saw that the schola was on fire.

I went back into the temple, and I barricaded the door behind me.

I went up to the room at the rear of the balcony and looked out over the forum once again. It was still deserted, but now the palatium was also on fire. Beyond the forum, the main road was crowded—people were leaving Urbis, I realized.

Downstairs, Palta had lit a few torches and collected blankets and cushions for us to sleep on.

I told her what I had seen.

"Perhaps the priests are burning everything."

Why not?

"And people are leaving they city because they have no idea what's happening," she went on. "They may not even know that Gallians are behind it all. Better just to leave Urbis and find someplace safe to stay."

"It may make Feslund's task easier."

"I don't think that Feslund is smart enough to win this war," Palta replied, "even with all the gants in the armamentarium."

And if he lost the war, then what? I couldn't imagine.

It grew dark. I'd had a chance to sleep earlier in the day, so I took the first watch.

Palta lay down on the cushions and put a blanket over herself, and soon her regular breathing told me she was asleep. I stared at her for a while. What would I have done if she had been killed? My last friend.

The long night passed. I thought about waking Palta to take her watch, but I wasn't tired, so I let her sleep. I thought about home. I thought about all that had happened to me on Terra. I tore off a hunk of bread, then washed it down with wine. All the while the portal was looming behind me. Finally I turned and stared at it.

Its glow was softer in the dark. It was beautiful, really. Enticing. I wanted to reach out and touch it. I felt my hand moving towards it, and then I pulled my hand back.

The portal had been nothing but trouble for me. In some universe, of course, the portal hadn't been there in the woods behind my house, or it had been there and I hadn't entered it, or I had traveled to Carmody's world but not to Terra…so many different universes, so many different me's, happy and sad, living and dead.

And in this universe, I was able to kill a person with my mind.

This was the universe I inhabited; this was the only me that mattered right now. I had made my choices, and here was where I had ended up, standing watch in the temple of Via while the armies of the Roman empire were probably massing to destroy me.

Haec Est Via.

This is the way.

It wasn't a path I should ever have taken.

I took another sip of wine. And then I heard a sound.

I raised my gant. It was the front door, slowly opening. I should have roused Palta, but I didn't. I waited.

I saw a purple-robed figure advance into the dim torchlight.

It was Gratius.

He bowed to me. I inclined my head slightly in return, but I didn't lower my gant. Maybe he had turned against me, as Tirelius had predicted.

"Larry," he greeted me softly.

"Gratius."

He ignored the gant and continued to advance.

"I knew I would find you here," he said.

I felt a lump rising in my throat. "Can you take me back to my home?" I asked. "That's all I wanted. That's why I'm here."

He nodded. "I can," he replied. "But there is something you need to understand."

"What's that?"

He stood in front of me now. "Affron. Valleia. Carmody," he said. "They are all alive."

CHAPTER 30

———◆———

"**W**hat?"

"Alive," he repeated. "I was afraid that you might not understand that. The morning they disappeared—I came to warn all of you that Decius was sending soldiers to capture you. He had discovered where you lived, but he made the mistake of telling one of his generals, who told me. Affron wanted to wait for you and the girl, but there was no time."

"Where did they go?" I asked.

"The only place they *could* go. Away from the priests and their power. We found a ship that would take them to Barbarica."

Barbarica. The name still gave me the chills. "Does Tirelius know?"

"Only I know. The other priests assume that Affron and Valleia are part of this attack—we just haven't seen them yet."

I remembered the pontifex's momentary confusion when I ordered him to take me home. I assumed that he had been taunting me when he asked me why Affron or Valleia wasn't going to do that. But he had in fact thought they were still alive—and they were!

"That's wonderful," I said. "But—"

"Before I left them," Gratius interrupted, "Affron said: 'When you find Larry, bring him to me.'"

"Why? Why did he say that?"

Gratius shrugged. "He said that you would understand."

I would? I realized that I was shivering.

And I found my mind ranging out across Terra. To a small room. To a person sitting cross-legged on the floor, making strange motions with his hands in the air in front of him.

I gasped.

"Larry?" Gratius said.

I brought my mind back to the temple, to the conversation. "Yes?"

"Wake the girl," he said.

He didn't much like Palta, I realized; she had stabbed his hand when she took the gant away from him to kill Hypatius. It didn't matter. I reached down and shook Palta awake. I pointed to Gratius. "He says they're all alive," I whispered. "In Barbarica."

She understood immediately and scrambled to her feet. "Affron is alive?" she demanded.

Gratius nodded. "We have no time to waste," he said. "The priests who haven't been captured or killed are plotting their strategy. Meanwhile, everyone else is fleeing Urbis, and no one is stopping them. By tomorrow the situation will have changed—you may be trapped in here. They may find a way to attack you. So we must go now."

Palta looked at me. "But Larry wants to go home," she said.

"That is his choice," Gratius responded.

"Affron needs me," I said.

"Why?"

I looked at Gratius.

"Before we parted in Roma, Affron told me exactly what would happen," Gratius replied. "He said that you would return to Urbis and destroy the power of the priests. I didn't believe him. I assumed that you would be caught and killed. But, you see, he was right. Here you are, in the heart of Urbis. Via is yours. Many of us have always thought that Affron was the future of Terra. But Affron apparently believes something different—he believes that Larry is the future."

This sounded ridiculous. But Palta looked at Gratius, and then at me, and I think at that moment she began to understand something.

"What do you want to do, Larry?" she asked. "Do you want to go home?"

I looked at her—her blond hair, her gray eyes. She was pulling at her ear lobe. She did that so often. We had been through so much together.

I thought about home. I had never quite understood why I had agreed to leave my world and come to Terra with Valleia. But even then, something had been happening to me, or I had begun to discover something inside me.

It is only by setting out that we can finally return home, Affron had said to me once. And what exactly had he meant by that?

Home, I thought, would always be a part of me. But now there was something that I had to do. "We must find Affron," I replied.

"Are you sure?" she asked. "What about Feslund and the rest?"

"They'll have to fend for themselves." I turned to Gratius. "We take our gants," I said.

He nodded in agreement. "The journey may not be easy," he said. "Terra will not be safe for us—or, perhaps, for anyone."

"All right," I said. "Let's go."

I turned and took a last look at the portal. This was as close to home as I was going to get for a long time. Perhaps forever. And then I took Palta's hand and followed Gratius out of the temple and into the night.

We walked quickly down the temple steps and across the empty forum. The night was cool and cloudy. The fire in the palatium was still burning. The smoke choked us. Gratius led us between two buildings and down another set of steps. At the bottom was a narrow path, and on the path was a horse and cart, much like the cart that had taken Carmody and me away from the palatium on our first night in Terra.

An old man sat cross-legged on the path next to the horse. His head bobbed up and down as if he was half-asleep but trying his best to stay awake. Gratius motioned for us to get back in the shadows behind a tree. Then he tapped the man on the shoulder. "I'm here, Calchus," he said. "You can go back to bed now."

He helped the man get to his feet. "Gratias, Domine," the old man said in a quavering voice. *Thank you, my lord.* "Terrible times, are they not?"

"Terrible times indeed," Gratius replied.

The old man shuffled off along the path. When he had turned a corner, Gratius motioned to us to come to the cart. He took some cloaks out of it. "Put these on," he said. "And put up the hoods."

He did the same, covering his purple robe with a dark brown cloak. Then he got up onto the bench at the front of the cart and motioned for us to join him.

"Will the city gates be open?" I asked.

"Some priests are trying to keep them closed," Gratius replied. "But they will not succeed. Too many people in the city are too afraid. They can't understand why the gods have deserted them. They blame the priests. As, perhaps, they should. So they are leaving Urbis, and the soldiers who might have stopped them have been killed or have left Urbis themselves."

He flicked the reins, and the horse started to move. "We didn't mean to kill all these people," I said.

He shrugged. "Of course you did. Or, it didn't bother you enough to change your plan. But no matter. If it had not happened now, it would have happened eventually. The world must renew itself, and you are apparently the agent of its renewal."

I had no idea what he was talking about. Gratius made his way out onto the main road. A thin sliver of moonlight lit the way. I could still smell the acrid smoke from the fires at the barracks, the palatium, the schola. Occasionally we passed families trudging along the road, all heading for the gates, many pulling small carts filled with their possessions. They looked up at us and probably wished we would let them ride in the cart with us, but no one asked, and we didn't offer. We were all just at the start of our journey. They would have friends or relatives in Roma or thereabouts. We had much further to travel.

Palta pressed herself up against me, and I put my arm around her. "This must be hard for you," she murmured.

"Yes," I said. "Very hard."

The walls of Urbis loomed in the distance. More people joined us on the road. The city was emptying out, and I was the cause.

I thought of my mom and dad, of Cassie and Matthew, of Kevin and Stinky Glover and Nora Lally and all my friends and relatives. Of going to high school and learning to drive and all the stuff that I wasn't going to do. It seemed so far away now. What did I care about high school or cars or baseball or movies? They were gone, completely gone. I was here in this cart, sitting between two people from utterly different worlds, going somewhere even more alien.

We could see the gates now. They were open, and people were streaming through them. "If anyone asks you a question, say nothing," Gratius murmured to us. "Let's not take any chances."

We didn't reply. We were safe enough, after all. If there was a problem, we had our gants. We looked around in silence as we passed through the open gates. We saw no soldiers, no priests, no officials of any kind. No one asked us anything.

And then we were outside the walls. I thought I spotted a bit of lightness beyond the hills; dawn would arrive before long, and it looked like the rain had finally passed. I held Palta tighter.

Urbis lay behind us now.

Ahead lay Barbarica.

PART VI

Barbarica

CHAPTER 31

———— ◆ ————

A s always, the women at the market stared at her suspiciously and treated her with contempt. People here didn't like outsiders, and they didn't mind letting outsiders know it.

Valleia didn't care. She had been a viator; she was used to traveling through strange worlds filled with strange people. These stout women with their muddy hair and weather-beaten faces seemed very familiar to her, even though she had never been to this place before. They were simple people living a hard life. They relied on each other to survive. And outsiders were a threat.

But they weren't bad people. They wouldn't descend on the outsiders and murder them in their sleep. They would leave the outsiders alone and trust that before long they would go away. Which, of course, the outsiders would. Because why would anyone stay here unless they had to?

Valleia bought bread, eggs, and butter and filled up a small jug with milk. There were no vegetables available, no fruit, no wine. After she left the market she walked down to the pier and bought fresh-caught fish from a wizened old man who touched his cap out of respect for her, instinctively knowing that she was more important than he was. Seagulls circled over the fishing boats, crying to each other. A cold wind whipped in from the ocean. Valleia pulled her woolen cap down over her ears; no robes and sandals here. It was hard to imagine how cold this place would be, come winter. She talked a bit about the weather with the old man in his native language; it wasn't hard to learn, although she didn't have the accent quite right yet. Viators were good at learning languages.

After buying the fish she walked through the town. Small shops lined the main street. Many catered to the needs of the sailors and fishermen who lived nearby. A few were for their wives and families—a clothing store, an apothecary, a shop that sold trinkets imported from Roma. None were very successful, Valleia supposed. People here didn't have much, and what they had they tended to make for themselves—they sewed their own clothes, they concocted their own remedies from plants and tree bark. This was not a bad way of living. She had been to many worlds, like the one that Larry Barnes came from, where people's homes were overflowing with objects—things that they didn't need and often didn't know they had. Were they happier for having all those objects? Valleia doubted it.

She kept walking. Soon there were no more shops, just small houses whose owners rented rooms to sailors, or where the craftsmen lived who worked in town—carpenters, masons, shipwrights. She smelled wood burning and fish being fried. She kept going till she reached the cottage they had rented at the end of a muddy road off the main street. It was a drafty, thatch-roofed place, lovely in the summer, but increasingly less lovely as the seasons changed. Winter would arrive early here; perhaps they would be gone by then, but she didn't know for sure. They had traveled far enough; she had little wish to travel any farther.

Carmody was chopping wood behind the cottage. He smiled when he saw her and put his ax down. "What's for breakfast?" he asked. "Wait, let me guess."

Valleia laughed. "I need to learn new recipes, William. Maybe the women at the market will teach me."

"They are terrified of you," he replied, picking up some of the logs he had split. "They believe you are a Roman witch. They make signs at you behind your back to ward off the evil you bring."

"They have every reason to be afraid of me, I suppose," she said. She held the back door open for him and then followed him inside.

The cottage had just a single larger room. It was dark and sparsely furnished. It reminded her a bit of the insula where the five of them had stayed when they first arrived in Roma—except that this place was private and quiet. And, of course, Larry and Palta were not here with them.

She sighed. Much had happened.

Carmody put logs into the cook-stove and the fireplace. Valleia took off her cap and set to work. Soon the eggs she had bought were frying in the butter she had bought, and a cheery fire was burning in the fireplace. She set aside the fish; they would eat it for lunch, as they did every day. She almost felt warm. Carmody cut the bread and poured the milk, and when the eggs were done they sat down at a small table before the fire.

They ate in companionable silence. There wasn't much to say. After so much turmoil and danger, they were safe, and they were happy. The priests might try to track them down here, but they wouldn't succeed. The local folk would give the priests no help; they weren't interested in rewards, or threats, from Roma. And anyway, why would the priests think the three of them would come to this place? For all the priests' power and knowledge, Barbarica was huge, and largely unknown to them. This little part of it was called Scotia. There was no reason for anyone to go to Scotia except an occasional merchant.

And of course they still had a weapon. A kind of weapon. Perhaps. When she and Carmody had finished their breakfast Valleia rose and cooked more eggs. She put the eggs and bread on a plate, poured milk into a cup, and placed the plate and cup along with a metal spoon on a small wooden tray. She took the tray outside, past the woodpile, to a small shed at the edge of the woods behind the yard. She knocked on the shed's door. There was no answer. There was rarely an answer. So she left the tray by the door and walked back to the cottage.

"Did you see him?" Carmody asked when she came back in.

She shook her head.

"He can't stay in there much longer. The cold will drive him out."

Valleia shrugged. "Who are we to say what he can or cannot do?"

She was tired of thinking about Affron. She had tried to understand him, and never could. She had tried to love him, and she had thought sometimes that perhaps he loved her, but the love never seemed to blossom into something real. She knew that he was special—beyond special. Unique. The kind of man who could change the universe. She wondered if he had seen the gods who had created Via; perhaps, she thought, the gods had always been there, inside him. But she found herself losing interest in such matters.

Because she was in love.

Carmody was *real.* Smart and strong and sensible. The kind of man who would respond to your affection, who would protect you and cherish you and not take advantage of your love.

"Let's not talk of Affron," Valleia said. "I'm sure he doesn't think about us nearly as much as we think about him."

"That's certainly true." He pulled her down onto his lap and kissed her ear.

She smiled. "You don't still want to go back to your home, do you?" she asked. "To Boston? To the United States of New England?"

"This is home," he replied. "Where you are is home."

That was a very good answer. And she was mostly sure that he meant it.

She felt a movement inside her. It was that other life, reminding her of its existence. The life that mattered more than all of Affron's concerns. She took Carmody's hand and placed it on her belly. "He moved," she murmured.

"He can't wait to join us," Carmody replied. "To make us a family."

Valleia placed her head against Carmody's shoulder, and he put his other arm around her. "Everything was worth it," she said, "to be here, together."

"Yes, it was."

Valleia raised Carmody's hand to her lips and kissed it, basking in the warmth of the fire, and his love.

She hoped—she trusted—that his love would never change.

Affron ignored the knocking, which registered dimly on his consciousness. He was too busy looking at his hand. The folds of skin on the knuckles, the tracery of the blue veins, the nails that needed to be trimmed. A tiny scar below the little finger. Dark hairs. He held it out in front of him. It moved in space, just a little. His hand was a remarkable thing.

If he tried, he could feel Terra moving in space, in the terrifying silence of infinite emptiness.

If he tried, he could feel Larry and Palta and Gratius moving ever so slowly across Terra—breathing, thinking, worrying. What will become of us? What is happening to us? When will we be safe? Where?

If he tried, he could do many remarkable things.

But why try? That was the question that baffled him. In a spinning, swirling, ever multiplying infinity of universes, what could one man accomplish? A man made of folds of flesh and traceries of veins and nails that needed to be trimmed.

The gods heard the question and shrugged their shoulders. A man does what he can do. And then the universes move on.

Affron moved his hand slightly to the left and, as before, it started to disappear. He kept moving his hand until it was totally gone. Gone from this universe, anyway. He felt nothing except a dizzying sense of oddness, looking at the lonely stump of his wrist. He could move his fingers, but he could not see them. They were somewhere else entirely.

So what did that mean?

He didn't know.

He wondered if he would live to find out.

He didn't know.

He moved his hand slowly back into this universe, into the cold damp air of the shed.

So strange.

If he didn't live, what then?

Then, he knew, someone would replace him.

And that person, he knew, was moving slowly across Terra. Towards Barbarica, and his fate.

*Turn the page for an
excerpt from*

BARBARICA

The Portal Series
Book Three

Richard Bowker

The boy went over to the shed. Arva followed. The boy stopped in front, and then walked around it. But there was nothing to see from the outside—just a small, windowless wooden building, barely more than a man's height. He raised the latch on the door and went inside. Arva followed, once again, although there was barely room inside for the two of them.

The place was dark and musty. It contained a few tools, as Arva had guessed. No logs, but some boards, and a few old chairs stacked in the corner. And one set down in the middle of the wooden floor. The boy sat in the chair. Why? He stayed there for a while, and then he got out of the chair and knelt on the floor and put his hands out in front of him. For some reason Arva started to become very nervous. What was the boy doing?

And then, just for a moment, Arva felt something else. He felt as if he were falling, falling, in emptiness that went on forever, that multiplied endlessly around him. And he too seemed to multiply, and every self was falling, and he knew he would fall forever.

It was the most awful thing he had ever felt.

And in an instant it passed. The boy was looking at him. "Me paenitet," he murmured. *I'm sorry.* But then he turned away and seemed to stare off into nothingness. And then

Arva seemed to *see* the nothingness—just there, above the wooden floor. And how could that be true?

Arva backed out of the shed. He wanted no part of this boy, or whatever he was staring at in the shed. He wanted to run away. But he forced himself to stay. He was not a child; he was not a girl. He had travelled across the world. He would not be afraid of emptiness, of nothingness. Of falling.

He noticed that the man and the girl were standing behind him, their cloaks wrapped tightly around their bodies. They, too, were waiting for the boy.

Eventually he came out of the shed.

"Well?" the man asked.

"Affron was here," the boy replied.

"We knew this," the girl said.

The boy shook his head. "It's different."

"How?"

The boy didn't answer her question. "We should go," he said. "He's waiting for me."

"Where?"

"North, I suppose." He gestured at Arva, as if to say: *We can trust what this man told us.*

They walked back to town. He left them at the stable. They politely thanked him for the trouble he had taken. He said it was no trouble; he was delighted to help.

He watched them head off north on the King's Road. When they were out of sight he went directly to Grillich's tavern and ordered a cup of whiskey, even though it was still morning. He drank it down and sat shivering by the fire.

He was not shivering from the cold.

And as he stared at the fire he found himself praying to the gods, for the first time in many years. Even though he had no idea what he was praying for.

The last person to see the three strangers was Corin the stable boy. He followed behind them as they rode, hoping for one last glimpse of the girl with the blonde hair and gray eyes. And yes, finally she turned and smiled and gave him a little half-wave before turning back to the road and her journey.

And that was enough to keep him warm for the rest of the long, lonely winter in our small town.

THE
PORTAL
SERIES

Portal
Terra
Barbarica

Richard Bowker is the author of *Replica*, *Senator*, and other novels. He lives near Boston with his wife and two sons.

You can contact Richard through his website: www.richardbowker.com